the

secrets
she keeps

the
secrets
she keeps

JOLIE MOORE

The Secrets She Keeps

This edition published by
Moore Digital Media Inc
1125 N Fairfax Ave
Unit #46071
West Hollywood, California 90046

ISBN 13: 978-1-64414-088-8
eISBN 13: 978-64414-087-1

Cover Designer: Damonza.com

The Secrets She Keeps/Jolie Moore. — 2d ed.

for those who have loved and lost

1 NARI

I was competing with a luau for attention. The hula dancers in grass skirts were winning. The bar had been packed
to the gills the first three nights I'd been there. Now it
was less than half-full. And there was nothing more pitiful
than drinking in an empty bar.

Every year the medical conference coordinator trotted
out the same tired luau, same hula dancers, same whole
roasted pig, same hollowed out pineapples filled with alcohol. And every year, my doctor colleagues flocked to the
flaming tiki torches like moths. Maybe I would be better
off picking someone at the luau for a hookup, but the
pseudo native display made me more queasy than poi.

I surveyed the bar again. Still pretty empty, but then
so was my glass. Signaling the waiter, I ordered something

called a Tai Chi from the twenty-dollar cocktail menu. The server offered up sushi, but I waved him away. So didn't need any rice soaking up the alcohol and killing my buzz.

It only took a few minutes before the first guy came over.

"Nice dress," he said. The man helped himself to one of the three empty stools at the high, square table.

"Billabong," I supplied.

"What?" He shook his head. Off-kilter. Good.

"The designer. They do great beachwear. I'm Nari Yoon."

"Dr. Colin Mann." He extended his right hand.

I looked down at his other hand. No ring on the fourth phalange. So far, so good. The name wasn't too bad either. His hair was on the longish side, and going a little bit gray. Ten years ago, I'd never have given a guy with salt and pepper hair a second glance, much less my real name. But I wasn't the only one getting older.

"How long have you been in practice?" I asked, trying to gauge his age and more importantly, his stamina.

"About ten years in Nashville," he said. Shifting on the stool, my mark leaned forward expectantly.

Dr. Colin Mann looked like he wanted to impress me with some incredible stories of heroic patient care. But I wasn't interested in medicine tonight. Not the practice of it, at least. I needed a balm of a far more basic form from him.

"You here alone?" I crossed one leg over the other. The cascading hem of the rayon dress revealed a significant portion of leg and thigh. He was pretty cool about the reveal, and I liked that about him. Maybe that control extended to the bedroom as well.

"Yep," he said, offering no more.

I drained the Tai Chi and closed my eyes for a long moment, enjoying the lightheadedness. For an instant, I wished I could float right out of my body.

After opening my eyes again, I gestured outside. "You going to the dinner?"

"Things look much more interesting right here," he said.

Right answer.

Forty-five minutes and two more Tai Chi's later, I gave Dr. Colin my room number. I excused myself for a trip to the ladies before coming back to settle the bill and seal the deal.

But when I carefully placed one foot in front of the other, completing the balancing act of walking while drunk and successfully making my way back to our table, I was disappointed to find my companion had disappeared. I looked around, making sure I had the right chair. In a room full of identical square black stools, and dulled mental acuity, perhaps I'd made a mistake.

"No mistake," Dr. Lucas Tucker said as if reading my mind. Eerie. "Dr. Colin Mann had an emergency call that took him away."

Turning my wrist toward my face in what I hoped wasn't too exaggerated a gesture, I peered at the little gold hands set against the blue mother of pearl. Ten-thirty. I had to be up in my room grinding it out before midnight, and I'd lost a sure thing.

Tonight, I needed sex like a fish needed water. It was the only way I'd ever made it through days like these without gasping for air, dying on land. And the night was escaping me quickly. I looked at Lucas a little differently. Cocking my head to examine him more closely made my head swim a little, so I straightened up. Alcohol was the second best path to oblivion. But the morning after was murder. Time to split my hand and double down.

"Well, I need another Tai Chi, then," I said, wincing a little at my slurred words.

"How many have you had?" Lucas' eyes narrowed in doctorly concern.

"Not enough." To the attentive server who appeared at our table as if teleported, I said, "Two Tai Chi's."

"Did you enjoy the luau?" he asked.

"Skipped it. Once was enough. You?"

Lucas hesitated for a moment. "It was...interesting."

"Seems a bit imperialist to me. But to each his own." Lucas turned his light brown eyes on me. Were they hazel? Under the clinic's fluorescent lights, I'd thought them brown. But now I could see that tiny flecks of green and gray dotted his irises. My heart gave an unexpected thud.

Damn.

I had never noticed he was a man before. I shook my head with exaggerated movements. No, that wasn't it. Of course I'd noticed he was a man. There seemed to be a great shortage of them in the primary care field these days. So a new one and a single one at that, in the office, had sparked weeks of speculation.

No, it was something much simpler. I'd never noticed he was a man who could possibly rock my boat. I took a glance at my watch again. My boat needed some serious rocking soon.

"Why are you shaking your head?" he asked, sipping cautiously at the drink. My sips were smaller this time around as well.

Like a light switch in my head, I turned off Dr. Yoon. "You look very good tonight. Nice to see you out of a white coat and comfortable shoes." I lifted my own three-inch Jimmy Choos and propped them on the chair next to him.

His eyes traveled the length of my leg, stopping only where the dress landed. I bent my knees, ostensibly to get comfortable, but in reality it revealed more leg. Lucas' eyes traveled farther up to the hem again. My criteria narrowed sharply to straight and interested. Dr. Lucas would certainly do.

Suddenly resolved, I stood, gripping the table for balance. "I'm going up to my room. I'd love it if you joined me. Maybe we can get to know each other better," I said, putting it frankly.

Assuming he was wired like most men, he'd close the tab and knock on my door in five minutes or less. I opened the tiny purse at my side and dropped a duplicate of my own keycard on the table. "Fourteen twenty-two."

I'd peed again, then artfully arranged myself on the chaise when the snick of the lock echoed in the room. Lucas' expression was somewhat wary, so I stood and took four long steps to close the distance. Simultaneously I pulled him toward me with one hand, and pushed the door closed with the other. Good coordination for the inebriated.

"Nari—"

I silenced his protest with a solitary finger against his lips. He needed no further prompting. He pulled me to him, pursuing my mouth for a kiss. I turned my head from the sudden intimacy.

His hot mouth was against my neck and moving down, seeking sensitive skin and a reaction.

This.

This is what I needed on tonight of all nights. By waiting so late, grief and memory had started to crowd in on the periphery. There was no time to waste.

Sliding a hand down his chest toward his khakis, I felt for and found his belt buckle. With a single hand I pulled the leather from its brass hold and slipped it from the loops. It dropped to the wood floor with a soft clink.

"Nari, slow down. I didn't expect for you to—"

I didn't want talk. I needed action. A flick and the button of his slacks was undone. Rubbing my hand along-

side the zipper I'd released, I realized he was well and truly aroused. No worries there. I'd only have to push past
any scruples he had. I'd played most of my cards, but not
all. Time to pull the ace from my sleeve.

Men were visual. Turning on the bedside lamp, I
grabbed fistfuls of fabric in my hands and pulled the thin
dress over my head, playing my trump card. Other than a
thong and three-inch nude heels, I was naked. Like iron
filings to a magnet, Lucas' hands were on my tits in the
space of a heartbeat.

Yes. This. I wanted to scream with relief.

Alternately, he squeezed and rubbed his fingers along
the engorged tips. Pleasure flooded my brain, and everything else left. Sweet, sweet oblivion was around the corner. I sat, pulling him down on the bed by his shirt.

"Take this off," I begged, pulling apart the stiff collar.
A button pinged against something metallic. He complied,
taking the shirt from my hands and releasing the final
closures himself.

Then I urged him over me. The heaviness against my
slightness, the rough body hair against my smooth skin
was almost too much to take. Almost. But not quite. Another kind of emotion was sneaking in. That had never
happened before.

Mentally squashing it like a bug, I plowed forward.
Feeling along the duvet, I found the condoms I'd stashed
next to the bedside clock hours earlier. Rolling over, I
tugged at his boxers, releasing the thick member. Were I
sober, I'd have been impressed.

But now all I wanted was to fill the emptiness. I swirled my tongue around the tip, earning a guttural moan from the man. He was mine now. I licked again, the smell and taste making me more buzzed than the alcohol. Slowly, I slipped on the condom, smoothing it with my hands. He pulsed and twitched against me.

God knew he felt hard as a rock and as ready as I was. We rolled over again and I notched him against my opening. Pushing out a deeply held breath, I guided him in.

"Ah!" he cried out, trying to stop the movement of his hips. "Is this okay? Are you—"

"More than ready," I said. Looping my heels on his shoulders, I urged him on.

What little control he'd had was gone in an instant. He grabbed on to the ankles by his ears and slammed home.

If I could have kept him hard inside me for a single hour more, that's what I would have done. But nature didn't work that way. Eventually, he pulled out and found the bathroom. In less than a minute, he was back.

Fuck me pumps off, I camped under the covers.

"Did you...Do I..." he stammered.

I shook my head. It wasn't about an orgasm as much as it was about making it past midnight. I looked at the glowing orange clock. It was well past. Lucas looked like he wanted to say something. Sleep, not words.

I pressed a single finger to his lips. "Sleep now. Talk later," I said.

I had no plans on talking later, but I didn't say that. I closed my eyes. Nothing flickered in my mind. It had worked. I let myself drift. The alcohol's sedative effect was strong and pulled me into unconsciousness.

I had a perfectly intact, completely non-mutated aldehyde dehydrogenases gene. In short, I could hold my liquor. I'd never sat at a bar, face beet red, one step away from falling down in the street, ass over tea kettle in my own vomit.

Genetically, I may have been fine, but I'd made a big mistake last night. I'd gone to sleep with a man on the wrong side of the hotel room's door. I'd have to rethink my liver's tolerance.

When I drank, my preference was for soju, easy enough to get in Los Angeles, even outside Koreatown. But last night, in the resort's hotel bar, it hadn't been an option. Instead, I'd downed too many of the house special: a Tai Chi, the Mai Tai on steroids.

The combination of coconut rum, spiced rum, and dark rum had tasted yummy the first time around. A second had been the start of a divine slide to oblivion. The third...well, the third was probably what landed me in this bed with a hulking bear of a man next to me.

I'd fucked up my hookup.

Waking up alone had always been my preference.

I moved my foot again one last time to make sure my sense of touch wasn't faulty—set off by alcohol-related hallucinations or psychosis. Nope, there was a hairy leg in the bed next to mine.

I cracked open a single eye, squinting. Maybe I'd dreamt the whole thing. But no, he was right there, half a day's blond stubbly growth shadowing his jaw. Slipping from the covers, I did my best not to shake the bed and wake the sleeping giant.

What happened in Kauai, stayed in Kauai, right? The *one* year I'd decided not to drag my best friend Daisy along, *this* had happened. My best friend had felt slighted by the absent invitation. After all, we'd gone on this trip together every year for the past three. But the conference had fallen on the tenth anniversary of Andrew's death. And I didn't want to have to battle heart-wrenching sadness, tears, all the while steering a best friend straight who was putting her own life on the path to ruin.

Once, maybe twice a year I craved, no, *needed* the oblivion only copious alcohol and anonymous sex could bring. It made the days bearable and the nights nonsuicidal. A dozen or so hookups in nine years with nameless faceless men, nothing I was ashamed of. In March, and sometimes in July, I waltzed into a bar and made myself an easy mark.

This year, Lucas Tucker had somehow slipped under my radar. I squeezed my eyelids tight, trying to remember what had happened to that other guy. Connelly, Conlin, something like that. Five hundred randy men away from home, and I'd been desperate enough and stupid enough to bed the only one I knew in Kauai.

Mentally I snapped my fingers. Colin from Nashville. That had been his name. He had been my intended target.

Maybe I needed to check *my* judgment too. Because now that my more sober brain thought about it, what medical emergency could the guy have had? Rum not only killed the liver, but brain function as well. Someone should have written that down in a medical journal somewhere.

I took a deep breath, and the nausea eased for a moment. All that mattered was that I'd made it. Today was March twenty-fourth and my world hadn't ended on March twenty-third, even if it felt like it would when the sun had come up yesterday morning.

I was alive. Andrew wasn't. Those fundamental facts would never change.

The pounding intensified in my brain, as I lifted my body and tiptoed to the bathroom, reminding me of my continued existence on this earthly plane. I pawed through my makeup case, looking for something to stop the pain.

Four years of medical school, several years of practice, and I'd yet to come up with a cure for a hangover, not that I was trying. Maybe I should have gone into research. Probably a billion dollars in that kind of cure. My parents would shout with pride from their Riverside rooftop if I made a big a success of myself off a patent like that.

Shaking my Tory Burch makeup case one last time, I had to accept the sad truth. The turquoise bag held nothing stronger than naproxen, acetaminophen, and ibuprofen. I contemplated taking a few of each. But mixing drugs was not a good idea. I pushed the Tylenol back into the bag. It was too easy to overdose on those, especially with the night my liver'd had.

Instead, I poured out four of the brown pills, a total of eight hundred milligrams, threw them back with rank tasting hotel tap water and hoped that would ease the pain, if only a little.

For some reason I couldn't put a French manicured finger on, this tenth anniversary of Andrew's death was harder than any of the last nine. And it showed on the reflection of my face in the stark bathroom light. Whomever said time heals all wounds, lied. I was living proof that hurt could be as fresh on day three thousand six hundred fifty one as the first.

Wrapping my hair into a tight twist, and jabbing in a few bobby pins, I winced at the pain in my scalp and my puffy face. For a regretful second, I wondered if having a real friend by my side last night would have helped me avoid the mistake I'd probably made.

For all the previous years, I'd been in Los Angeles when this day came. And being in the nearly four million strong City of Angels was the equivalent of being alone. With a one-week shift in the dates, instead of flipping through photos and letters in the privacy of my own bedroom, I was in Kauai rubbing shoulders with disorderly doctors and brushing up on pre-diabetes indicators.

But I'd avoided spending the week with Daisy because I didn't want to have to put on a pretty face for my best friend. If I told Daisy the truth about my yearly pity party, there wouldn't be any sympathy. I expected I'd hear the same thing my pragmatic Yankee friend had intimated only once, *Your college boyfriend died. It's time to move on. Get over it.*

But the sting still remained like a thorn in my heart. Even if Daisy had never said those cold and exact words aloud, the message was the same. Because I was supposed to have gotten over him if not ten years ago, then at least by now.

"Nari," a hoarse voice called.

Lucas.

With the sound of the shifting bedsprings, heat suffused my face. I looked in the mirror again. Post coital awkwardness made my face red in a way alcohol never did.

What sounded like a foot thumped on the floor. The bed squeaked. Another foot hit the wood floorboards. He sounded like he was shuffle-walking in my direction. I steeled myself for what needed to come next: a gentle nudge or big shove out the door.

"Ow!" was followed by a curse. "Shit!" The bedsprings groaned in protest.

Damned healing instincts kicked into gear a nanosecond later. Against my better judgment, I wrenched the faucet shut and ran around the wall separating the vanity and sink from the four-poster. Lucas was back on the bed, holding his foot in his hands.

"Toe broken?" I asked, skipping the medical history and differential diagnosis.

"No." He worked the digit back and forth carefully. "Got any aspirin?"

"Tai Chi hangover?" I tried for nonchalance.

"Not quite. But I'd rather avoid the headache." Except for the foot, he looked none the worse for wear. I'd seen him finish the drink, in fact I'd encouraged it. I'd never wanted my partners to remember any more than I did. But of course six foot whatever inches of solid man did not go down easily.

I left him massaging his large foot, and rummaged through my bag again. Aspirin wasn't the kind of thing pharmaceutical reps handed out. Acetylsalicylic acid had gone off patent more than a century ago.

"Ibuprofen is the best I can do," I said. Coming back around the corner, I put two pills in his hand, snatching my own back like I'd brushed fire. Touching him had sent something akin to an electric current through my body. He was concentrating on the pills and didn't feel it or didn't notice, thank goodness.

Lucas swallowed them dry. Water, damn. I went back to the bathroom to turn on the taps. I threw the remaining paper cover on to the counter and filled the other small glass. Bringing it to him, I was careful not to touch his hand this time. Once burned and all that.

While his Adam's apple bobbed, I stepped toward the floor-to-ceiling window, reaching for the sparkling blue of the Pacific Ocean. Smooth cold glass halted my progress. How could this be the same dull gray, cold water of Santa Monica?

How could Lucas, whom I'd long ago planned to set up with my best friend, have ended up in my own bed? I turned around to face the naked man. Keeping my well eyes above his neck, I found his face was open and smiling.

"You want to grab breakfast?" he asked. Didn't he know the hookup code? He was supposed to have been dressed and absent. No, I didn't want eggs. I wanted to crawl under the nearest rock and sleep off the shame of boinking a co-worker, not break bread. As if the nausea in my gut from the rum wasn't enough, the thought of breakfast nearly pushed me back to the bathroom with the aim of a bigger porcelain bowl.

"I'd rather die," I admitted.

"Food will soak up all that stuff you drank last night," he said conversationally. Didn't he realize he was naked? All six foot three, four, whatever of him...totally and completely clothing free. In the light of day, I could see that his curly blond hair did not end at his shirt collar, nor his belly.

My gaze continued its downward slide. Because I had to see.... Yep. Well, everything was where it should be, including his foreskin. That assessment was only clinical, of course. The gut churning that turned to nervous flutters could be and would be studiously ignored.

Overwhelmed by a dozen conflicting emotions and a sudden urge to be alone, I started picking up his clothes from the floor and thrusting them at Lucas. I'd seen thousands of nude bodies in my life, but I didn't want to see his now. Didn't want to remember tangling my hands in that springy hair and tugging hard. Wanted to forget the pleasure his hands and mouth had brought, even when it hadn't been about that.

He didn't say anything else, but acceded to my silent request and pulled on his boxers. When he bent to add socks to his ensemble, I folded my own clothes and put them on the chaise at the foot of the bed. Pulling the hotel robe closer around me, I sat. Cleared my throat for the brush-off. "I have some things to do. So...."

"What do you have to do?" His question was so earnest, I didn't have the heart to give him the hard shove through the door.

Instead I used the old stand-by—pretending to misunderstand. "Pardon me?" Maybe he'd take the hint.

"What—"

"I heard you." I had to put an end to this. I had candles to light. A ritual to endure. "I know this trip is on the clinic's dime, but I need to take a day alone." My voice was properly cool and detached. It was a persona I'd cultivated, no, *perfected* over the years. Every vowel was perfect, every consonant enunciated. I always made sure my meaning was absolutely clear.

Lucas wasn't clueless, thank goodness. Rejecting men was not in my wheelhouse. Sure, I'd perfected the art of rebuffing come-ons. A woman in Los Angeles had to. But rejecting a nice guy who'd only made the mistake of swimming in the toxic waters of my life, that I hadn't done—ever.

I stepped back toward the windows again, pretending to enjoy the view after I snuck a glance at him. Damn, he looked like I'd kicked his puppy or something. I hated that I'd put that look on his face. It wasn't even seven in the morning and I'd already violated the first of our profession: First do no harm.

Out of the corner of my eye I watched Lucas shrug into his button-down shirt, pick up his shoes in one hand and his pants in the other. When he emerged from the bathroom a minute later, I made no pretense of watching the ocean. I tried to arrange my lips in some semblance of a smile—an apology. He was all but dressed. The belt buckle clinked shut. I watched him walk to the door. Slowly, he turned one lock, flipped back the safety bar.

I looked down at my fingers. Cuticle scissors, that's what I needed. How had stray skin separated from the middle finger of my left hand? I was usually very careful with my personal hygiene. I'd probably overlooked it in the rushed mani/pedi I'd gotten the day before the flight. It would have to be fixed.

"I guess I'll see you at work on Monday morning then," Lucas said with a slight hesitation. I did nothing to halt his progress. He let himself out.

2 LUCAS

I worked hard to banish Nari from my thoughts. A couple of fellow conference goers patted me on the back as I walked through the lobby in last night's clothes. I wondered, not for the first time, if the hotel had set the conference attendees up like co-eds, with women in one building, the men in another, as a way to humor the staff. It was like the freshman walk of shame all over again.

"Had more than a Mai Tai," one guy said with a playful punch to my shoulder.

"She was cute even without beer goggles," another said.

I unballed the hand I'd chivalrously fisted, resisting the urge to punch these guys out. Doctors at a medical conference were like a bunch of frat boys during spring break.

Slightly drunken sex with my very pretty co-worker had not been the plan. If I were being honest with myself, I'd have to admit I'd had my eye on Nari ever since I'd joined the practice. For a while, I'd even thought she shared my interest until she mentioned something about her best friend.

Nari wasn't all that good at spinning, though. She'd have failed miserably at politics. Her friend sounded like someone in need of rescuing. I liked to confine my heroics to work where writing a prescription or making the right diagnosis could save someone's life. I most definitely did not want to be set up with some prim and proper New England girl without a real job. I'd met enough of those during my time in Vermont. I'd wanted Nari.

Weeks ago, I'd decided the best way to get to know Nari would be to ask her to dinner, maybe to a swank place on Third Street or in Beverly Hills. Buy her some wine, maybe take her to a show of some kind. The women in the office were always going on about one production or another at the Pantages. I'd bookmarked the site, and was going to buy tickets to the newest show once they'd gone up for sale. But Nari's bare leg so close to that other doctor's hand had blown my carefully laid plans to smithereens. Stupid as it might seem, I hadn't wanted the guy to take advantage of her. I wanted to be the only one unwinding that hair from those bobby pins. Slipping those skinny straps from her shoulders. But I judged that all wrong. Very, very wrong.

Drinking had fucked up the whole thing. She couldn't push me out of her room fast enough. She must have thought I was no different than half the guys here, looking for a drunken hookup. It wasn't as if I'd done much of anything to invalidate her opinion.

Sex, no matter how good an idea it had seemed last night after that Tai Chi and holding the keycard of my fantasy date, was not supposed to happen. Not like that, at least. Her swift shove out the door told me all I needed to know. She thought I'd seen her as a conquest. Just another mouse playing in paradise while the cat sat aloof at home.

Conquest was the name of the game this week. It wasn't my game, but I didn't need to start a fight with another one of these doctors to prove that. Instead, I avoided the eyes of everyone else throwing knowing looks my way and peered at my watch instead.

All thoughts of chivalry and fights were forgotten as I got a closer look at my watch. Damn, I was gonna be late. If I didn't hustle, I'd miss my appointment. Later, when I got back, I'd have to figure out how to fix the big mess I'd made. But I hadn't come to Hawaii for sex or the latest miracle drugs. The latter had been an excuse for my family's sake. I'd come to Kauai for a single reason—to gather information.

With renewed purpose, I jogged to my hotel room. A shower and a shave later, I grabbed a free coffee from the lobby and made my way through the revolving door to a waiting taxi. Nari wasn't the only one planning a skip day.

Before I could lay my hand on the front door of the lawyer's office, thirty minutes of winding roads later, my phone rang. I stepped back into a tall stand of bougainvillea near the front door.

"Lucas honey, how are you?" Mom. It was as if the woman had a sixth sense. A blood relationship couldn't have made us any more attuned to each other.

"Enjoying Kauai," I answered cautiously. She'd seeded my room with condoms the first time I'd had sex. I didn't put sniffing out my night with Nari past her. But that was a no-go area. She must have gathered that from my tone.

"What are you up to today?" she probed instead.

"I think I should ask why you're home in the middle of the afternoon?" I looked at my watch and added six. It had to be, what, four in the afternoon on the east coast. My mom was a dedicated teacher who worked it like a nine to five job. She was usually at school meetings with parents planning fundraisers, or hand deep in sorting through natural fibers preparing for the next day's lesson.

"I couldn't get anything done today with everyone at the school running around prepping for the yearly fundraiser. Your dad has an early day anyway. So I came home to make his favorite dinner. While I was breading the pork chops you popped into my head."

Guilt flooded my veins. I couldn't get anything right today. First I'd botched things with Nari, now with my mom. It wasn't the time, though to make amends for my first son disappearing act or talk to her about my impending appointment. I looked at my watch again. "I'm actually going into a session about treating patients with compromised immune systems," I lied.

"Well, okay," my mom said, her disbelief evident. "Call us back when you get a chance. We miss you now that you're so far away."

I rung off.

I hadn't exactly hidden the fact from my mom and dad that I was looking for my birth parents. But I couldn't really share each leg of the journey with them either. They'd looked so nervous when I'd finally admitted my plan. Briefing them on each and every step along the way would have been agony for everyone involved. I wasn't so dense that I couldn't see that. But closing them off from nearly aspect of my life was hurting them as well. Striking the right balance was hard.

I was still smarting from the fact that I'd probably ruined the family's last Christmas dinner when I'd announced my plans to find my birth parents. The one where my brother had pronounced me self-involved, and my sister had called me dense.

"But why, Lucas?" my sister Brooke had asked. I'd looked at her face, tiny and sharp featured like my mom. She topped out at maybe five foot three, barely squeaking by Joyce.

My brother didn't ask a single question, but I could feel Christian's judgment across the long pine table. My brother looked like a male version of my mom and sister.

Taller, broader, but still as different from me as night and day with stick straight brown hair and the Tucker face.

At six foot four with curly blond hair and brown eyes, I was a giant in their Lilliputian universe. I needed to find my own Brobdingnagian clan.

My dad had paused while cutting the ham. My mother had nearly dropped the basket of biscuits, the dog snagging one before my mom saved the rest of them from Angus' waiting mouth.

Bringing dinner to a grinding halt hadn't been what I'd intended. But I'd wanted to announce my plans when everyone was together. I didn't think I could do it twice. And with me in California, holidays were the only time we were all in one place nowadays.

"Because I need to know my background," I punted. Expressing the need to find out why my birth parents had abandoned me was more than I was willing to admit in front of everyone. "Every day I treat patients who know their medical history. I don't really know mine," I'd offered.

"You could fork over the money for DNA analysis, couldn't you?" Christian said.

Count on brother Chris, the biologist, to come up with that recommendation.

"I've seen patients bring in those so-called analyses. They can't tell you if your dad had cancer or your mother had diabetes." I tried to ignore our father's squint, my mother's trembling hands. "Nothing is greater than firsthand information. You and Brooke have that. Why can't I?"

Dad swiftly cut off the discussion. "There's no reason you shouldn't have all the answers you need, Lucas," he said. My dad's reasonableness cut more deeply than an angry lash of words would have.

Recovered, Mom passed me the biscuits. "I agree," she said, taking one big swallow of air. "We support whatever you need to do."

Nothing like unconditional love to bring on the guilt. They'd pulled me aside when they'd dropped me off at the airport to assure me that I had their full support. But I would have to have been blind not to see what that support had cost them.

Nida Vara was a chatty one. I drank the lawyer's chai, endured her small talk, and tried not to cringe at the clashing floral prints of her walls, furniture, and clothes. But after ten minutes of being nice, I wanted the bottom line.

"Can you open my adoption records?" I asked.

"The short answer is no." It was the most succinct sentence she'd uttered in our limited acquaintance.

My intestines tied themselves into knots. Coming to Hawaii, the place I'd been born, I'd thought there was a crack in the door to the past. The lawyer had been so optimistic on the phone. Now that same door was slamming in my face, a key twisting in the lock. The thought that I might never know the origins of my birth set the acid pouring into my gut. I wished I could articulate why this was so damned important–to myself, to my parents, to anyone. But I needed to know. I leaned forward, eager to accept whatever help she could offer.

The lawyer grasped my hands. She spoke before I could think what to ask. "But I do have some information and a few questions." Nida Vara pulled a single sheet of paper from a slim manila folder. Its thin presence paled in comparison to the thick brown accordion files practically spilling their contents on the shelf behind her. "You were born on April seventeenth at Kauai Veteran's Memorial Hospital," she said.

I grasped onto the one new shred of information. "Does that mean my parents were in the military?"

"Yes. Probably the birth father. Women weren't enlisted in the numbers they are now."

"Were they married?" So many scenarios had run through my mind since the day my parents had told me I was adopted. From a teen girl hiding her pregnancy, to a mom with one kid too many, all the way to the tragic situation of a rape. But I very much hoped my birth and existence didn't start from an act of violence and bring grief to some woman every time she thought of me.

"Can't say. But probably. That would have been the reason she was admitted there versus a county or state hospital. Both parents were named on the birth certificate."

"Why can't you tell me who they were?" If I was in Hawaii, and the solution to the mystery of my birth was here, why could I not put those two together like puzzle pieces and get to the truth?

"I received a non-identifying document," Vara said.

I could feel my eyes going crossed. Throw a complex diagnosis my way, no problem. Legalese I couldn't stomach. "What does that mean in plain English?"

"In older adoptions like yours, courts and agencies are happy to provide adoptees copies of the birth certificate, but they redact anything that would give a hint about the birth parents. That's what I have here."

She handed me a blurry copy of an old microfilm record. I pinched the bridge of my nose. I wondered if the sudden headache was from the lawyer in front of me or the rum from last night.

Nida Vara looked a little uneasy. I gestured for her to continue. Might as well swallow whatever bitter pill she had to offer. "Well, Mr., excuse me, Dr. Tucker, have you asked your adoptive parents for the records they might possess?"

Gut churning started again. "No. I'd rather do this any other way than that. It was hard enough for them to support my search," I said.

"I've seen this before," she said. Vara's headshake of disapproval was so slight I might not have noticed if I hadn't been watching her so closely for clues about my background. I wanted to stop and ask her why my parents couldn't understand that my love for them had nothing to do with this. But I needed legal advice, not therapy from

Ms. Vara, and I had the wisdom to know the difference. Wish I could say the same for some of my patients.

"Let's try a different question. Where were your parents living when they adopted you?" she asked, her voice a bit softer.

"Vermont..." Damn. I had no idea. I paused for a long moment, searching my memory. Came up blank. "Maybe New Hampshire. Why?"

"Your birth state is where you'll need to start. Each state handles the opening of records differently. Your case is a little more complicated as you were born in one state and adopted in another. It's doable. But I'm not the lawyer to do it for you. You can do it yourself—"

I shook my head. Seeing patients, dictating files, making referrals, and wrangling with insurance companies was already more than a full-time job. Throw on that heap fixing what-the-hell-ever had happened with Nari and I was all out of time. "I can't. Maybe. I don't know."

Vara pushed a thick soft cover book into my hands, making my choice for me. She had my next few weekends sewn up. "Read this. It'll tell you where to start."

3 NARI

One hundred thirty dollars and two cab rides later, I was ready. I drew the curtains, thrusting the sun-soaked room into early dusk. After I pulled matches from my pocket, I lit the candles one by one, each representing a month we'd been together. Then I extracted the box from my suitcase. Trying to hold back the tears that would blur my vision and make this more difficult, I sucked in gulps of air.

The album was always first. Pictures of me, Andrew, and our friends filled the polypropylene sleeves. I traced their tiny paper faces. We'd all looked so young then. Andrew, Daisy, Isabella, even me.

Then I opened a smaller book, its leaves gilded, and looked at the pictures of my wedding day. I'd worn a white wool dress that hid my expanding belly. Andrew had worn his tux. He was the first person I'd ever met who owned a tuxedo.

I hadn't come to college looking for love. The fact that I'd found it had galled my parents. They had told me time and again they weren't paying for courtship. They were paying through the nose for me to get my pre-med bona fides. That as their only child I was subject to certain expectations. That I was coming close to failing to meet any one of their goals for me.

Getting more comfortable on the rug, I leaned back against the front of the couch and let the memories do what they always did, soothe my grief. Bring me back to a time when everything was headed in the right direction. When the future had seemed brighter than the past.

On that single night in his Owen dorm room more than ten years ago, I'd changed the course of both our lives.

I had laid back on the extra long twin bed, my arm reaching for the pillow. I'd tucked it under my head and turned toward the dingy wall that was probably supposed to be white. New England was nothing like California. Sometimes I wondered if Yankees were allergic to paint. Every campus building I went into looked like it could use a new coat. My parents had painted their walls nearly every two years. Owen did not use the biannual refresher plan.

The bed dipped; Andrew had come back from the bathroom he shared with three other seniors. He shucked the boxers he'd pulled on to dispose of the condom with some kind of modesty. At least he had some manners.

Owen sometimes reminded me of the cable movie *Animal House* with all the drinking, burping, farting. The girls were marginally better, but I'd spent nearly all my time on the boys' side.

"Ri?" His voice was a question. A single finger bumped down my spine.

I turned toward him, our fronts nearly touching. Avoidance never got me anywhere. "I...got into USC," I blurted.

"That's great!" Andrew's hug was a tackle. We bumped against the springs under the thin, lumpy mattress.

"I didn't get into Perlman." Not that I'd put much effort into the interview. The whole time we'd been in Philadelphia, I had twin thoughts running through my mind. Life in leafy Philly with Andrew, idyllic. My parents' ire at not returning home, less than.

"Anderson or Marshall, here I come," he said, laughing.

"Your dad wants you to go to Wharton." Where Andrew's dad and probably a thousand generations of Clarkes had gone to school.

"My dad will get over himself," he said.

Andrew's nonchalance was foreign to me. I tried to imagine telling my dad that I'd chosen something other than what he'd wanted. I closed my eyes for a second, blinking away that image. Owen had only been a go because a few other churchgoing kids had blazed the path years earlier, otherwise I'd have been limited to Cornell or Riverside. But at either of those schools I'd never have met Andrew.

My heart nearly stopped at the thought. I closed my mind to that possibility.

"Do you think we should go to separate schools?" I asked, testing him.

Andrew sat up, unselfconscious. I matched his movements, but with the duvet firmly wrapped around my own body.

"What's going on, Ri?" He blinked his blue-green eyes at me. My heart did the same skip it had been doing from the first day I'd seen him singing on the rush line. Simply, I adored him like I had no other boy or man. The floppy dirty blond hair he gelled into a sleek pompadour on performance nights. The smooth, lean swimmer's body that ended in goofily large size thirteen feet.

My mouth opened and closed, but no words came out. I imagined I looked like a koi gasping for flakes of food in a backyard pond. Instead of searching for the right words, I pulled a small plastic stick from under one of the pillows.

"What's—"

I pushed the human chorionic gonadotropin test into his hands.

"You're pregnant?" Though he made an attempt to mask his shock, it was still palpable.

"I don't know how—" My arms flailed uselessly under the covers.

"I do," he said, his smile crooked. Blunt tipped fingers snaked through the covers, spanning my waist.

I looked down between his legs. Did nothing turn him off? Boys. Batting his hand away, I said, "This is serious."

"So is this." A half-smile played around his lips.

I gave him my scary serious face.

Andrew sobered, draping the free end of the comforter over his erection. "What do you want to do?"

I scrutinized his face. Was he suggesting I have an abortion? Would he dump me if I didn't get rid of the baby? What did *he* want? Gawping fish mouth, again.

Words had never failed me. Not since I'd entered kindergarten and realized the children spoke a language different from my parents. Not since my attempts at play were rebuffed when I'd asked politely in Korean. Since then, knowing the right words and having them always at my fingertips had been very important to me.

I took in a lungful of air. He wasn't asking if I wanted to see an action movie or eat at the four dollar Indian buffet, both of which I'd tolerated for years while smiling. I needed to tell him the truth.

Another deep breath. "I want to have the baby," I finally admitted. It was an irrational, career-limiting, possibly relationship-ending decision, but I wanted the baby anyway. I'd always wanted to be a mom. If it was meant to be now, then so be it. A child could be worked around. After all, wasn't I going into a profession predicated on saving human lives? Adding one more life to the mix couldn't be a bad thing.

Andrew leapt from the bed like the sheets were on fire. He hopped back into his boxers, then pulled pants and a button down shirt from his small closet. I glanced at the clock on his desk. Where was he going five minutes from midnight on a Friday?

"Andrew—"

"Wait." He held up a hand, then pulled open drawer after drawer, making a mess of the contents.

I spied my clothes on the back of the desk chair. Should I get dressed as well? When I slept in Andrew's room, I slept naked. The heating system in the century old building only had two settings, off and hot. Hot avoided hypothermia. But right now, being nude put me at a distinct disadvantage.

Caught between keeping tonight's sushi down and making a run for the room I shared with my longtime roommate Daisy, I remained immobile.

Satisfied with whatever he'd found, Andrew stopped moving. Sometime in the last minute while I'd been planning my escape, he'd added a sport coat to his ensemble.

I made a quiet study of my feet, flexing them and mapping out the metatarsals and phalanges. It was never too early to get a start on Gross Anatomy. I'd heard it was the hardest course.

"Ri, babe." Andrew's voice was tentative, which wasn't at all like him. I looked up, then down. He was on one knee. A navy blue velvet box in his right hand.

The shakes started then. I put my hands in front of my mouth, stifling both the scream and the dinner that threatened to erupt.

Andrew shook his head. "I totally planned to do this a different way when I asked Mom for Grandma Maude's ring. Me and the Spizz have been practicing for weeks. But here goes: Nari Yoon, will you marry me?" He'd sang the last in his smooth baritone. I imagined the *a capella* group practiced a three-part harmony for this moment.

I swallowed. Tears leaked onto my hands. Then I nodded. With each bob of my head I became progressively more certain. This is what I'd wanted when Andrew had come for me tonight. When I'd picked through dinner, looking for fully cooked fish. When I'd made love to him.

"Yes. Of course. Yes," I said.

"I know we're young," he said.

"Yes," I said again.

"But my parents had us in their twenties, and I'm here today," Andrew continued.

Why was he still talking?

"My brother and I turned out—"

"I said yes, Andrew."

He stopped speaking and lifted me into the air, duvet and all. For a moment I was flying, then he tackled me back onto the bed. Then we were kissing all over again.

"That's why you weren't worried about USC," I said when we came up for air.

Andrew's navy wool clad shoulder lifted and dropped.

I wanted to cry with relief. "I've been worried for months that you were going to dump me at the end of the year."

"Nari. Never. I love you so much. I thought you knew that." Mingled with the happiness in his voice was hurt at my lack of faith.

"I did. I do," I said, smoothing over the bump quickly. "It's just that you never mentioned anything about marriage."

"I wanted this to be a surprise. The Spizz. A serenade. You deserved all of that."

I'd have loved the other. What girl wouldn't? But this was okay too. This was just us. Andrew had slipped the small diamond on my finger. "I'd planned to follow you to wherever you needed to go," he had said, full of youthful confidence in the future.

It had been the happiest moment of my life.

Bolstered by Andrew's faith in us, I had even been nearly ready to have that conversation with my parents. That conversation where I talked about going to Penn instead of my dad's alma mater. The conversation where I finally told them how serious I was about Andrew and how a future with him was nearly as important as pursuing medicine.

I'd still have to have that talk, but it would be supported by an engagement...and a baby. Self-consciously I'd patted my still flat stomach. Maybe I'd save the baby for later and let them get used to the engagement first.

Quickly, before I lost my nerve, I flipped through the rest of the scrapbook, the memories bittersweet. Thank God I hadn't known then what was to come. I arranged my legs into a crisscross position, braced my hands on my knees, and let the memories take me away once more.

An hour later, I blew out the candles, tucked the albums carefully in my carry-on bag, and opened the curtain. I'd survived another year without him. It was time for some retail therapy.

4 Lucas

"I give 'em the meds," Dr. Rami said. We were sitting in the hotel lounge in full sight of every guest coming and going.

"How do you justify that?" I asked, only half focusing on him, although he sat right in front of me.

"They're only going to doctor hop. Maybe this way, I can keep an eye on them. I'm talking zolpidem and alprazolam, not oxycodone," he said defensively.

Shapely legs and glossy bags turned my head. Nari, saucer-sized sunglasses firmly in place, white dress setting off her tan skin, swished into the lobby. I looked down at the shopping bags again. Well, she didn't go cheap. I might be new to the west coast, but I recognized the sheen of ultra high end boutique bags. Nari had them in spades.

Forgetting my manners and Dr. Rami, I rose and moved toward her like moth to flame.

"Let me help you," I offered, matching her pace.

Closer up, I could see her eyes through the dark lenses. Warmth was not the word I'd use to describe the emotions radiating from them. "Got it," she said, not breaking her stride.

Tripping over my feet, I tried to keep up with her. "Going up?" I asked when we reached the gleaming brass elevator doors.

At her barely perceptible nod, I pushed the up arrow call button. I followed her into the empty elevator and pushed '14' for her floor. She didn't protest, so I picked up the bags when she dropped them to wrestle the key card from her tiny purse, covered in a rainbow of designer logos.

"I don't really need—"

I was determined to do this one thing for her. So I pushed through the door and put the bags on the floor by the bed. What the hell? I'd never seen so many half burned red candles. Each wick was dark. How had she not set off the fire alarms? Her room smelled like an apple pie had exploded.

For a single moment, jealousy shot through me like an arrow. She hadn't gotten it on with another guy in here, had she? I looked around. Nah, this wasn't seduction. It was something else entirely. Had she done a human sacrifice in here? Was she Wiccan or what?

"Thanks for your help." Her cool voice penetrated the fog in my brain. I was being dismissed for the second time that day. But I wanted answers before I was banished this time.

"Are you okay?" I asked. My hand did a Vanna White flourish encompassing all the half-burned candles in a single gesture.

"Fine, Lucas. Burning candles won't cause cancer."

With a sigh, she sat, her back ramrod straight on the white chaise. Nari pushed the glasses on top of her head. For the first time I looked at her closely. Her eyes were bloodshot. Fine lines kissed the corners. Smudges of fatigue lined her lower lids. For someone who never had a hair out of place, it was telling. I didn't know though, what I should be gleaning from it.

"Last night didn't go the way I'd planned," I started. Matching her posture, I took a seat on the accompanying love seat. I sat up straight, hands braced on the pillows at my side in case she changed her mind and wanted me out quickly.

A small smirk played around her lips. "What *did* you plan?"

"I didn't plan anything. Wait, that's not what I wanted to say. I...didn't plan for us to end up in bed together...at least, not last night."

"What if I did, Lucas?"

"Did what?"

"Plan to end up in bed. I'm not a helpless victim. I went down to the bar looking to get laid. I never meant to sleep with a colleague, but the rum ruined my judgment, I guess."

Like a punch in the gut, her answer hit me. Preconceived notions flew from my head. "You were planning to have sex with anyone?"

She pulled her sunglasses from her hair and carelessly threw them on the table. Rhinestones glinted in the sunlight streaming through the windows. The sparkling blue waves stood in sharp contrast to the gray mood in the room.

Her sigh was world-weary. "Yes."

I looked around to see if I had walked into an alternate universe. Everything about this was a little bit off. Conservative Nari Yoon who minded her manners and was nice to nurses had been looking to get laid. Her formerly pristine hotel room was littered with half burned candles as if she'd adopted an unknown religion. Her normally immaculate appearance was frayed around the edges.

I tried to gather my straying thoughts into one coherent picture. "So you were looking to sleep with anyone who wandered by?"

"That's about the size of it, Lucas. I needed to blow off some steam. A convention full of oversexed doctors didn't seem a bad place to start. At least I wouldn't have to convince them that a condom was a good idea."

Because like everyone else, it had been drilled into my head that a barrier method was the least any sexually active couple should do. But she'd have been sexually active with or without me.

I needed to get out of there. This was going nothing like I'd expected. On the ride up here, I'd been wishing that maybe we'd talk, get to know each other, share a meal. Maybe fool around again. At that moment, though, I realized my fantasy Nari had little to do with the real woman in front of me.

"I have to stop confusing expectation and reality," I said.

"Come again?"

"Nothing." I rose. I'd flown to Hawaii to learn about medical advances and find my parents. Maybe I needed to get back to my original plan. "Have a good rest of the conference, Nari."

"Thanks for understanding." Relief softened the body she had held rigid. If she really wanted me gone, I would go. "See you Monday?"

I needed to get the hell out of here.

I nodded. On Monday we'd be colleagues again, nothing more. Then I turned and headed for the door, all the while wondering how in the hell I'd misjudged that so badly.

5 NARI

Three months later

Turning my second bedroom into a full-sized closet and dressing room had been the best decorating idea I had ever devised. Rolling garment and shoe racks made getting dressed a breeze. I took a final glance in the full length, three-way mirror of my dressing room.

Hair. Check.

Fingernails and toenails. Check.

Not that my appearance mattered much. Asian woman plus L.A. bar equaled hookup. Every. Single. Time. That math was easier than anything I'd tackled in college.

After knocking back three glasses of Chamisul soju in quick succession, I was ready. By the time I made it down the elevator and covered the half mile to the bar on Melrose on three and a quarter inch heels, I was feeling pretty damned good.

The red wine I ordered as I got comfortable at the bar was an attempt to look modest and demure while the soju went straight to my head, making me less of each of those things.

I relaxed my face. I tried to make it stern and serious during work, now replacing it with a smile, and soon a man approached me. I was tempted to look at my watch and see how many minutes I'd been there for comparison's sake, but I resisted. Especially since the hand lifting the watch was none too steady at the moment.

"Tim," he said. I shook his outstretched hand. Grip firm. So far, so good.

Since I wasn't marrying him, I sized up Tim for what I needed—a night of wall-banging sex. He topped out at an even six feet probably. If I stood, he'd be about eye to eye with me in my wedge sandals. That could work.

"Nari." I introduced myself. "Where are you from?" I asked. Native Californians were more rare than diamonds.

"Texas," he said. "Out here trying to get into the business, you know."

Yes, I knew. Of course I knew. Every other person who'd come out here was trying to get into entertainment. It was stiffer competition than medical school.

"You?" he said.

"I work at a doctor's office." I was careful not to lie. I didn't dumb myself down to get laid, exactly. But doctor wasn't sexy to anyone. Paper pushing, insurance processing back office girl was bland enough that everyone glossed over it like I wanted.

"Where are *you* from?" Tim asked. Could I take that drawl in the middle of sex? Would he call out "howdy" when he came? I tried not to let my eyes stray around the bar. Eliminating prospects one at a time was the best method. I'd learned that from experience. Sometimes I was amazed at the number of things twenty years of schooling glossed over.

"Riverside," I said. If he hadn't been here too long, he wouldn't think too poorly of my unglamorous Inland Empire roots.

"No, really," he said. "Where are you *from?*" I stopped twirling my wine glass in my hand and sat it on the cocktail napkin on the bar. Strike one. Tim was out. It was too early and I wasn't desperate enough to give him two more chances.

"Fort Lee, New Jersey." My voice was flat. "If you'll excuse me," I said like I'd seen someone I was meeting. Tim wandered off back to a group of guys in the corner. I turned my back to the room, ordered another glass of wine. After drinking about half, I turned again, making another survey of the bar area.

I nearly toppled my wine when I saw a lean guy with dirty blond hair sidle up to the bar. The resemblance to Andrew couldn't be overlooked. When he looked down the bar, I raised my hand in salute. Craft beer in hand, he approached. One point for a halfway decent drink choice.

"Nari," I said.

"Perry," he shook his head ruefully, laughing. A cowlick popped up in the front of his head. "Forrest."

Resisting the urge to smooth back the bump of hair, I laughed along with him. "Is it Perry Forrest or Forrest Perry?"

"First name's Forrest," he said.

"That's a lot of 'Rs.'"

"Sure is. My parents were pirates."

The joke was all kinds of preschool silly, but after five drinks I couldn't stop laughing for a good two minutes. Forrest of the four "Rs" didn't even blink an eye at my high-pitched snort. Another point for the Andrew doppelganger.

With a wave of my hand, I gestured for him to sit on the empty bar stool next to me. He took the invitation. "You here alone tonight?" I asked.

"I'm supposed to meet my friend Jason. He's running late. Should I cancel on him?"

Forthright, I really liked that. Another point. He was up to three. Five and I'd take him home. I nodded. Signaling the hostess, I said, "Join me for dinner."

Forrest Perry of the four Rs looked like he'd won the lottery. I held out my hand and he did the right thing, helping me down from the stool, keeping his hand at the small of my back, guiding me to the intimate table for two at the edge of the bar the hostess had indicated. I held out my hand again. He took it, lifted me back on another stool. Another point for chivalry. Warm tingles went up my spine. This Andrew look-alike was doing mighty fine.

"Want to split antipasti?" he said, glancing at the menu.

"That would be perfect," I said. The waitress took our orders for meatballs, calamari, burrata and another glass of wine for me.

When the server walked away, I had to satisfy my curiosity. Find out how big a cradle I'd be robbing. "How old are you?"

Forrest looked down, pink rising in his cheeks. Ah, a young one. "Twenty-four," he said.

A seven-year age difference wasn't so bad. He'd have stamina, if not skill, that's for sure. Plus, after an hour, give or take, I realized he was funny, and kind of sweet. He'd earned the full five points two times over. I leaned forward, ready to make the offer of a single night he'd never forget, when a big hand landed on my shoulder.

"Dr. Yoon, fancy meeting you here."

I turned, seeking the source of the deep voice. Lucas was standing right behind me, three other guys in tow. If they were filming an ad for cargo shorts, there would be no need to go outside the bar for casting. I hadn't seen so many variants on khaki and bulging pockets since I'd left New England.

"You're a doctor?" Forrest went from confident to intimidated very fast. Damn, he was losing points by the second. I didn't want this one to slip through my fingers. I didn't have the time nor sobriety to search for another prospect.

"This is my colleague, Dr. Lucas Tucker. I'm sure he and his friends will be getting dinner in the restaurant very soon." Far, far away from me and Forrest, I wanted to add.

Thank God Lucas got the hint and stopped the round robin introductions in their tracks. He and his little entourage made their exit from the bar area, crossing over to a noisy and crowded area full of rough-hewn tables and well heeled patrons. Time to get my own show on the road.

"So," I leaned forward. I didn't have much in the way of cleavage, but the low cut maxi dress put all I had on full display. "What do you think of—"

"Do you have a moment, Dr. Yoon?" Lucas? Again? He was like a bad penny. I turned around and sure enough, there was my giant blond colleague. The inside flap of my childhood book of Norse mythology, that's what he reminded me of. Momentarily distracted from my profound annoyance, I wondered where the curly hair had come from. They didn't have a lot of curls in Scandinavia, did they? Maybe one day I'd ask. Out of purely scientific genetic interest, of course.

"What do you need, Dr. Tucker?"

"It's a bit of a clinic emergency," he said. "It'll only take a moment. Then you and—"

"Forrest," the kid supplied on cue.

"Forrest can get back to...whatever."

"Fine," I snapped. "Let's step outside."

Lucas steered me through the thickening happy hour crowd toward Melrose Avenue. Late model cars as shiny as the day they came off the assembly line streamed by.

"What are you doing in there?" Lucas asked.

"Excuse me," I tried to fill my voice with as much incredulity as I could after six drinks.

"I asked—"

"I heard you. Since your name is not on my birth certificate, I'm wondering exactly how it's any business of yours."

"First it was that guy, Colin in Kauai, and now it's this guy on Melrose."

"Is this a safe sex talk? Because as you may remember, I have condoms covered." I turned toward the traffic paused and idling at a stoplight, and away from whatever emotion had made him wince.

"You were going to have sex with that guy? He's what, ten minutes out of high school."

"You're harshing my buzz. Good night, Lucas." I took a single step towards the bar before I felt a single hand on my upper arm. I turned, ready to face an assault charge.

"I'll go with you," he said.

"Go where?"

"Home. That's where you were taking the whippersnapper, right?"

I laughed then. I could hear that my pitch was slightly askew. And my laugh was an unattractive half-drunken snort of a laugh. I could hear how ridiculous I sounded, but couldn't stop even with both my hands in front of my mouth. "Whippersnapper? What are you, sixty?"

"I'm serious," he said.

My laughter ceased immediately. Something tingled between my legs "What about Forrest?"

"Who?"

"My date?"

Lucas handed a claim ticket to a valet along with a small fold of bills. "Wait here."

For the first two minutes, I wanted nothing more to go back in there and pick up with Forrest where I'd left off. I was violating a lot of hard and fast rules. Some mine, some society's. I never did the same guy twice. Anyone with half a brain wouldn't do their colleague. What was that stupid saying, don't shit….

I couldn't shake the last part from my alcohol-soaked brain before a lime green Subaru drove up to the street. Of course he'd drive something like that. It was my second guess. My first had been a used Volvo wagon. Both had been popular with cargo pants and Timberland-wearing guys when I'd been in college. I'd met more outdoor en-thusiasts in Olde Haven than I'd ever met in L.A. with its picture perfect weather. Ignoring life's ironies, I watched Lucas emerge from the restaurant door alone.

He exchanged a folded bill for the keys from the valet and opened the passenger door. I slipped in with as much grace as I could muster.

Even with all the early evening traffic and stoplights, it took Lucas no less than ten minutes to get to my house. I produced a garage door opener from my purse and the huge iron gate pivoted open. Three minutes and one elevator ride later, we were in my apartment.

Lucas pocketed his keys and stood in the living area, looking a little helpless. I didn't know what he was nervous about. I was a sure thing. *I* was the one who should be nervous. I never did the same guy twice. I hoped he didn't think this was some kind of prelude to a relationship. I didn't do boyfriends. Ah, hell, he really had dulled my buzz.

Needed to fix that first. Leaving him standing and twirling, I pulled the soju from the fridge. Got two glasses from a cabinet. First I poured one for him. I left my own glass empty.

I wandered into the kitchen and sat on a stool. The untouched drink lingered in front of him.

"You put two hands around it and drink it in a single shot," I instructed.

He did. "Now you pour for me." He did. I downed it, not ashamed to rub away the alcohol on my lips with the back of my hand.

"Why were you going to bring that guy here?"

I rolled my eyes in a way that said *ob-vi-ous*. But he didn't rise to that bait. Damn. Here goes, I thought, letting the soju act as a truth serum. "To forget," I answered truthfully.

"What are you trying to forget?"

Now that, I wasn't going to answer. "Something I don't want to remember."

6 LUCAS

Nari stood up. With two flicks of her wrists, the silky tie-dyed dress pooled on the floor. She stood before me in the skimpiest underwear I'd ever seen, her shoes, and nothing more. My inner fifteen-year-old wanted to stand and clap.

My thirty-something-year-old self cursed softly, but hopefully under my breath. When I'd intercepted whatever was going on between Nari and the twenty-something guy she'd been breaking bread with, I promised myself, I wouldn't have sex with her. Not again. Or at least not without dinner, a date, a talk–something.

When I'd pulled her from the restaurant, and when I'd guided her into the car and entered her garage, and even when I'd rode the elevator up to her apartment, I promised myself each and every step of the way that this wouldn't happen again. Yet here I was, primed and ready. Unable to control my lizard brain response.

I had only been trying to save her from making a mistake I was sure she'd regret. Plus, how did she know that guy wasn't some serial killer, some stranger she was going to invite to her bedroom? Forrest could have stuffed her into a garbage bag and the murder case would have remained unsolved forever.

But when Nari turned and strutted from the room, I forgot that I was trying to be a savior. Instead, I turned into as big a predator as the other guy. Calling myself all kinds of an asshole, I had no choice but to follow the hard dick in my pants. It was as if the damned thing had a mind of its own.

By the time I got to the bedroom, a study in white from the walls to the rug to the duvet, she was sitting on the edge of the bed, carefully unstrapping her shoes. First one fell to the rug with a soft thud, then the other. I must have been closer to temptation than I thought, because all Nari had to do was reach out her hand to slide the belt buckle from the loop.

"Nari, this isn't why I came here," I managed to say in protest, making one last-ditch attempt at chivalry. But all bets were off when her hand came to my fly and the noise of my zipper parting filled the room.

My shorts, heavy with a brass compass, hiking map, keys and wallet fell to the floor with little resistance. Reflexively I stepped from them, damming the hiking boots that made it difficult to disrobe. Her fingers were in my boxers. In an instant, all thoughts of talking or putting her to bed poured from my mind like water from a colander.

Two hours later with her snoring softly next to me, I called myself ten times a fool. Why was I trying so hard to save someone who didn't want to be saved?

My altimeter watch read ten. I was sober and in my colleague's bed—again. My pants did a shimmy on the carpet. A quiet buzzing filled the room. Damn it, my phone. I'd said a hasty good-bye to my hiking buddies. Maybe they wanted to catch up. Careful not to disturb Nari, I rolled from the bed and retrieved my shorts from the floor.

I pulled on my boxers and walked down the hall to the living room.

"Hello," I answered, keeping my voice low.

My mom's soft voice greeted me. I patted my bare chest. Somehow I wished I could jump into my clothes as quickly as Superman. At least I had on underwear.

"Are you on a date?" she asked.

How should I answer that? Say no, and I was in for a long family chat with the phone passing between my mom and dad. If I said yes, then they'd get their hopes up for marriage and grandchildren. Two drunken hookups didn't exactly make *that* a possibility.

"Lucas? Are you there?"

"I'm here, Mom." I sat on the couch, resigned to ninety minutes of Vermont gossip.

Somewhere between high school politics and university shenanigans, Nari must have entered the room.

"Who are you talking to?"

I nearly dropped the phone. Nari had come in noiselessly. Her hair was in disarray around her shoulders. Wrapped in a long white silk bathrobe and not much else. My stomach did a little flip flop. Maybe all the talk of high school and college was making me feel like a teenager again, in my pants and in my judgment.

"Is that a woman at your house, Lucas?" my mother asked.

"I'm not home."

"Oh...oh. Why didn't you say something?"

"I think you should hang up now, Joyce." I heard my father in the background. Dad must have taken the phone from my mom because all I heard after that was silence.

"Your parents?" Nari raised an eyebrow on her way to the kitchen. She pulled open the fridge and pulled out a large Britta pitcher. A glass appeared from the cabinet and she filled it to the brim, surface tension the only thing keeping it from spilling.

A thin trickle snaked its way down her neck, making the robe partially see-through. I tossed the phone on the table and tried to look anywhere but at her.

Even without watching her, I could feel her cool and assessing gaze on me.

"Your mom calls to check up on you?"

I turned toward her again. There was none of the snark or sarcasm I'd expected with that comment.

"She's up all times of day and night working on dyes. She loved to call me when I was in residency because I was never asleep either. Habit she can't break, I think."

Nari opened the refrigerator again. Poured herself another glass of water, and perched on a kitchen stool. "Did you say dye? Like color?"

I nodded. "She spins wool into yarn and dyes it for her students. She also does silk."

"Is she some kind of art teacher?"

"Yeah. She loves those kids."

"Did you get the art genes?"

My heart sped up, then slowed down in rapid succession. Why did those kinds of questions still throw me after thirty years? They were innocent enough. No one was pointing a finger at me, singling me out. I did not have a scarlet "A" tattooed on my head that said my parents had picked me up at the airport or church or wherever they'd retrieved me from. She couldn't know the mother she asked about hadn't birthed me from her womb. I cued in to Nari's quizzical gaze and realized I'd probably been quiet far too long.

"I'm adopted. My genetic makeup is a mystery." I tried to smile like it was a joke. But neither of us were laughing.

Nari was quiet for a long time. Her assessing look was back.

"Go home, Lucas."

For a single interminable minute, I wondered if she was rejecting me because my biological parents hadn't raised me. But that was ridiculous. "What about—"

"There's nothing to talk about, Lucas." She stood, paced around the small table, then took up the same seat she'd just vacated. Nari bowed her head. She shook it from left to right, her hair hiding her face. Pulling a band from her wrist, she did that magical girl thing I'd seen my sister do a thousand times. One minute Nari's hair was on her shoulders, the next it was up in some kind of bun thing. "This is why I never do the same guy twice," she said.

The comment was like a slap in the face. I couldn't help rearing back. "I thought...I hoped." Truth sputtered out.

"Stop, Lucas. Please stop. If you hadn't sent the Kauai guy away—"

"His name was Colin—"

"Or the young one from tonight."

"I didn't get his name—"

"Forrest. What did you say to make them go away?" she asked matter-of-factly.

"I told them we'd fought and you were trying to make me jealous."

"Oh, God." She hit her forehead with a fist once, then again, then again. "Why?"

"You were going to sleep with him, right?"

She shook her head. For a long moment, I thought maybe I'd gotten it all wrong. "Sleep isn't quite what I was planning to do." A rare small smile escaped. Odd that I was awash in vindication.

"It seemed like a bad idea," I said. "I didn't want a stranger to take advantage of you."

"So it was okay if you took advantage?" she asked.

"No." This was going all wrong. I'd done the honorable thing, right? "I was trying to keep you safe from randy doctors and possible mass murderers," I justified.

"You achieved one of those."

I cursed my fair skin that was no doubt becoming ruddier by the minute. "I like you, Nari." There. I'd put it out there. No more beating around the bush. Half of my brain had been thinking that I didn't want her to get hurt shagging random guys. But the other half of me had taken advantage of the opportunity that I was sure was down the dating road a ways.

"Okay."

She wasn't going to make this easy. I was starting to think that nothing about this woman was easy. "Will you go out to dinner with me next Friday?"

"No," she said without hesitation, almost without thought.

Caught up short, I scratched at the hair on my chest. "No for next Friday, or never?"

"Never, Lucas. I don't think I led you on."

"So you were going to have two one-night stands?"

"Yes."

I wasn't an idiot. Objectively I'd known that. But I'd wanted to think she'd slept with me for a reason other than being horny. "Are you going to...I don't know...go out to a bar next week?" Why did I think she'd only done this twice? I was so naïve. The rules were clearly different in California. New England felt like a completely different planet.

"No Lucas, not next week. Please don't worry about me." She raised her hands as if she were swearing out an oath. "I promise I'll be celibate for the next nine months."

I should have listened when she'd told me to go home. "I'm going to get my stuff," I said, lifting myself from the couch and heading back to the bedroom. Shoving my hiking crap in my pockets, I pulled on my cargo shorts, shirt, wool socks, hiking boots. When I emerged from her very white bedroom, Nari hadn't moved an inch.

I jingled the keys in my pocket. "Do you need a ride to your car?"

"I walked to the bar. Drinking and driving is a big no-no for me," she said.

Something wasn't quite right about this picture. She was clearly comfortable with her sexuality, and confident in her ability to land a guy. But why was it a different guy every time? Didn't most women want relationships? To nest? Except for the white lab coat she wore at work, she wasn't any different than most women, right?

"Is it just me, or do you date anyone?" I wanted to kill myself right then. I'd emasculated myself with that needy question. She didn't want me. Why didn't I pick up my car keys and get the hell home?

I was an Ivy League-educated doctor. The list of women willing to give me a shot wasn't short, by any means. My medical school classmates certainly had their pick of mates even if they didn't have the time to date. But my parents had always focused on the importance of leisure and a life outside of work. So I'd picked a nearly nine to five specialty. I'd always wanted to have a serious relationship. And foolishly I'd thought Nari a candidate.

Her sigh was long, drawn out. "I don't date."

My hand was on the door, but I didn't want to go home with this mystery unsolved. "Why?"

Nari's head snapped up. The way she smiled then, it was as if a light were coming from inside her. It was the most beautiful I'd ever seen her. "Oh," she started as if she were answering a question as easy as what a patient's vitals were on rounds. "I'm in love with someone."

7 NARI

I had a single *kimbap* slice at my lips when a knock came at the office door. Without waiting for an invitation, Lucas entered, brown bag in hand. I put down my chopsticks when my hand shook a little with a quick surge of heart-pumping adrenaline.

"Can I join you?" he asked from the doorway.

I looked right, then left dramatically. "I don't think there are any men you need to save me from in here."

A small smile ticked up both sides of his mouth. He leaned back toward the hall and looked both ways. "I promise to stay the hell out of your sex life," he said. "Seriously, though. It's been awkward the last few days around here. I'd really like everything to go back to the way it used to be. Can we be at least amicable colleagues, maybe friends?" He lifted a single shoulder in question.

For a reason I couldn't quite pinpoint, that amicable friends idea bothered me. I mentally brushed away the feeling. "Sure," I said. "Friends." I extended my hand. He came in and shook solemnly.

After closing the door behind him, he sat in one of the chairs I usually reserved for patients in imminent receipt of bad news, and pulled out his lunch. From the looks of it, he had a large ham and cheese sub, an apple and a brownie. It was so all-American I had to laugh.

"What so funny?" he asked, opening his bottled water and taking a swig.

"I don't know," I said, shaking my head. "The brown paper bag and the food is just so you."

His brow furrowed, but he unwrapped and took a bite of his sandwich anyway. "What do you have there?" he asked after chewing and swallowing a few bites.

"Kimbap, kimchi, chapchae," I answered.

Lucas looked uncomfortable for a long second. "Is it okay if I ask you what all that is?" His naïveté was kind of endearing. It was a far cry from the know-it-all Los Angeles guys I was used to. Single guys in this town loved to lecture me on the history of Japan or Korea as if being born in New Jersey made me ignorant about Asia. I could never tell if it was supposed to be some kind of pickup maneuver or if I were being condescended to. I didn't really care to figure it out.

"*Kimbap* are the rolls. It's like Korean sushi," I said, cringing inwardly. My mom would have smacked the back of my hand if she'd heard that answer. My parents hated being compared to the Japanese as if Korea didn't have a distinct and arguably more influential culture. "The *kimchi* is cabbage fermented with red peppers, and *chapchae* is vegetables and rice noodles."

After taking and swallowing two more bites of his sub, he looked longingly at her plate. "Can I—"

I swiveled in my seat and pulled a small paper plate from my desk drawer. I gave him a bit of everything and an extra pair of disposable chopsticks. Game face on, he did the best he could with the chopsticks, and tried everything. "This is good," he said, rapidly cleaning the plate despite nearly dropping his utensils more than once. "Wanna switch lunches?"

"Nope, I had my fair share of mayonnaise heavy sandwiches in high school."

"You didn't eat like that in school?" he asked, gesturing toward her container. "That had to be better than school lunches any day."

"I went through a phase where I was kind of embarrassed at how Korean my family was," I said matter-of-factly.

"I kind of had a phase like that," he said.

"Seriously? Or are you just trying to empathize?" I asked.

"No, seriously. I told you how I was adopted, right?"

I put down my chopsticks for the second time since he'd breached my inner sanctum. My stomach churned a little. Appetite, gone. "Sure," I said, the word almost sticking in my throat.

"I went to the high school my mom taught at," he said. "It was really cool when I was in nursery, kindergarten, even the lower grades. But by the time I got to middle school, kids' powers of observation were much better. Or they'd paid attention through Medellin genetics. At one time or another, every single person asked me how a tall curly-haired kid had come from such short brown-haired parents."

"You were a tall kid?"

"I eclipsed my mother by the time I was ten, my dad by fifteen."

"How big was this school?"

"Probably three hundred kids."

"In how many grades?"

"Nursery through high school."

"Jesus, no anonymity there. Was it a religious school or something?"

"No, Waldorf."

"Is that the guy who doesn't believe in children reading?"

"Rudolf Steiner? Not exactly. I was literate enough to make it through college and medical school."

"Ah, yeah. Sorry about that. My high school probably had sixteen hundred kids, easy."

"I really liked the school, otherwise," he said. "Once I told them I was adopted, the subject was dropped."

There it was again, that word. Adopted. I quickly searched my mind for a way to change the subject. I was about to launch into gossip about the pharmaceutical rep, a dead ringer for a Dallas Cowboys cheerleader, when Lucas started talking again.

"I'm thinking about looking for my birth mother," he said.

Okay. Wow. There was no way to back out of this. I lifted my gaze from the chopsticks I'd been fiddling with. He was looking at me, waiting for a reaction. I'd hidden the real one long ago. What should I put on my face?

Even though I wasn't hungry, I picked up some kimchi and stuffed it in my mouth. I washed it down with a long drink of green tea. After all that, he was back to eating, but still looking at me. Lucas reminded her of a cocker spaniel, from the curly golden hair to the look of open neediness dogs had a knack for. Looked like he didn't have anyone to talk to about this.

"Thinking about or actually doing?" I finally managed.

"A little bit of both. I met with a lawyer in Hawaii who was able to get me a copy of my birth certificate," he said.

I made a huge effort to control my inhalation, exhalation. "What about privacy laws? The state just handed over your birth parents' names?" Please let him say that they couldn't do that.

"No, I wasn't that lucky," he said. My breathing eased just a little. "Their names and identifying information were blacked out." Normal, my breathing was almost normal again. Some secrets were meant to stay that way.

"What's your next step?" I asked. My voice was nearly conversational. He didn't know me well enough to tell the difference.

"I'll have to talk to my parents. I need to find out where I was adopted."

"That seems easy enough," I said cautiously.

"Well, yeah, sort of."

"Did you tell them you're looking for your parents?"

"Birth parents, and yeah, I mentioned it at Christmas. They said they supported me, but seemed nervous all the same. And my brother and sister have each asked me not to bring it up again."

"Brother and sister? They're not adopted as well?" I paused. "Sorry if that's too intrusive." I was used to asking intimate and personal questions about fifteen times a day. Sometimes I forgot that a person couldn't do it in casual conversation.

"It's okay. I brought it up," he said. Big sigh. "After they adopted me, Mom got pregnant with my sister then brother in rapid succession." Lucas fished his phone from his pocket, flicked at the screen and leaned forward.

I peered at the tiny faces. Damn, he was right. It was like a game of What Doesn't Belong from Sesame Street.

Panic nearly closed my throat a second time. Taking as deep a breath as I could without appearing to do so, I pushed out the question burning in my brain. "So why do you want to find your birth parents? Your mom sounds awesome. You probably had all sorts of craft projects in your kitchen." Because craft projects made up for a mom leaving a swaddled baby on a church doorstep.

"My family *is* awesome. They love me. I don't doubt that. It's hard to explain, but it's just, something's missing. I want to see the people who look like me. Find out why they gave me up."

"If they didn't do an open adoption, maybe they don't want to be found."

"There was a statistic in this book the lawyer gave me that said ninety-five percent of birth mothers would like to reunite with their children."

What about that five percent, I wanted to shout. Weren't they worthy of consideration? Instead my question was calm. "Can I give you some unsolicited advice?"

"I've doled out my share. Shoot."

I thought carefully before I spoke, trying to get the phrasing just right. "Women's lives are complicated. Pregnancies only happen to them. Be careful. It could be a Pandora's box you're opening up."

Lucas nodded, but didn't look dissuaded. I handed the rest of my lunch over to him, my appetite long gone. He quickly abandoned his food for mine. "You want my apple? Brownie?" he asked between bites and a lot of sips of water.

"No, I'm good," I said, shifting the patient files around on my desk. I thought he'd taken the hint when he packed away his lunch remains in the paper bag. But he made no move to leave. He sat forward, his hands hanging loosely between his legs. I closed my eyes for a long moment trying not to think about what else lay between those thighs.

"What?" I asked finally. Damned open book his face was. They were on their way back to her unorthodox sex life.

"How does your, um, boyfriend feel about your, um, bar hopping?" he whispered, leaning forward. The walls in the clinic were thin, but at his volume no one would hear the question. I was oddly grateful for his discretion.

"Boyfriend?" I asked in reply. I'd never told him I had a boyfriend. I was as single as a mateless sock fresh from the dryer.

"Oh, I get it. I'm sorry. It was a brush-off." He started to rise then. The open face closed with hurt and disappointment. I didn't want him to think I'd lied. That I didn't do with people I cared about. Not that I cared about him more than a friend, of course. I rose and tugged at his free hand, making him face me again.

"Oh, you mean Andrew. No, no, no. That wasn't a brush-off. I wouldn't lie about that."

Disappointment and hurt turned to confusion. "So where's Andrew?"

I dropped his hand and looked toward my window, blinking back tears. "He's dead."

8 LUCAS

I closed my laptop browser. The book Nida Vara had given me suggested several high trafficked websites where I could register my particulars and seek out my birth parents. But I hit a wall every single time I scrolled down the past the box that asked for my current name and e-mail.

I had my date of birth and location, but beyond that, I was in the dark. I felt stupid when I realized I didn't even know what state I was adopted in. My dad had worked in New Hampshire for as long as I could remember. But my parents had always lived in Vermont—probably. Slamming down the metal lid in frustration, I cracked my knuckles. I didn't have half of the information I needed.

I rolled the chair away from the desk and looked out the modern government edifices and helipads that surrounded my place. The apartment in the 1899 building had been a rare find. I loved the living quarters, if not the location.

The "heart of downtown" had seemed brilliant when I'd made the weeklong trip to find a place to live. I'd lived in the heart of downtown Brooklyn during my residency and had loved it. In Los Angeles, though, I may as well have been in no man's land. Spring Street was not a happening place for a single doctor.

Putting aside the mystery of my birth for a moment, I thought about my love life, such as it was. I flipped open the laptop again and went to the clinic's website. I typed in Nari's name, and there was her picture. My heart sped up a little faster. She was smiling at the camera in her white lab coat, the clinic's logo emblazoned above her left breast. I tried not to think of her left breast, or the right one for that matter. She was pining for someone who died, who she still loved? There was no way I could compete with that. I rolled back and forth on the chair's casters for a solid fifteen minutes of indecision.

If my life was full of roadblocks, it was time to knock one down. I rolled back to the desk and lifted the handset of the cordless phone from its base.

"Hey, Dad," I said when I heard my father's voice come on the line.

"You want to talk to your mom?"

I almost said yes then thought better of it. Maybe this would go down easier with my dad. Matthew Tucker had always been the more dispassionate of my parents. The horrors of human history had probably done that to him.

"I wanted to ask you a couple of questions. No need to bring Mom to the phone."

"Oh, okay." My dad's voice was hesitant, something that was unusual. Professor Tucker hadn't been a yeller or a rager like other dads I'd met. But as a long-tenured history professor at Dartmouth, he had a way of getting his point across.

"I need to know about my birth and adoption."

My dad's sigh was long. I could hear the springs of the old wooden desk chair creak. "Let me close the door," he said, placing the phone down. I could practically see my dad gently laying the old corded phone down and rising to close the office door of his wood-paneled study.

The pool table green carpet would be muffling the sound of his preferred footwear, top-siders if he'd been outside today or moccasin slippers if he'd been working in his office. The clunk of wood as door hit jamb, then the sound of my dad's wedding ring clicked against the plastic receiver. "I don't want your mom to hear this if she doesn't have to. She's having a hard enough time as it is."

Guilt made my heart thud. "It's not about you guys. I love you and am glad that you took me in," I said. My paltry reassurance sounded awkward and distant, even to my own ears.

My dad's bark of a laugh was unusually harsh. "You weren't a kitten we rescued from under the porch, Lucas."

"Why did you adopt?" I asked for the first time. The story I'd been spoon-fed about them wanting a child to love and me needing parents wasn't enough anymore. It hadn't been enough for years, but I'd never had the guts to probe further. I pushed away my resistance and readied myself for the answer.

"Your mom and I were together for five years and she hadn't gotten pregnant," he explained. "Not for lack of trying."

I turned off the part of my brain that knew my parents had sex. The single biggest upside of being adopted is that I didn't even have to acknowledge they'd done it the one time it would have taken to produce me.

"In the late seventies, it wasn't like now with all the doctors and specialists and tests. Time and again, they told us to go home and try harder. Your mom had her heart set on a family of her own." My father didn't need to say any more about that. My mother's own mom had died when she was six. Joyce had been raised by her aunt and uncle, almost, but not quite belonging to her adopted family.

"When she started talking about adoption, it seemed like the perfect solution. We registered with an agency, and waited."

"How long did you wait?" I asked. Why had *I* waited so long to ask these questions?

"Not as long as we thought. We didn't care about gender, background or disability. So when they called and said there was a baby about to become available in Hawaii, we borrowed money from my parents and flew out there. A week later, we went to the hospital and picked you up."

The line was quiet. I had already heard some parts of the story. Like how they thought I was perfect. How they counted my fingers and toes. How they worried because they hadn't brought any cold weather clothes. How I'd cried for much of the return trip on three airplanes, with two layovers, one in Los Angeles, the other in Chicago.

But now that I was older, had seen babies born during my obstetrics rotation, I wondered if I'd cried because I was suddenly alone. Because their voices were different than the ones I'd heard for nine months. Because I'd been without the mother who'd been my lifelong companion up until then. Of course, I didn't share a single word of those thoughts. Instead I went for the pragmatic, the practical. I asked for the one thing my father could give me with the least effort.

"So I was born in Hawaii, right?" I wanted to confirm what I'd already pieced together on my own.

"Yes." Dad sighed. "A hospital on Kauai to be exact."

"Do you know which hospital?" I rushed on. I didn't want my father connecting the dots about the true purpose of my trip there in March.

"Veteran's Memorial."

"Did you meet my...birth parents?" I got my hopes up during the long moment of silence. Maybe finding them would be as easy as asking my father for their names.

"No. We didn't want to know. As far as we were concerned, you were ours the moment they handed you over."

I didn't push. I didn't have a right to. I switched gears, ready to fill in another gap in my knowledge. "In what state was I adopted?" I was hoping it was New Hampshire. From what I'd read in the book Nida Vara had given me, it was one of the states that was making it easier to link adoptees to their birth parents.

"Vermont."

My heart sank. "I thought you were living in New Hampshire back then."

"We were. But when we got serious about adopting, we bought that first house on Elm Street."

"Can you send me what information you have?" I asked.

My father was nothing if not orderly. Writing books about the Depression and the New Deal, he had to keep his research and notes organized. From my adolescent exploration in my dad's office, I'd found a stack of Playboy magazines, and a fire proof lockbox. Sneaking a couple of the former had been easy. I'd never figured out how to open the latter. The keys to my past probably laid in there next to passports and insurance records. "Dad?" I spoke into the faint static after getting no response.

"What do *you* have?"

"I don't even have my birth certificate." Because if I did, maybe I'd have known what state to start in.

"Didn't you get a passport?" my dad deflected.

"Mom got it for my junior year abroad. I never renewed it."

"Do you really have to do this? Your mother couldn't love you more if you were from her womb."

This kind of guilt trip should have worked, like it had when I was fifteen and asked questions, or even at twenty five when I was leaving medical school with more questions than answers about my own history. But I was thirty-five and no longer an easily distracted child.

"I need to do this, Dad. I'd appreciate your help, but if I have to I'll do it without."

The silence was longer this time. "I love Joyce, dearly," my dad said. "I'll think about this and let you know."

"I love you too, Dad," I said but didn't know if my dad had heard it before I was greeted by the unbroken monotonous sound of the dial tone.

For two weeks my phone was silent. I didn't hear a single thing from my mother, my father, or my siblings. I couldn't remember having ever gone that long without seeing, touching, or at least talking to them.

My phone messages and e-mails went unanswered. On this, yet another solitary Saturday, I sat in my office, trying to battle the feeling of abandonment that threatened to engulf me. My nuclear family had closed ranks based on blood and genetics. Two things they'd always told me didn't matter—suddenly did.

Turning on the computer, I got down to the business of reconstructing my life story, from the beginning. Two hours later, I'd started the ball rolling. I'd requested a copy of my birth certificate from Vermont's Vital Records department. In a week, I'd have that.

Next, I waded through the morass that was Vermont Adoption law. And for one single moment, I wished I'd gone to law school instead of medical school. Although truthfully, being a lawyer seemed like being in permanent health insurance hell.

From my research, the bottom line was that I'd been born too early for the big swing toward adoptees getting information. It was all about open adoption now, keeping in touch, sending pictures, sharing genetic information. Laws weren't likely to change for people of my generation.

Without help from my parents, I was at square one. So I dutifully put in my request to ask some faceless state employee the name of the agency that had handled my adoption. Every scrap of information was going to be a fight.

Having made at least a start and finding the truth, I looked at the clock. I'd long missed the Sierra Club's weekend hike. I could probably track down some of the guys and join them for a drink, but I didn't want to watch them rehash details of a day I hadn't shared. Stories about bobcat and coyote sightings weren't the same if you hadn't been there.

I briefly considered having a look at internet porn, but there was too much out there that could scar me for life. I hadn't figured out a way to filter the clinically misogynis-tic crap from a good looking rack and butt. I missed the days when peek-a-boo Playboy was all I could get my hands on.

I shut off the laptop, not even making an attempt to find release. The frustration I was feeling wasn't only sex-ual. Slamming the door to my office, I paced the rest of the apartment. Thanks to my long working hours and my once-a-week housekeeper, the apartment was spotless. The refrigerator was empty, but I'd stock it after a visit to the farmer's market in the morning. I wandered the living room and lifted the remote. My television wasn't the big-gest I'd ever seen. But even with forty inches there wasn't much to watch. I put it down the channel changing wand. Sports or reality television wasn't going to cut it.

I needed a friend. One who could understand. So I called the only one like that I had on this coast.

Nari answered on the first ring.

"It's Lucas," I said.

"Is there some kind of work emergency?" she practical-ly yelled into the phone. I could barely hear her over the techno music thumping in the background. Had she found the only nightclub that operated in the middle of the day? She'd said something about being celibate for nine months, but maybe she was on the prowl again.

Maybe I shouldn't have cribbed her cell number from the emergency call list. "No, nothing like that."

There was a long bass-filled interlude before she an-swered. "Oh, okay. Hold on a second." Muffled talking was followed by the sound of a cash register. Then the hum of cars starting overtook the earlier sounds of commerce. "What's up?" she asked.

"Did I catch you at a bad time?" I asked, sounding lame even to my own ears.

"I was just returning some stuff to Abercrombie."

Before third guessing myself, I spoke. "Want to share an early dinner? I was thinking—"

"Sure, where should I meet you?"

I was silent a long second. I'd never expected her to agree so readily. "My place downtown. I thought we'd walk."

"Okay. Give me your address. I'll see you around six?"

I was over the moon. It was hell on the adoption side of things. But maybe, just maybe I was finally getting somewhere with Nari after all. I dropped the phone haphazardly and took myself to the shower, singing all the way.

9 NARI

Following the directions Lucas texted me, I inched my Range Rover into the tiny visitors' parking spot. As the elevator creakily ticked off first one floor then the next, I considered turning around and getting myself the hell out of there.

Lucas probably thought we had a date, and all I wanted to do was probe him further on the adoption issue. I no longer thought I could dissuade him from trying to find his own birth mother, but maybe I could somehow clue him in on the possible hurt he could cause someone. Giving up a child for adoption wasn't like some cable movie with a teen mom in pursuit of college and a teary-eyed good-bye to the baby. It was hard and messy, and impossible to forget.

Smoothing out my halter top, I pushed my sunglasses onto the top of my head and surveyed the long corridor of nearly identical wood doors. Peering at the door of the corner apartment, I finally saw "4G" inscribed on a narrow brass plate. I knocked and waited.

"Glad you came," Lucas boomed, opening the door wide. His dress shirt was unbuttoned, blue tank stretched across his broad chest, his feet bare.

I swung the large faced oversized men's watch toward me. "Am I too early?"

"Nope, right on time," he said, gesturing welcomingly.

I stepped into the entranceway cautiously. "Can I—" I waved a hand toward the upholstered wood chair.

"Sure. Make yourself at home. Are you hungry?"

"Very. I haven't eaten anything. Had a very busy day."

Lucas sat opposite me on a carbon copy of my chair. Neither of them looked like they'd ever been occupied by a human.

Making no move to button his shirt, he leaned forward expectantly. I tried to ignore the tingle in fingers that were itching to slide under his tank and touch his chest again. I wondered if the hair there was as soft as I remembered. Then I banished the thought.

Uncomfortable in my own skin, in the silence, I searched for something to say. "Nice place. How'd you end up downtown?"

"Had a week to look before I moved out here."

"Is shopping hard? Seems like a food desert out here."

"I end up going to Hollywood a lot. That's not too bad. The commute to work, though, sucks. New York was much easier to navigate."

I searched my memory. "You were at Brooklyn Hospital, right?"

"Yep. Did my residency. Stayed on. Biked in the summer. Walked in the winter."

"Sounds ideal. Why move to California?"

"Seemed like a good idea," he said. Then changing the subject abruptly, he asked, "What did you do today?"

"Shopping."

He clasped his hands between his knees. His pants hugged his muscular legs all too well. Making an effort, I looked into his eyes. Meeting them, my heart skipped a beat. I'd been wrong about the brown. Hazel. They were definitely hazel. Everything chafed, my clothes, the chair, my skin.

Lucas looked as uncomfortable as I felt in the silence. He said, "The places around here are mostly craft beers and high end sandwiches. Or I was thinking we could order in Chinese?" He paused, looking at me. "Do you eat Chinese?"

"The food yes, the people no."

He smiled. His full lips hid perfect teeth. God, I'd slept with him and hadn't even noticed how good looking he was, even if oversized blonds weren't my type. "Is that a yes, then?" he asked, looking uncomfortable under my scrutiny.

"Sure. I'll have Chow Fun or any kind of noodles, really."

While he went away to the kitchen to tackle the menu and ordering, I decided to investigate the rest of the apartment, to uncover more about the man I'd had inside me—twice. It was pretty much what I expected once I got past the entertainment-focused living room. I peeked into one bedroom. It had a bed, a dresser, and not much else. The room smelled faintly of cologne, soap or something that reminded me of being horizontal with Lucas. Hazy memories of his hands on my breasts, breath in my hair, tickled at the edges of my mind. Thank God I hadn't been sober. When my heart beat faster, I quickly backed out of the room. I poked my head in the other. It was an office. As a man, he didn't need the kind of storage space I did.

I backtracked to take a second look. Most of the books on the narrow floor-to-ceiling bookshelf were many I had. He'd saved some of the textbooks from medical school. An old copy of the Physician's Desk Reference joined them. He'd probably moved to the PDR online like most of our younger colleagues.

Alongside novels with dragon and troll covers, there were a few dust jacket covered volumes on FDR and labor unions. He liked history? I looked at the authors. All were the same, Matthew Tucker. Pulling one down, I read the inscription: for Lucas, Brooke, and Christian.

"Those are my dad's books."

I startled at the sound of his voice. Heat radiated from his body, enveloping me in a citrusy scent. I tamped down the strong urge to lean back against him. "Oh, sorry. I was—"

"It's okay." His voice soothed me. "They're just books. My dad's a professor at Dartmouth."

"Where you went to school," I said more to myself. Maybe he didn't have some great love of New Hampshire. He'd probably done seven years in Hanover because it was free or nearly. "Your brother and sister go?"

"Yup," he said. His "Go Big Green" was halfhearted.

I looked at his chest and the strong column of his throat, and wanted to ask him to button his shirt, maybe back up just a little before I made a fool of myself. But there was a loud knock at the door before I had to say anything.

"Must be dinner," I said superfluously. I needed to say something to push past the closing of my throat. Push him back.

He disappeared and I stopped to take a deep breath. I'd never noticed a guy's smell before, or yearned to touch him, not in years anyway. Certainly not while sober. I refocused and went out to the dining area with determination not to get waylaid by hormones. That's all it was. I was a woman of childbearing age. He was a man with healthy sperm. It was fate, biology, evolution, pheromones even, that pulled me toward him, nothing more.

"Wine?" he asked.

"Just water for me." I perched on the corner of one of the barstools opposite the cook top and accepted a large glass of ice water. Sober Nari was a celibate Nari.

Lucas took plates and utensils to the dining room table. If we'd stuck to eating at the counter it would have been easier. The lighting, ambience, and dining room table were starting to make it feel like a date. I didn't date. Fucked yes, dated, no.

Reluctantly I made my way over to the table and accepted a seat opposite his. Remembering my manners, I opened the containers and doled out servings of the steaming sweet and spicy chicken and rice for him. Noodles for myself.

He sat and tried to wrap his oversized hands around the chopsticks. He dropped one, picked it up, dropped the other.

Oh God. I couldn't watch an hour of this. I stood and walked toward the kitchen. "Where are the forks?"

"I can do this." His face was set with determination. I imagined he didn't give up on much in his life. But this, he should probably let go.

"No need to try on my account."

Frowning slightly, he pointed me toward a drawer. I pulled out a full place setting and brought it to him.

"I wanted to impress you," he said, blushing.

I swallowed all the snarky and cutting remarks that came to mind. Nice wasn't something you should crush like a bug under the heel of a spiky shoe.

"Why do you want to look for your birth mom?" I asked, finally getting to the point of my visit.

Lucas ate a few bites, his eyes focused somewhere in the middle distance. "Do you know your origin story?"

"You mean like where I was born?"

"Not just that. But how your parents met, how they fell in love, where you were conceived, their wedding, all that jazz."

"Some of it. My parents are a little conservative so I don't know all the details, but the big picture, sure."

"In addition to their medical history, that's what I really want to know."

"But don't you have that from...the Tuckers?"

"Matthew and Joyce."

"Your mom and dad? They had to have met, fell in love, had a reason for adopting. I mean half the female patients I break the news to about pregnancy are less than thrilled. Your parents went out of their way to add you to their life. That has to be worth two origin stories."

Lucas' smile was small. "Are you in cahoots with them in the guilt-making department?"

"No, it's just that you might want to think about who you're hurting on your quest to find out." I fiddled with the wide rice noodles, watching them get cold, gelatinous, and unappetizing. "Have you considered that the circumstances of your birth mom may not be roses and sunshine?"

Lucas put down his fork, and planted his chin in his hand, elbow propped on the table. "Yes." He winced a little. "I've thought about that as well."

I pushed my plate aside. "I'm not saying it has to have been something violent or sordid. But maybe it's the kind of thing that will unearth heartache a woman might try to forget."

He pushed himself away from the table and stood. "I'm going to get something a little stiffer than water, if you don't mind." I heard cupboards open and close. A glass clinked against the counter top. When he came back, his glass held something dark swirling among the ice cubes.

"Tell me it's not rum," I said, trying to lighten the mood I'd singlehandedly tanked.

"Nope, not this time around," he said, taking a healthy sip, but offering nothing further.

Despite the cool reception, I pressed my point nonetheless. "All I'm saying is that it sounds like you're hurting the mom who put her heart and soul into raising you. You're a tall, attractive, single doctor. Most moms would kill for a kid like that. And the woman who gave you up made a choice thirty whatever years ago. However she may feel about it, that choice was hers and it's in the distant past. If you contacted her now, you'd be a very hard secret to hide."

I took it upon myself to box up the remains and deposit them on the kitchen counter. When I came back Lucas was sitting on the couch, sipping at his drink. Avoiding the chairs that looked unused, I settled next to him on the sofa and watched dusk settle over the city.

Lucas put the glass, empty save for ice, on the table and turned toward me. "You look really nice."

It was like the air crackled around us, charged with static. Not this again. I had already slept with him twice.

All that sexual energy should have been used up by now. I didn't expect there to be this remaining awareness between us. But there it was, filling the air. I didn't move for a long second, my body suspended between fight or flight. Taking a deep breath, I looked him straight in the eye and played polite. "Thank you."

I should have looked anywhere but at those eyes. He made no attempt to hide what he was feeling or thinking. He'd get eaten alive in this city. He'd look at a woman— all that want and desire in his eyes. Next thing he knew, he'd be looking for a second job to support the two million dollar mansion, designer purse habit, and private school tuitions a woman would heap on him.

But he wasn't thinking about another woman. He was thinking about me. That was as plain as the nose on his face. He was going to kiss me. I had about five seconds to push him away, talk him out of it, give in. It was the last thing that I did because while my head wanted the former, my heart wanted the latter.

When he leaned in those first few inches, I met him in the middle. His touch, at first, was tentative. As if he were giving me a chance to get used to the smell and feel of him. One of his large hands cupped my jaw, the other pulled the clip from my hair. I didn't know which made me feel more vulnerable, the tip of his tongue sweeping along mine or the feel of my own hair around my shoulders. I never took my hair down outside my own home.

His hands were in all that loose hair, molding my skull, pulling me closer. Guilt banded my arms to my sides. He wasn't that easily dissuaded. A hand left my hair and bumped along my naked spine. Until his hand had touched my skin, I'd forgotten the halter had no back. With only a brief pause, he slanted his head the other way. No man's mouth had claimed mine in years. I'd deliberately forgotten how good a man's lips felt against mine. How the lingering sting and sweetness from his drink could made me heady.

His hand slipped further down my back and pulled at the bow holding the scraps of the blouse's fabric in place. Heat seared my skin as his hands skimmed up my sides, near my belly button, tickling against my ribs. Lucas' thumb brushed against my nipple. I heard a groan from him, and an answering moan that must have been mine.

All of a sudden my arms got very mobile and pushed against the center of his chest. The only sound in the room was the smack of our lips coming apart and labored breathing, mine and his.

"I'm sorry, I can't do this." The room slowly came back into focus. "This was such a fucking huge mistake, my coming here."

Lucas took in air. I could see his erection straining against the thin fabric of his pants. "Why?"

"I'm not drunk enough for this," I answered obliquely.

He stood, finally buttoning the shirt he hadn't closed earlier. The shirttails covered the zip front of his pants, hiding his uncontrollable reaction from my view. He stalked through the living and dining area to the kitchen.

He turned on the tap, pulled down a large glass, filled it, drank it, repeated the motions again.

I turned away from him, trying and failing to tie the bow. I'd used my dressing room sized three way mirror to do it the first time.

I hadn't heard him behind me. "Here, let me," he said, pulling the fabric from my hands. His touch was clinical as he pulled the cotton firmly into place. His hands grazed my shoulder and turned me toward him. "Why do you need to be hammered to be with me?"

"It's not you, it's me," I punted.

He pulled a face appropriate for that crappy excuse. But I didn't want him to feel as bad as me. "It's the only way I feel like I'm not cheating on Andrew."

10 LUCAS

Great. I was competing with a dead guy. Talk about a contest I could never win. But I wasn't dumb enough to say *that* out loud.

I stood and turned my back to Nari again, looking out on the parking lots and helipads that distinguished Los Angeles from older, prettier cities. I willed my erection to go away. I needed to think. Getting the blood back up to my brain would be the first step.

"Why did you come here today?" It hadn't been to get laid, or even make out. It came to me now that nothing about her demeanor suggested seduction. I'd seen that side of Nari, drunk Nari, and it wasn't here tonight. Not one tiny bit. I'd let my desire to be with her—sober—overtake reading the cues she was broadcasting.

I turned toward her, waiting for an answer. Her back was against the couch, her eyes closed. She opened them and looked at me. There was so much going on behind those brown eyes, confusion, hurt maybe. But through all that emotion, I still couldn't get a read on what was going on in her head.

I repeated my question. If I hadn't been looking at her, I'd have missed the quick flicker of her eyes down and to the left. She was going to lie to me. Taking a deep breath and bracing my hands on my hips, I got ready for whatever crap was coming down the pike.

"I thought we were trying out being friends. Sounded like you needed to talk."

The "friends" word relieved me of my arousal. Grateful, I sat on the couch, making sure to keep more than a foot between us.

"Tell me about Andrew," I said. If I was going to have a chance, I needed to know what I was up against.

Her face got that look again, like a light was shining from inside. Thinking about her dead ex took ten years off her face. It was like she lived in two parallel universes, the one with Andrew and the one without him.

"My senior year in college was the hardest of all four years. I was planning on medical school and couldn't slack off like my classmates. Andrew had joined the Whiffenpoofs, so he wasn't around as much."

She paused, rubbing the empty space on her ring finger absentmindedly. "By December, we'd been engaged a couple of months, but Thanksgiving had been a disaster. I didn't know if my parents would ever come around."

Engagement, marriage. This had been more serious than some college boyfriend. I crossed my ankle over my knee. This was going to be more than I'd bargained for.

"After classes ended in December, Andrew thought it would be great if we could spend the weekend together before we went back to our families and faced a litany of questions about getting married so young. So he drove us to this little Westport Inn. It was the cutest little place. Anyway, I woke up Saturday morning to a surprise. Andrew had planned for us to elope, if I was game. My best friend Daisy was there. Russell Curry was there, too."

"Did you get married?"

"Yep. Right there on the water. Everyone got dressed up and the Justice of the Peace married us that morning. We had a champagne brunch to celebrate. That weekend was our honeymoon. So when I went back home I had a little more ammunition than an engagement ring."

I knew nothing about her parents. She'd never mentioned them more than in passing. But even my very liberal east coast parents would have been less than thrilled if I'd eloped in college. Joyce and Matthew had encouraged dating around, but not relationships that interfered with education. Marriage had never been on the table.

"How did your parents take their twenty-one or two-year-old daughter getting married?"

"I never told them," she said.

"Seriously? Why not?"

"When I got home for holiday break, they were armed and ready. You could have filled a book with the warnings and dire predictions they had of my life ahead."

"Didn't they notice the wedding ring?"

"It was small, meshed with the engagement ring. And after they started in on me, I took it off."

"To this day, you've never told them?"

Slowly, Nari shook her head. "I thought maybe during spring break, or after graduation even. Or..."

"Or?"

"Later, I thought they'd understand and accept him. But then in an instant I wasn't married anymore."

Nari rose and went to the windows. The lights of the city made downtown attractive at night. I stood and fiddled with my shirt. It took nearly everything I had not to go to her, lay an arm across her shoulders, pull her into a hug. She rubbed her bare arms. Goose bumps. Swiftly I unbuttoned my shirt and draped it across her shoulders.

She slipped an arm into a sleeve, and followed with the other. Nari came up to my shoulder. Despite her height, she was very slender. The shirt dwarfed her, hanging about her like a homemade ghost costume. I took a deep breath, then went for it. She was being unusually candid and I didn't know if the opportunity would ever arise again.

"How did your husband die?"

11 NARI

The word husband jolted me. Other than Daisy and Russell, no one knew we were married. But that's what he'd been—my husband. Only the death us do part had come a little too soon.

In order to save my sanity, I'd relegated thinking about those days ten years ago to one day a year. But I'd had my day in March. After Hawaii, I had planned nine months of relative peace. Chancing a look at Lucas, I saw nothing but warmth in his eyes. No wonder the nurses said he had a great bedside manner. He could probably get patients to reveal all of their bad habits.

"The Spizz and the Whiffenpoofs had this tradition of traveling and performing at every member's home town," I started.

"I've been to my share of a capella concerts," he said.

"So, it was Andrew's turn. The group did a performance at Penn on Saturday night. I was going to go with him, but…"

"But?"

I'd been at the tail end of morning sickness. The mere thought of a three-hour car ride made me queasy, so I had begged off. It wasn't as if I hadn't seen him perform a thousand times. And I'd hoped he'd get somewhere with his parents. Not going to Wharton was one thing, but a marriage and baby were altogether different.

"We were getting close to graduation and needed to lay it on the line for everyone. Needed all four of our parents to understand that we'd chosen each other over everything else. But most of all that we wanted and needed our parents' support. Marriage, baby, and graduate school weren't going to be easy.

"But I wanted to give him some time alone with his family," I said in an edited version of the truth.

"Okay."

"Usually, the group traveled together, by plane, by van, whatever, but Andrew had driven separately."

"Because he'd planned for you to be there?"

That had been part of it. But the other part was that I'd had my twelve-week ultrasound scheduled for first thing Monday morning when neither of us had class. And it had been important that both of us be there. We'd wanted to see the baby together. Though we'd both agreed it was corny, we'd wanted that stupid x-ray printout with an outline of our baby's head, nose, finger, toes.

"So he made the three-hour drive to Olde Haven alone. He called before he left to say he'd be back at school by dinner time, and to wait for him. But six o'clock came and went. I tried his parent's house, but his brother Simon said he'd left late, so I went to dinner with Daisy. But when I got back to his room at eight, he still wasn't there. When I called his parents' house a second time, the phone was busy. I started to panic. Finally at nine, they called Daisy. She walked over and we called them together."

"How..."

He didn't need more than that single word. His question was clear. "Drunk driver. Some woman had a few too many, got on the New Jersey turnpike. She had a Ford Expedition. He was driving a Honda. In the SUV versus car fight, he lost." I reported it to Lucas clinically, like I was talking about a patient during grand rounds. It helped to speak about it that way.

Not in a way that mattered. Not in a way that had me thinking of crushed steel, broken glass, and blood. Not in a way that had me imagining his last moments. Was he afraid? Did he scream? Was his death swift or protracted? Had Andrew known that his life was about to end, that the proverbial light was about to go out? I felt dampness on my face. I pinched my wrist hard to end the thoughts before they spiraled out of control. Thought stopping was a technique I'd learned during my psychology rotation.

Without cutting off this walk down memory lane, I truly feared a descent into madness.

I used Lucas' sleeve to wipe a tear that was close to dripping from the end of my nose. In so many ways it was like the whole thing had happened yesterday.

The weeks after *it* were a blur. There had been a memorial at school, and another at his graveside in Pennsylvania. The Whiffenpoofs had sung at the funeral. And I'd cried and thrown up through the whole thing. When I got back to school and back to the doctor two weeks later, it was too late for a first trimester abortion. Not that I would have necessarily done it. That Catholic upbringing still had a strong hold on me even if I wasn't a believer any longer.

Without Andrew, I hadn't wanted to raise the baby, even though I'd been committed to giving birth to her. The idea of having a little one who served as a daily reminder of what I'd lost made me crazy. But the only alternative I could come up with was adoption. That semester I only had two goals, graduate without flunking out, and find parents for our child.

I didn't know when Lucas had put his arms around me, but one minute I was standing at the window, the view blurred. And the next minute, I was soaking his blue cotton tank with my tears.

"I'm so very sorry," he said. I could feel his chest vibrating with the words.

Pulling back a little, I looked up at him. His throat was working as his eyes locked with mine. I pushed a curl behind his ear. With a single finger, I traced his jawline. It scraped over weekend stubble. Even from here, I could smell him. It was the same scent I'd briefly caught a whiff of in the office, in his bedroom, from his shirt. But now he was in high definition. Musk, menthol, and citrus filled my nostrils. My pinkie continued its bumping—down over his Adam's apple, clavicle, and landing against his pectoral.

Rising and falling, rising and falling, his chest moved under my hand. The ribbing of the tank followed his narrowing torso to the top of his greenish-gray pants. Giving in to my curiosity, I molded my hands on those little indentations between abdominal muscle and the ilium bone.

Lucas gathered my hands in his, stopping their exploration.

"What are you doing?" he asked, his voice a rough burr.

"I thought it was obvious," I said. I shrugged off his button down shirt. We both watched it fall to the polished wood floor in a heap of starched cotton. Reaching behind, I pulled both ends of my halter's perfectly tied bow a second time. Never taking my eyes from his, I flicked the two buttons at the top and lifted the starched cotton over my head.

Cool air swirled around my chest. Lucas' gaze zeroed in on my nipples. I could feel them tightening.

His hands hanging loosely at his sides tightened into fists as he fought what was happening between us. I picked up his right hand, uncurled his fingers and laid the open palm against my left breast.

"This isn't a good idea," he hissed through his teeth.

"I think it's a very good idea," I said, picking up his other hand and doing the same.

"I'm not Andrew," he said.

Pulling his head toward mine and brushing his lips with mine, I said, "I know very well who you are." Then I kissed him. Brushing each of his palms over a nipple, he left my breasts and pulled me to him. He walked me backwards, kissing me all the time.

When we got to his bedroom, I had on nothing more than my underwear. He'd lost his own pants along the way.

Standing by the bed, Lucas took in gasps of air, as if trying to regain his equilibrium. I didn't want him to have control. His tank top went next. I used my lips and tongue to follow the lifted shirt hem, through the whorls of hair to his nipples, which seemed as sensitive as mine if his gasp was anything to go by. With one index finger, I hooked on the side of his waistband, and the other index finger spanned his waist until I had a good grip on his boxers. And with a single forceful tug, his erection sprang free.

Damn. I couldn't wait to feel that length and thickness inside of me. I took him in my fist, sliding the foreskin back and forth, watching the shiny swollen head come and go, in and out.

"Can we slow down?" Lucas panted, his breaths coming out in uneven gasps.

I didn't want slow. But I didn't want him to walk away either.

He ran his hands along my arms, pulling them away from his penis, instead looping them around his neck. Taking his time, he kissed the top of my head, each temple, my forehead. He touched the rest of my face and neck before landing on my lips.

He brushed his mouth across mine, once, twice. I tried everything I could to capture his mouth, focus him on kissing me—hard. But he was not as easily persuaded as the last two times.

He was on to me.

Gently, he lay me on the bed, skimmed off my panties and looked at me like a man ready to enjoy a feast. But he didn't look famished, maybe mildly hungry. His heavy lidded gaze suggested that languorous lovemaking was on tap. I tried not to let my impatience show. Instead, I closed my eyes and tried to get lost in the sensation of his hands and mouth tasting my neck, nibbling at the vulnerable concave armpits, the sides of my breasts. My breath hitched when his stubbled jaw grazed my navel. Anticipation made my skin feel almost too tight.

"I've wanted to taste you," Lucas whispered. His breath fanned along my pubic hair, giving me goose bumps again. Then he did, each flick of his tongue brought me closer and closer to the edge until my world shattered into a thousand tiny pieces.

When I opened my eyes Lucas was braced above me, his erection sheathed in tight latex that did nothing to hide its length, width, or hardness.

Of their own accord, my thighs fell open and he seated his hips between them. With a single hand he notched himself at my opening. I hooked my heels behind his back, trying to urge him forward. He would not be moved.

"Nari," he said. "Look. At. Me."

I opened my eyes, taking in the room streaked with shafts of lights leaking through the blinds. Looking anywhere but at him, I gripped his wide shoulders, silently pleading. He didn't acquiesce.

"What's my name?"

I sucked in air, wondering if he knew what he was asking of me. "I..."

"What's *my* name?"

"Lucas." My puff of breath made his name barely audible in the silent room.

One long thrust filled me. I turned my head to the side, closing my eyes, praying for the moment when the sensation would overwhelm my thoughts, and for long blissful moments, the past would disappear.

A single hand turned my face back. "Open your eyes," he said. "Look at me."

With the help of the sodium vapor street lamp, I could see his unblinking eyes, lips pursed in arousal. One thrust followed another, his hand settled near our joining, his thumb brushing against my clit in counterpoint. Every time my eyes dared drift closed, he paused. So I had no choice but to look at him when my breath hitched, when my muscles grew achingly tight, when I came apart, unable to hold back my cry at the rush of pleasure.

"Nari, oh God," he said, his face dropping to the pillow next to me as he thrust his way home. For a long moment he lay on me, using his arms to take some of his weight. When he finally slid from me and went to the bathroom, I turned toward the window, feigning sleep.

Some time later, I turned my head toward the man next to me. I wondered if Lucas was asleep. He hadn't said a word when he'd come back to bed. And now, his breathing was even, his arm heavy on my waist. I faced the windows, looking out at the glowing orange lights of the city. Every breath was labor as I tried not to let the guilt of what I'd just done crush my soul. It was the first time I'd *made love* with someone after Andrew died, not just had down and dirty sex. The first time I'd been stone-cold sober. There was no wine, whisky, rum, or vodka I could blame for my actions.

Lucas' intake of breath tickled my ear. "The Hawaii conference came on the anniversary of Andrew's death, didn't it?"

I nodded. My cheek scraping against the pillowcase was the only sound in the room. His lips moved near my ear. It sounded like he was counting. I tried to puzzle out what he could be thinking. Then I got it. Sweat broke out on my brow, under my breasts. He'd followed the same path I would have. Develop a hypothesis. Suggest a diagnosis. Test.

"What happened on June twenty-fourth?"

Adrenaline made my movements swift and jerky. I was out of the bed in a flash and in the living room, searching for my clothes. Underwear and pants on, I stuffed the stiff white fabric of the halter in my purse and wrapped his discarded button-down around myself instead.

"Nari," he called shuffle-hopping into the room at the same time he was trying to pull up his boxers.

But I had a firm hand on the front door.

Andrew.

I could talk about him in limited amounts, maybe even more after tonight. But the baby girl I'd handed over in the hospital. That memory I never wanted to exhume. It needed to stay buried deeper than spent nuclear waste.

"You can't leave." His voice was full of firm rationality.

"But I am." I had to. If I stayed, he'd learn all my secrets. I'd bared enough for a lifetime.

"After tonight. How can you?"

I twisted the knob. "I don't know what's happening here, but I need space." I knew exactly what was happening. But I wasn't ready for a relationship, shared confidences. It was a betrayal I couldn't live with.

"From me?"

"Yes." I'd wounded him again. I was becoming toxic to everyone around me. Leaving would be the kindest thing I'd done all day.

"Before you go, tell me what happened in June."

Pain rose from the depths. I had to swallow three times before I could say what I should have said hours before. "Good-bye, Lucas."

12 Lucas

Rejection had been my companion since the first day of my life. There was no way in hell I was going to invite it in. Nari had kicked me out twice, and run away once. I didn't need to be told a fourth time that she didn't want me. That first day of work after she left was hard. Every time I saw her slim silhouette bent over a chart at the back counter, I wanted to snake an arm around that waist. Tuck a finger under her chin and raise her head so I could see the truth in her eyes.

The truth of whether Andrew was in her past. The truth of her feelings for me. The truth of what in the hell had happened in June that had her running to that bar on Melrose Avenue.

Instead, I inclined my head and moved on to my office or an examination room. The press of patients and pre-authorizations made ignoring her, if not simple, then doable. When I got a spare moment at work, or the thought of Nari arching under me wouldn't shake from my memory, I focused single-mindedly on prying my birth records from the clutches of bureaucrats. I needed to find my mother.

Sitting at my desk during my lunch break, I clicked lazily through adoption reunion websites, reading the stories, imagining what my own would be like.

"Is this Lucas Tucker?" a voice asked on the call that had been patched through from the front desk.

"This is Dr. Tucker," I responded expecting a long drawn out rejection for a procedure from an insurance company rep or someone double checking on a prescription from a pharmacy. I always injected the title when I answered. It made the calls shorter. No one wanted to waste a doctor's time.

"This is the Department for Children and Families, Agency for Human Services," she said.

"How can I help you?" I asked. My mind was wandering all over the place. I was a mandatory reporter of abuse for the state, but I never saw children and hadn't thought much about it. Wildly, I wondered if I'd missed something critical during my tenure at Westside Medical.

"You contacted the Vermont Adoption Agency several weeks ago regarding your placement," she continued.

The plastic phone receiver nearly slipped from my grasp. When I'd left messages all over New England, I'd hardly expected a response. Who did? I thought most government agencies were black holes where money and information went and little emerged. The public equivalent of health insurance.

"Hello," she said more insistently. "*Is* this Lucas Tucker?"

I must have been quiet for a long time. I repositioned the phone by my ear, steeling myself for what was going to come next. "Yes. I'm sorry," I said.

"Because you were born prior to nineteen ninety-six, your adoption records remain confidential," she said.

I hunched over my desk as empty of hope as a deflated balloon was of air.

"Thanks for calling," I said mustering all the politeness I could. I pulled the phone from my ear ready to place it back on the cradle. But she was still talking. I quickly placed it back against my ear. "... so I suggest you contact them. If your birth parents are interested in contact, they may have left information with them."

"With who?" I asked.

Crinkling of paper came over the line. "The Hope Agency in Montpelier." She rattled off a number. I scribbled something I hoped I could read later.

"Thank you," I said before I really hung up this time.

I had to see three patients before I could get back to the phone. I was nearly five in the afternoon east coast time when I was finally able to steady my fingers long enough to push the right combination of numbers for The Hope Agency.

"Completing families for fifty years, how can we help you?" a voice answered.

I introduced myself. "I'm looking for my birth parents," I said. Before she could give me the brush off, I plowed ahead. "I know records for babies born before nineteen ninety-six are confidential," I said. "But I was wondering if either one of my parents may have contacted the agency looking for me?"

"Please hold," she said, putting the phone down rather than mute me. I heard doors opening and closing and people saying good bye and good night. Even if you were "completing families" for a living, I guessed you probably wanted to get home to your own at the end of the day. "You're in luck. Your mother has been looking for you. Do you have a pen and paper?"

I pulled a pad advertising some kind of anti-fungal cream closer to my pen. I'd never in a million years thought it would be this easy. "Yes, I'm ready," I said.

"Alice McGee," she said, then spelled the last name for good measure before giving me an e-mail address. "Double luck that you got us before we closed. Nearly everyone's out the door for the weekend. Let us know how it goes," she added conversationally. "We sometimes like to include reunion stories on our website."

"Thanks," I think I said before hanging up the phone. I hope none of my afternoon patients were dying of cancer. I tried my hardest to concentrate of the parade of sore throats, irregular coughs, and the vague aches and pains. But it was no use. Skipping dictation or cleaning up the day's files, I was out of my office at six on the dot.

All the way home in stop and go traffic, I wondered what in the hell I was going to say in that e-mail.

Even though I knew I should probably have slept on it to temper my eagerness, I was at my desk computer, not three seconds after I dropped my keys and wallet on the kitchen counter.

I pressed the button starting the laptop. Clicked to open the e-mail program. Started a new e-mail. Typed in her address. Words failed me then. I stood and paced. The room was dark by the time I'd figured out what I wanted to say.

```
Dear Ms. McGee,
    My name is Lucas Tucker. I'm a doctor liv-
    ing in Los Angeles. I think you may be my
    birth mother. I received your name and e-
    mail from the Hope Agency in Vermont this
    afternoon. I was born April 17, 1979 in
    the state of Hawaii.
Sincerely,
Lucas Tucker.
```

Simple. To the point. I pressed send. I snapped on the light. It was only seven thirty. A long lonely Friday night stretched out ahead. It was too late to call my parents. What could I say to them anyway? My brother and sister were out for the moment as well.

I lifted the receiver ready to call Nari, try to bridge the gap between us. She seemed to understand my quest. I had dialed the three-two-three of the area code when the computer pinged. I looked to see who'd sent me e-mail.

Alice McGee's name was the only one in bold in the upper left hand corner. My hand shook.

When my mother had finally acquiesced to me and my sibling's ceaseless demands for store bought bandages, Christian, Brooke and I had rushed home to try them. But two days later, we couldn't get them off. Tiny hairs and skin had fused with the adhesive. Mom had taken us all out on the back porch and ripped them off in less than a second ignoring our whelps of pain.

That lesson had hurt at the time, but was probably one of the best ever. I clicked the e-mail ready for whatever was coming my way.

> Dear Dr. Tucker,
>   I live in San Bernardino County in a city called Twentynine Palms. I think there are probably more than twenty-nine palm trees here. I'm home all day tomorrow. I'd love to meet you. Here's my address:
>   6568 Indian Cove Rd, 29 Palms 92277
> Alice.

She'd left no phone number. I credited her with sparing me the embarrassment of possibly crying on the phone. I e-mailed her back promising to be there at ten a.m. at the latest.

If I hadn't woken up with sun streaming through my window, I wouldn't have known I'd slept. I'd tossed and turned for what had seemed like hours imagining what our reunion would be like.

With the workweek and disaster of the previous weekend with Nari in my rearview mirror along with the skyline of downtown Los Angeles, I drove to the desert ready to unlock the secrets of my past.

During the traffic free three hour drive toward San Bernardino County, I mentally mapped out how the day should go. Would my mother hug me? Yes. Tell me why she gave me up? Without hesitation. Would she have my hands, eyes, height? Of course. We were of the same flesh and blood.

After I pulled onto Indian Cove Road, I waited three doors down from the address scribbled on the paper wilting in my hand until I could catch my breath. Whether it was the scorching desert heat or corresponding lack of humidity, I could scarcely bring air into my lungs.

For a full ten minutes, I considered backing up my car, making a three-point turn, and driving home. I tapped at the steering wheel weighing the possibility. This was what I'd wanted, I reminded myself. What I'd fantasized about while staring out the window of my childhood bedroom while heavy snowflakes fell. Resolved to meet my past, I started the car once again and inched toward the house number that had been emblazoned on my mind since Alice's e-mail.

I hadn't seen a single lawn since I'd pulled off the freeway and into the town. This street was no different. The tan stuccoed house was barely distinguishable from the sand surrounding it; a far cry from the green oasis of Palm Springs a few miles south. Turning off my phone in case my parent's called, I pushed open the car door and made my way to the house before I lost my nerve.

A small dark-skinned woman was out the door and down the walkway before I had a moment to get my bearings and ground myself in the biggest moment of my life so far. The woman, only half my size, nearly tackled me with a hug.

"Jared?" The question was a shriek. "Could it really be you?"

"Jared," I said to myself as much as to her. I waited. There was no instant connection. No zing of recognition of her voice, of my name. Nothing. Emptiness remained.

"That's the name I gave him...you. I know I wasn't supposed to, but I had to call you something."

I stood stock still. Beads of sweat trickled down my neck making me itch in the early morning desert heat.

"Come in. I made some iced tea," she said.

I walked behind the five-foot tall woman, her dead straight dark hair, streaked with gray, swinging behind her. Was there some big strapping soldier in the story? Alice McGee looked as different from me as my own adoptive mother. Maybe this whole thing was a fool's errand. Tentatively, I sat on a small couch while the woman bustled around the kitchen, humming.

Handing me a glass and paper napkin, she sat on an easy chair opposite.

"Tell me about yourself. Did you grow up in Hawaii?" Her voice was low and husky. Had my dad met her singing in a lounge—love at first note? I refocused. Tried to answer her question.

"My parents..." I paused, uncomfortable with that to call Matthew and Joyce in the face of the woman who'd really given birth to me.

"That's okay," she said leaning forward to give my leg a few firm pats. "They were your parents. The Tuckers, was it, provided food and shelter and love where I...couldn't." Alice's cough was close to a chocked sob. In a moment, she'd pulled herself together, cleared her throat.

"Joyce and Matthew only came to Hawaii to pick me up. I was raised in Vermont."

"And you're a doctor now," she said with no small amount of awe.

I nodded. "I work at a clinic in West L.A." Quiet descended while I sipped at the astringent drink. "We don't look anything alike...you and I. Is my...father tall, blond?"

"He was a Marine, jarhead and all. But not as tall as you. His hair was light brown and stick straight like mine." She sat forward like she was going to touch he, my hair, but resisted. "Your curls are a mystery."

"What happened to him? Did you...Do you...?" I stuttered to a stop. This was the part I'd worried about most. The last thing I wanted to do was bring up some unspeakable pain for Alice.

She laughed, a hearty full-of life sound. "Me and Joe were on and off for nearly thirty years. We gave up a few years ago. Finally."

Relief surged through me. No tragedy here. "So he's alive?"

"And kickin'. Have no doubt about that. He's too ornery to die. He went back to Georgia, though. Left me out here with Joshua trees and desert sun."

"Did you have other children?" My hands itched in anticipation of holding a photo or shaking a hand of another kid who looked like me.

"Just one." Alice stood and plucked a picture from the shelf next to the television. She passed the golden frame into my hands. It was a formal portrait of a little family. Alice, Joe and an adolescent who looked like a mix of them stood formally in front of one of those marbled gray backgrounds so familiar in family pictures. Something clenched in my gut. Joe was big, square, and nothing like me. I'd never fit in with the Tuckers, but I wouldn't have fit in with the McGees either. Maybe it was all a trick of the imagination—family resemblance and belonging. I racked my head about the odd genetic combinations and recessive genes that could have produced me.

Harder than asking my patients about drug use or sexually transmitted diseases, I worked on a way to ask the single question I needed answered. I swallowed then pushed it out. "Why did you give me up?"

Silent tears coursed down Alice's cheeks. She coughed, swallowed twice before she spoke. "We were eighteen and not yet married when I got pregnant. I went to the priest at Joe's church and he recommended I see a Sister at a child services agency. She helped me make an adoption plan."

"But you got married anyway?" But hadn't kept me.

"Giving you away was the stupidest thing I ever did. It was so overwhelming. Joe was about to get moved from Oahu to Cuba. There was a bunch of political trouble in

Central America. The nuns told me that we were too young. That even if we married, Joe might be killed. And I only had a few days to decide. At least that's what I thought." She shook her head. Regret was etched into lines on her nut brown face. "Joe and I got married right after. I curse that woman, Sister Paula Mary." Alice mimed spitting on someone's grave. Then her face crumpled.

I let her cry, but made no attempt to hold or comfort her. I had my own issues of abandonment to process. It was the best and worst of what I could have expected. My parents had loved each other and stayed together. They'd had another child. Alice and Joe just hadn't kept *me*.

"If you were on Oahu, why did you give birth on Kauai?" I asked, trying to unravel the first knot in the story.

Her head lifted from her hands, Alice's brown eyes held mine steady. "I didn't give birth on Kauai."

My heart sped up, nearly pounding out of my chest. Quickly I assessed myself. Not at risk for a heart attack, I didn't think. I said, "But my parents picked me up from Veteran's hospital in Kauai. My redacted birth certificate says I was born on April seventeenth of nineteen seventy-nine in Kauai." I lifted my messenger bag from the floor and pulled from it the Photostat copy Nida Vara had given me.

Alice reached for the smudged copy, scrutinizing it closely. "Oh holy mother of God...this isn't...you aren't...my baby." She took a few hiccoughing breaths. "I had a baby on the same day, but he was six pounds, five ounces. You were eight and a half pounds." She looked at me from sad, reddened eyes. "Someone gave you the wrong information. I'm so very sorry."

"No, I'm sorry," I said standing suddenly, upsetting the coffee table. Tea spilled everywhere. Alice ran to the kitchen returning seconds later with a roll of paper towel. I took it from her, unwinding a large wad and swabbing at the speckled carpet.

"I don't think it will stain," she said bundling the sodden mess in her arms and disappearing out back.

"I'm sorry," I said "This...I don't know what to say." What I wanted to say was that I was relieved that she hadn't given birth to me. There was still someone out there who looked like me. Who shared my DNA. I sat back on the couch staring at the dark, wet patch on the carpet. Tried not to feel sorry for myself. This had been, in many respects, too easy. I'd have to go back to the drawing board...do all this...a second time. Maybe Nari was right. Maybe this was something I best leave alone.

Alice's choked voice intruded into my thoughts. "Tell me about you. Do you like your job? Are you married? Have kids yet?"

I was so far from a kids, wife, and family that it felt like another planet. I answered, "I enjoy my job. Seeing different people every day and trying to figure out how you can help them is certainly interesting." It was my stock answer. My brain was too crowded to come up with anything new and original. Not now.

"But no girl...in your life...or boy?" Her words were diplomatic, her open face accepting.

Nari. "Girl, woman. Maybe, I don't know." I stammered out.

"Why not? Do you love her? Take it from me, you do not want to have a life full of regret. I'm living proof, that's not a good idea."

"She's a widow. I'm not sure she's over her husband." Nari would kill me slowly if she knew I was spilling her secrets. She'd never sworn me to secrecy, but she was so very private and interior.

"How long dead?"

"Ten, eleven years or thereabouts," I said.

"Maybe she needs to find someone worth replacing that memory for." I didn't know if I could be that person. Not if sleeping with me sober made her run like a gazelle from a hungry lion.

"How are you going to find your son?" I asked her. I couldn't fix what was going on in my world, but I was well trained in fixing others.

"I'll call that place. The Hope Agency?" When I nodded confirmation, she continued. "Tell them they got it all wrong. Maybe someone mixed up my Jared's information with yours? Some of the private agencies took files when the Catholic charities got out of the adoption business. It's a start, at least" she said hopefully. "The agency we were with had everything buttoned up like they were housing a map of the nuclear stockpile. I may have to figure a way of going at it sideways. I thought with these agencies certified and everything, mistakes like this couldn't happen. Who knows? Maybe my Jared was meant to go with your family, and you his."

That hurt, bad. The idea that my parents could have been anyone. That there was no cosmic rhyme or reason to adoption placement except maybe happenstance. The idea that Matthew and Joyce could have been mine on a whim or mistake churned my gut, burning a hole in my intestines. "I should go," I said. If I stayed any longer, I'd work myself into an ulcer. "It's a long drive."

I stood. Alice walked me to the door. On the threshold, as I was about to turn, she grasped my upper arm. "I hope you find what you're looking for."

Doubly resolved, I knew that I wouldn't stop until I found the people who'd made me. "Same for you."

13 NARI

Lucas was holding a small vial of liquid and a padded envelope when I passed his office early Monday morning. I
hadn't had the guts to call him over the weekend, though
I'd fingered the phone a million times.

What would I have said anyway? "Thanks for the sex
and lending an ear to the story of my husband's death. I
like you, but don't like you like that. Couldn't ever like
you like that. It's not you, it's me." Or one of another
million bad clichés.

I'd have scurried away when we made brief eye contact, although I wasn't a scurrier. But he lifted a hand to
beckon me in.

"Do you need me to call in a nurse to help you with lab work?" I asked, looking at the paraphernalia on his desk.

"It's not for a patient."

Oh God. I practically admitted that I'd probably slept with at least twenty different men. Mortification overtook me. He probably thought I was a Petri dish of disease. "Are you testing for HIV?" I laid my hand on the knob, already backing out. "I've always used a condom," I said, ready to turn and head to my own office where I could stew in mortification—alone. Wait, that was physically impossible. "I mean the men. The men used condoms." Except for Andrew, but that didn't count. Not at this late date.

Composed, he thrust the type-filled page toward me. "Nope. DNA."

With shaking legs, I walked toward the desk, looking down at written instructions. "It's a basic cheek swab. I can call in one of the nurse practitioners—"

"Can *you* do it?"

"My clinical skills were never my strong suit." I'd injured enough patients with errant needles to last a lifetime.

"*Please.* I don't want this to be another item of office gossip."

I wondered if he knew how much speculation there already was surrounding the fact that he was a healthy, attractive, single male. "Hand me some gloves," I said, regaining some composure. A cheek swab wasn't a scalpel. This I could do.

He pushed a box of latex gloves across the desk. I snapped on a pair. Unscrewing the cap, I took out the damp swab. "I can't do this gently."

"I know," he smiled ruefully. "It's going to cause some discomfort."

I scraped first with one swab, sealed it in solution, then did the other cheek. I snapped off my gloves and tossed them in the red hazmat bin. I backed away from him to a zone of safety. "All done."

"I'm trying to find the origin of my genetic make-up," he said.

"I understand," I said, sounding like an automaton, all bedside manner gone.

"I drove to San Bernardino to meet my birth mom on Sunday."

Feeling like I'd been kicked in the gut, I fell hard into one Lucas' chairs. "What happened?" Maybe he'd assuage my fears that your only living child coming out of the woodwork wouldn't be the worst thing that could ever happen.

"It was a mistake. She wasn't the right person."

"How…. Oh my God. I'm so sorry. That had to be hell."

"It was," he said matter-of-factly.

The anguish on his face shot straight to my heart. This was why, I wanted to say with a wagging finger, digging up the past was always a bad idea. Why couldn't adoptive children leave good enough alone?

Why did so many advocacy groups and cheesy talk shows push for reunions? But having seen all those crying people in online videos and on cable, I tried to extend him a tiny bit of sympathy. "Did you call anyone? Were you alone last night?"

Exasperation joined anguish on his face. They must not learn to hide their emotions up there in Vermont. He'd be hash for a savvy woman.

"Who would I call, Nari? For most of my life, my parents and brother and sister were my confidants. We all lived together and shared almost everything. Since I've been out here, since I decided to look for my natural family, it's been a little strained, to put it mildly. My parents are hurt. My siblings are mad at me for hurting my parents, *their* parents."

"You could have called me," I blurted out. "We're friends, right?"

A large hand dusted with fine blond curls came to his forehead, smoothing away the worry lines. "Are we? Or are we people who have sex that you're ashamed of?"

"It's not...I explained—"

"I like you and want to be friends with you, more than friends. But you can only get naked with me if you're drunk. And if you're sober you run away in a guilt-induced panic."

"That's not fair," I said fiercely, lowering my voice to a whisper.

He didn't use the same volume control. "Isn't it? Would you go out on a date with me, in the light of day, to a restaurant, to the movies, for a walk on the promenade?"

"It's not you," I said again. Why was he deliberately misunderstanding this? I looked out his small window at the red taillights of the stop and go traffic along Sawtelle Boulevard. "I don't date."

"You have a very active sex life for someone who doesn't date."

The cruel accuracy of his remark felt like a bullet between the eyes. "I have to call in some prescriptions," I said, fleeing his office and the truth.

The absolute last person I wanted to ask for advice was my best friend. Despite our fifteen years of friendship, the favors had always flowed one way. Daisy fucked up, I helped out.

I credited myself with single-handedly saving Daisy from having to go home after college, unemployed tail between her legs, resigned to working for one of her father's Wall Street friends. Years later, I'd done it again—found my best friend a legitimate job and a path out of the adult entertainment industry.

I was the smarter, prettier, thinner, more together one.

But there was one thing Daisy knew more about than me, and probably every other person on the planet—men and sex. So here I was, fending off men in a Korean pub on West Third Street. Because fresh *ahn-joo* in K-Town would make my friend materialize faster than a Starfleet officer.

I looked around the bar, trying to figure out the exact word for a person obsessed with Korean culture. I'd been trying to pin down the right adjective for Daisy for the last decade. There were Anglophiles for people who pretended warm beer and minted peas were gourmet fare. Francophiles who swore the only good coffee and wine could be found in Paris. Daisy was that about Korea. She watched more Korean dramas and ate more Korean food than I could ever consume in a single lifetime. And now my best friend was putting up with a lot of asshole behavior from her new boyfriend, probably because he was half-Korean.

"I'm waiting for a friend," I said to the bold Korean guy who'd tried to buy my drink. He had to be at least forty. He was either married or his recently divorced self hadn't tanned over the pale line encircling his ring finger.

"I heard they have awesome *honghap tang*." That was Daisy's entrance line as she pulled up a chair under the paper lantern casting weak light on the hewn wood table. Of course she'd know the specialty of the house. My friend had a near encyclopedic memory of restaurants in the area between Vermont, Kenmore, Third Street and Seventh.

I didn't ask how Daisy had heard of some obscure Korean pub I had picked for its missing signage and accompanying lack of patronage. "So you want mussel soup and what else?" I bribed.

"*Yangnyeom,* and *pajeon* if they have it."

I raised my hand for the waitress and fired off an order for the soup, spicy Korean fried chicken and the seafood, green onion, and egg pancake. "*Soju* or *makgeolli?*"

"*Makgeolli* of course. Do they serve it the traditional way?"

I didn't ask the waitress that. Ordered the fermented alcohol and watched the woman skitter off. I was done with my Korean for the day.

"I can't believe you called me about coming here. I usually have to twist your arm to get you to K-Town."

That was true. Eating food my mom could make for a tenth of the price and twice as good was not my idea of great dining. Sitting in a bar and not drinking wasn't any fun either, so I got right to it. "I slept with Lucas Tucker."

I could see the gears turning in Daisy's head. *Nari had a sex life. Nari had a sex life after Andrew. Nari was talking about her sex life.* I waited one beat, two. Right on cue, Daisy executed a double take. Forget her comedian boyfriend, *she* should be the one working on a sit-com.

"That's the doctor, right? The one you mentioned setting *me* up with."

"The very one."

With that revelation, she couldn't get the questions out fast enough. "Are you guys dating?" *Without telling me,* was implied. "Or was it a one night stand?"

"I slept with him three times."

"Oh my God. Nari! I can't believe it!" Nor could anyone else in the bar from their startled looks at her uncontrolled volume.

"Daisy. I'm not interested in all of Los Angeles knowing my business," I said as cool and calm as one of the pickled cucumbers on the table.

Her whisper-shout was conspiratorial. "It's just that you've never, you know talked about sex before. All these years, it was like you were growing your hymen back or something."

"That's physiologically impossible," I said without a hint of the humor I knew was expected.

"It was just a joke, Nari," Daisy said. She took a long pause to inhale half the food on the table. The girl would die of a kimchi overdose if she ever went to Korea.

I took a sip of the green tea I'd ordered, and a bite of the *pajeon*. Ugh. Not half bad, but not half good either. But I wasn't here for the food. "What should I do?"

"About Lucas?" Daisy asked. I wanted to shake her. I wasn't asking about investing in stocks, real estate, or how to succeed in the adult entertainment business. I'd kept a single minded focus during the conversation. Maybe the bar with its attendant alcohol hadn't been such a good idea. *Kimchi* was like catnip for Daisy. In five minutes her eyes would be rolling back in her head and she'd be swaying to the barely audible music, praising the Korean food gods. I needed answers now before I lost my friend to a food coma.

"Yes, about Lucas."

"What do you want to do about Lucas?" she asked, waggling her brows suggestively. Was it me or was Daisy being particularly juvenile today? I'd slept with a guy. Big deal. It wasn't like we were thirteen or even twenty-three.

"I need to know how to handle him."

"Sounds like you already have a handle on him," she said. At my less-than-amused face, Daisy backpedaled. "Look, I'm sorry. I just don't know how to talk to you about this. Do you like him?" She paused. "Ugh. I feel like I'm on one of those awful kids' shows asking if you, 'like him, like him.'" She put down her chopsticks and cleared her throat. "Do you envision yourself pursuing a future relationship with him beyond sex?"

Well, now. Daisy wasn't joking anymore. She'd gotten to the crux of the issue pretty quickly. "I'm not sure," I said. I needed her help to figure that out. Not that I'd ask outright like that.

"But you've slept with him more than once?" Now that she was paying attention, her questions had the precision of a surgeon's scalpel.

"The first time was in Hawaii. I was drunk."

"Maybe if you'd invited me, this wouldn't have happened."

I knew Daisy would go there. But I didn't want to talk about Hawaii *or* Andrew.

"Can't go back," was all I said, closing the subject.

Daisy leaned forward. "So what about the second time?"

"I was drunk. He drove me home."

Impeccable manners forgotten, Daisy's elbows hit the table with an audible thud, palms bracketing her face. "When are you doing all this drinking? Since...Owen, you haven't really had a drink. You're like a MADD zealot. You hate it when anyone drinks who could possibly be getting behind a wheel."

I wanted to shake Daisy and make her say his name. "I still never drink and drive," I said instead, underscoring what she was avoiding.

"You're ducking the question. When are you drinking?" Her voice had gone all Al-Anon.

"Sometimes I need to blow off steam," I said. Not everyone is an alcoholic. But saying that aloud would have been cruel.

Daisy looked hurt even without my candor. "Why didn't you call me? You know I'd do anything for you."

And that was the rub. Daisy was my friend. I had no doubt the girl would have taken a bullet for me. Yet I didn't trust my friend with my biggest secrets. I was the only one who knew everything, had all the puzzle pieces. I'd made sure to dole out information among friends and family on an as needed basis. A few knew about the wedding, only my mother about the baby. No one knew about my particular twice-yearly brand of solace, except maybe Lucas now. But the whole story? I'd probably take that secret to the grave.

"It's about Andrew," I finally revealed.

Daisy abandoned her chopsticks. That's how Nari knew her friend was taking this seriously. "I thought we were talking about Lucas."

"I slept with Lucas on the anniversary of Andrew's death."

"Oh, Nari." She got up from the bench across from me and scooted next to me instead. It was Yankee awkward, but my friend slipped an arm around my shoulders anyway. "I didn't know you still had a hard time in March. You haven't said anything for years."

"It was the tenth anniversary. That's what was hard," I said, swallowing before the lump closed up my throat.

"Why didn't you tell me?"

"This is one of those cases where talking about it doesn't make it better."

"So you drowned your sorrows in alcohol and Lucas took advantage of you. So typical of men—"

I stopped Daisy before she went on one of her little tirades about the horrors of the half of our species with a penis. Without stopping her, she'd spew her dad's crap for a good long time. Instead of saying it was all me, I equivocated. "It was mutual."

"What happened after that?"

"We went our separate ways. Things were fine at work...until the second time."

"The second time? How'd *that* happen?"

"I was at a bar with someone from work and he came in. She got a better offer so he volunteered to drive me home." I said in my version of the truth. "I may have come on to him. But the wine made it a little hazy."

"You obviously like *something* about him."

"So last weekend he invited me over for dinner," I continued. If Daisy had been sitting any closer to the edge of her chair, her linen covered butt would have hit the floor. "One thing led to another."

"Out of bed, what's he like? Do you have a lot in common?"

More than I would ever let on. But what Lucas and I had in common wasn't the kind of thing that would make for fun car trips or romantic dinners. "We haven't really talked about music or books or television." The *normal* bricks that made up the foundation of a relationship. "He's been going through a hard time."

"Why? Please don't tell me he's in the middle of a breakup. Rebound men are the worst. They—"

"He's not on the rebound that I know of. He's adopted."

"Okay." Daisy drew out the syllables like there was a joke in there somewhere and she was in search of a punch line.

"He's been looking for his birth mom," I said with some finality.

"Wowza. That's heavy. And he wants a relationship on top of that?"

"I have no idea on that last one." But that wasn't entirely true. It was the fact that he *wanted* a relationship that was scaring the hell out of me.

"Sounds like it, though. Maybe you should try normal dating. Dinners, movies, walks on the beach," Daisy said in a perfectly reasonable tone.

The stab of betrayal nearly stopped my heart. "But what about Andrew?"

"What *about* Andrew?"

"He was my husband, Daisy."

"He's dead, Nari."

"Dead doesn't mean I don't love him anymore."

Daisy was quiet for a long time. I could practically see my best friend fighting not to throw out all the old clichés about getting over it, about what Andrew would want for my future, about moving on. Instead Daisy wrapped two hands around the ceramic cup and drank deeply.

"He can't love you back from the grave, Nari," she said. The words hit me like a kick in the gut.

"Daisy, that's not—"

"Do you ever plan to get married or have children?"

Daisy had forgotten the operative word—again. Been there, done that, I wanted to scream, wail, shout from the rooftops. But I knew Daisy was asking about the future, not the past.

"I don't know." Until recently, I had never thought about trying again. I'd gotten my chance, lost the two people most precious. I didn't deserve to try again.

"That's a pretty basic question. Most people know where they fall on this."

"Where do *you* fall?" Despite all the linen, khaki, and summer wool she owned, Daisy wasn't exactly little-miss-traditional-Connecticut. If my best friend could ignore her doom and gloom father, and see past her own dysfunctional family, maybe there was hope for me.

"I'm not sure I want either. Pushing a stroller through Griffith Park seems a little bit boring. I'd take adult conversation over talking to a toddler any day."

"Does *Raphael* want to get married?" I asked.

"I don't know. We haven't talked about it, *ever*. But *you're* avoiding the question."

"Why do I have to answer it?"

"Because it's probably not fair to fuck this guy—fuck *with* this guy—until you know what you really want."

"I thought you of all people understood casual sex." It was an unfair dig. But Daisy wasn't dishing up enough empathy. She didn't rise to the bait. It was very mature of her.

"If both parties are on board," Daisy said, stating the obvious rules of the hookup.

I sat back in my seat, frustrated. I didn't need a primer on normal relationship progression. I'd fallen way too far outside normal boundaries. This wasn't helping. Maybe I needed to know how to talk to Lucas. How to make Daisy understand that while I wasn't ready to leave this man alone, neither was I ready to *date* and *talk about the future* like so many of our peers did. I signaled the waitress and asked for a doggy bag and the check. This wasn't going how I'd imagined. Maybe I'd been watching too many *Sex and the City* reruns. Daisy wasn't full of sage advice or wisdom. Not that she'd ever been—about love or relation-ships. She gave great investment advice, though.

I pulled my Burberry tote bag from the purse hanger I carried everywhere. I tucked the heavy brass disc discreet-ly in an inner pocket. Little metal purse feet were not great at keeping the canvas free from the flotsam and jet-sam of restaurant floors. What was the point of having a dust bag, keeping everything clean in the closet if I didn't keep it clean anywhere else? Not to mention the supersti-tion of having your handbag on the floor.

"You can't just leave because I'm not saying what you want to hear," Daisy said, scooping leftover rice into a Styrofoam container.

"That's not why I'm leaving," I lied. I pulled the thin jacket around my shoulders, ready to brave the cool desert night. Daisy's phone rang as she stood, and despite all her play-it-cool nonsense, she was smiling and whispering into her phone. I suspected it was some kind of secret conver-sation between her and that comedian. With a twinge, I remembered having those kinds of whispered conversations with Andrew. For hours, days, or weeks at a time, a new relationship is impervious to the outside world.

It's a girl, her lover, and nothing else in the bubble. A sharp pang of envy sliced through my heart. Even after three years, Andrew and I had rarely left that bubble. Then with the single careless act of a drunk driver, our bubble burst.

Still on the phone, Daisy snatched up the doggy bag, and waved good-bye when the valet handed her some car keys. Patiently I waited my turn. After tipping the vested guy, I rolled up my windows, shutting out the noise and smell of Koreatown. At the stop light on Sixth, I looked around the cavernously empty SUV.

"Maybe I can try again," I whispered to the wood and leather cocooning me. At the green light I accelerated dangerously into the thick traffic, ignoring the blaring horns and squealing brakes. With that one thought, I felt like I'd cursed God. If lightning came from the cloudless sky and struck me dead, I wouldn't have been the least bit surprised.

I wanted Andrew *and* I wanted a future. I feared I couldn't have both.

14 LUCAS

Sometime between the end of medical school and now, my brain had left my body. Everything was upside down in my life and I couldn't figure out how to tilt it back in the right direction.

Spinning around in my chair, I stared at the map of the world. Lines blurred on the sand-colored map as my eyes crossed. But I could make out the curved edge of the continent where Los Angeles lay. Vermont was a smallish trapezoid well on the other side of the country.

Standing, I decided I'd conquer the near before the far. I fished around in my closet and determined that casual was the way to go. Khakis and a two-tone sweater my sister had gotten me two Christmases ago made the final cut.

I didn't call until I was parked outside her building. Nari was a little flustered on the intercom, but buzzed me in nonetheless.

The girl who answered the door looked about fifteen and was not Nari. Indecisive, I stood there for a long moment.

"Are you Nari's daughter?" I finally managed. Single-mom had not figured into the speech I'd rehearsed on the way over.

Backing away from the door, the girl laughed behind her hand. "No."

I took two steps inside the apartment, and the girl closed the door behind me. "I'm Eun-ji, her cousin."

I noticed the accent then. This cousin hadn't grown up anywhere near here. I thrust out my hand for a shake. It took a moment before she grasped it. "I'm Lucas Tucker," I said. "I work with Nari at the clinic."

Eun-ji winked at me. "Riiiiight. Work. That's why you're here on a Sunday. All those primary care physician patient emergencies."

"My cousin was just leaving to head back to her dorm at USC. Isn't that right?" Nari asked, full of "shove off, there are adults talking here" in her voice.

"I've been in Los Angeles long enough to know that's my cue," the cousin said. She hefted a heavy backpack onto her shoulders, took an envelope from Nari and let herself out.

"Did you just give her money?" I said, sticking my nose in where it didn't belong.

"She used to live with me. And now she doesn't."

That was all the explanation I was going to get on that one. "Eun-ji." I stumbled over the name. Mortified, I plowed on. "She looks like you. For a minute, I thought she might be your daughter." My laugh was pathetic. Rewinding the clock fifteen minutes wouldn't be a half bad idea. Why weren't scientists working on time travel along with cancer treatments? At this moment both were equally important.

"Is that because we're both Asian?"

I tried to bring her cousin's face to mind. I was sure they'd shared the same cheeks and chin, Nari's thinner, but still the same. I looked at faces and features every day at work. Maybe clinically or pathologically, but I thought I was more observant than the average guy. Backpedaling, I walked around the back of the couch. Gripped the cushions for support.

"I, uh, wanted to talk about us."

"Us?"

Five feet separated us, but it was more like a chasm as wide as the Grand Canyon. Though I knew she was the woman who'd lain under me, called my name while she'd come, this version of Nari looked as cool and out of reach as mist on a pond.

"I..." I faltered. The rehearsed lines fell out of my head like an actor with stage fright. Unfortunately, I couldn't call, "line," to the director. I cleared my empty throat. "I think we should go out, you know, date."

She looked over her shoulder out her kitchen window. I couldn't see much beyond the blinds. Didn't know if there was anything to look at. "As in go steady?" Nari asked, turning back, her eyes unblinking.

I didn't know if she was being snarky or serious. I decided to keep the conversation on the serious side. "I was hoping we could be exclusive, yes."

"Have you ever dated someone Asian before?"

And there it was, my greatest fear realized before I'd even been invited to take a seat. Forget the invitation, I sat heavily on her couch, placing my shoes on her all white rug. I could see the slightest frown lines between her eyes. My crimes were stacking up this morning. If she were judge, jury, and executioner, I'd be dead before lunch.

"No," I answered honestly. I leaned forward, my elbows on my knees. "What difference does that make?"

"Cultural differences can be hard to overcome."

I racked my brain for what was different about us, other than the superficial traits like different eye color and hair texture. She was tan, I wasn't. But in my family, I was used to that. "Like what?"

"I eat mostly Korean food," she said.

"I thought your lunch was good."

"You nearly died from the *kimchi*."

"Spicy food isn't what I grew up with in New England, but I'm open. What else, Nari?" I hoped she could tell from the tone of my voice that I wasn't convinced.

"Do you know what it's like being a Korean woman in Los Angeles?"

"That's a rhetorical question, right?"

"There's not a day that goes by when some guy isn't hitting on me. At gas stations, they'll pay to fill up my car. I've had men pay for my parking. In bars, they buy me drinks. I could have gone through my twenties never buying a single thing for myself."

"You're an attractive woman."

"You think that's it? My best friend is cute, and men aren't falling all over themselves to pay her way through life."

"Is she blond? Is she, um, endowed up top?"

Nari looked at me sharply. "No. Why?"

"Sometimes men like to look."

"And what, if she doesn't have breasts the size of melons, she isn't worthy of a second glance?"

"I didn't say that. All I was saying is that you're very pretty." I wanted to kick myself for the backhanded compliment.

"I think it's more than looking. I think they want to take me home. They have some fantasy of a docile comfort woman catering to their every whim in and out of bed."

I wanted to say she should talk to them for five minutes. They'd know in an instant that she wasn't that kind of woman and wander off in search of easier prey. I was starting to wonder why I wasn't one of those men.

"So if this is all so awful, what are you in bars looking for?"

Her nose flared and her eyes shifted away back toward the window again. "That's not fair."

"Why?"

"I'm there to make myself forget," she whispered. "You know that."

I stood and walked over to comfort her from the low blow I'd delivered. She was perched on the kitchen stool again, though this time she was dressed in skintight jeans and a blouse that was made for a man's easy access. But I didn't say that. Prying my foot out of my mouth, I spoke. "This isn't going at all like I planned." I took her hands in mine. "I really like you. I want to explore this."

"But..."

"But what?" I'd come ready to refute all her excuses. "You're Korean. I get that. We work together. I get that too. We're adults who get along and have..." I swallowed. "...great sex. We know all of each other's secrets. That's a better start than most couples get."

I nearly let go of her hands and patted myself on the back. One by one I'd knocked down her defenses. I'd even taken on the mammoth in the room, Andrew. I wasn't afraid of him anymore. On the way here, I realized a very important difference between us. He was dead. I was very much alive, very much here, and very much in like with Nari.

"Are you here only because you want to sleep with me?"

I could feel the heat creeping along the sides of my neck. At this moment, I hated being pale. I'd grown up with an open, liberal, sex-positive family. Enjoying melding my body with Nari's was one thing. Talking about it was something else altogether. But she was baiting me, and I needed to rise to it. Embarrassment be damned. "That's not the only reason." Damn, I'd punted. "I'd be lying if I didn't tell you that I was very much physically attracted to you. But that's not the only part of you I want to know better."

"I don't know what to say."

Finally something had gone according to plan. She'd said the one thing I had known she was going to say. Now I leaned in and did the one thing I was planning to do to convince her. I'd never been one of those guys who kissed a woman without invitation. Asking first was a drumbeat from my mother to my college resident advisor. But today wasn't about asking.

I pulled her to me, reveling in the fact that she was tall enough to kiss without breaking my neck. I looked down, taking my time. We were both sober, and I wanted us to both be present in the moment.

She licked her full lips in what I could only hope was anticipation. I didn't wait one second longer. Pressing my lips to hers wasn't enough. Brushing against hers wasn't enough. Only the mating of tongues—hers silken and reminiscent of melon—satisfied the craving she'd ignited last year, last week, in the last minute. Only that would prove enough.

Nari relaxed into the kiss. I had all of her—for a moment. One of my hands had slipped down her back and cupped her ass without her protest. I hadn't come here for sex but was ready to follow up on this impromptu make-out session. While I was mentally counting the condoms in my wallet, she pulled away.

"I got it. We're sexually compatible," she said, unaffected by our kiss.

I took a deep breath. Half of me, the semi-hard bottom half, wanted to stay and fight. The other sane, brain-heavy half wanted to walk out.

Maybe this was too hard. Maybe Nari wasn't ready. Now that I knew I wanted a relationship, maybe it was time to find it with someone else who was willing and able. I didn't hold fast to the soul mate theory. Or the fated theory. There were, I figured, hundreds if not thousands of people with whom I could be compatible. It was only a matter of meeting one of them—outside this apartment's door.

"Why are you pushing me away?" I asked instead of opening her front door and getting into my car. I should have been leaving, but something kept me rooted to this apartment and this woman.

Instead of turning just her head toward the kitchen window, Nari turned her whole body away. She stood that way for a long time. Clouds passed over, casting the room in shadow, then moved away, letting in light again. Her shoulders shook slightly. Was she laughing? I put a hand on either shoulder and turned her around.

Tears coursed down her cheeks.

I brushed one, then another away, but my thumbs could not keep up with the deluge. I could withstand lots of things, missing limbs, a blood-soaked emergency room floor, even death. But Nari's silent tears nearly did me in. No scalpel or suture could fix what was broken.

I put my ego aside before I asked the next. "Do we have any chance?"

After an interminable pause, she nodded.

"Then let's take this one step at a time," I said. I kissed away every single salty tear before I took myself home.

15 Nari

"Why are you shaking?" Andrew had asked.

I looked around the small airport, already missing the little cocoon of Olde Haven that buffered us from the real world outside. Sometimes I thought I could live in that ivory tower forever as long as Andrew was with me. "This is going to be dicey."

"You told them I'm coming, right?"

"Of course I told them you're coming. I'm not springing you on them. It's that they haven't said a single thing. Not about sleeping arrangements. Not about what's for Thanksgiving dinner. Nothing. When Daisy first came, they asked about every possible preference from pillows to *banchan.*"

"Those are the little dishes of food right?"

I nodded. He was learning, if slowly.

"Have you ever had a boy over?"

I cut him a look. He knew the answer to that. Dating and my parents' expectations did not mix. Any boys I'd "dated" in high school were a secret I'd held more closely than the Secretary of Defense kept hidden the location of America's nuclear stockpile.

"You're not just any boy. You're my fiancé and the father of my soon-to-be-born child." Not that my parents knew any of that. Not that those facts had gotten the chance to make any difference.

"Do they celebrate a traditional Thanksgiving?"

The way he asked, I knew he was pretty relieved to be away from all the turkey, trimmings, and relatives that usually bombarded his holidays. I'd enjoyed it when I'd gone with him last year, but it had been a novelty. I could see how all that eating, the flag football, not to mention the endless social niceties could be tiring. The holiday at his house hadn't been so much of a family event, but co-ordinated chaos. "Kind of. But there won't be a turkey or anything. Just a lot of Korean food."

"I can always eat rice." He bumped his hip against mine as we shuffled in line toward the airline agent. "You think they'll let us sleep together?"

"Never." I laughed and curled my hand into his. "A girl could get pregnant doing that."

He was instantly sober. "Are you going to tell them?"

"About which?"

"Either. Both. The baby. Us getting married."

I looked down at my engagement ring. The ticket agent called us. While Andrew plopped down the e-tickets, confirmed our seats, and checked our luggage, I slipped off the ring and wrapped it in a small rose printed handkerchief my mother had brought back from one of her Korea trips. I tucked it into the interior pocket of the Vernis bag my mother had bought as an early graduation gift.

Andrew gave me the window seat on our short propeller plane ride. He hated take off and grabbed my left hand in his as the metal machine defied gravity and lifted from the ground.

"Where's the ring?" he asked, mild panic in his voice. I hadn't removed it in the two months since he'd presented it to me. Not for a single second.

"It's in my purse." I said. "One thing at a time." He'd had to tell his parents as they're the ones that had pulled the family heirloom from the safe deposit box. As soon as we got engaged, his mom had called to congratulate me. I hadn't heard anything from his dad yet. I knew he was still sore about Andrew's decision to forego Wharton in favor of school in California.

Seven hours and two "formatted to fit this screen" movies later, we landed at LAX. Compared to the blustery cold of late November in Connecticut, Los Angeles was breezy and balmy. I pulled off my down jacket and reveled in the temperate air. Sometimes I really missed this. I'd follow Andrew anywhere, but I'm glad we'd agreed to start our lives in California.

I couldn't wait to be with Andrew and our baby in the land of perpetual summer. I didn't have the slightest idea how people wrapped babies up in winter. Did they have tiny little down coats? How did you get on little boots? It was hard enough getting my own snow boots on—after a lifetime of zero practice.

Glad I wouldn't have to figure it out, I shed my sweater and let the car, bus and plane exhaust caress my shoulders. When we got to my parents' house, it would be even warmer. Summers may have been miserable in the Inland Empire, but winters were divine.

"Doesn't seem like a holiday with palm trees and seventy-five degree weather," Andrew said, reluctantly unwrapping his blue and white striped scarf.

My toes in these leather boots were craving sandals. "You get used to it. Thirty-five million people can't be wrong."

Our bags finally came down the carousel. Andrew hefted both without me having to ask. I pulled sunglasses from my bag and took a deep breath.

"Ready?" I asked.

He nodded and we headed out to the pickup lane. Not ten minutes later, my dad pulled up in his big old Audi sedan. Apa loved that car as much as I hated it. I'd liked the Mercedes he'd had, but this car had been bigger. He could ferry around Mom and her friends or their fellow parishioners in comfort. Noncomplaining Koreans were more important than status, I guessed. When I got out of school, I promised myself I'd get the best car I could—as a reward.

"Mr. Yoon," Andrew said, dropping one bag and extending his hand. My dad picked up the dropped bag instead, and pulled the other out of Andrew's hand.

"Apa," I whined in four syllables. It was the voice I'd used all of my life to get what I want. "*Chin-jol-hag-ge al-as s-ji.*" Be nice, I begged. I wanted the two men I loved most in the world to get along. Ahead of us all was a long life—together.

Though I sat in the front, I couldn't get more than a few words from my dad. Usually a taciturn man, he wasn't exactly effusive. But I counted on these rides back from the airport to hear how my mother was doing, pry something from my father about his various businesses.

Today, I wasn't going to get a single thing. I couldn't see Andrew in the back, but heard him shifting, the chafe of denim against leather. We changed from one freeway to another, the rubber of the tires on the road, the only other sound in the car for the two-hour drive home. Andrew and I hadn't lived in each other's pockets, but this propriety forced distance was already starting to wear on me. Four days of not being able to touch my fiancé would be an eternity. I wanted nothing more than to recapture that closeness we always shared.

I knew my mother had to have been watching from the window because she was almost at the curb the minute we pulled up to the little cul-de-sac where my parents' house sat among two acres of grass in a thirsty desert.

"Andrew." My mother shook his hand and bastardized his name in a single movement. I tried not to be embarrassed. Immigrants had built this country, and they'd all come from somewhere else. My parents had gotten here a lot more recently and it showed. Andrew's family had gotten here on those first boats. World of difference, that was.

"Mrs. Yoo—, I mean Ahn," he said, looking at me, guilt pursing his lips.

My mother didn't even blink, used to the American idea of a wife taking a husband's last name by now. She'd been called Mrs. Yoon more times than I could count outside our little insular Korean community. She took his hand, but stood mute. I knew she was mortified by her English. They'd been here nearly twenty-five years. I thought it was good enough.

"I have lunch," my mother finally mumbled. I grabbed my purse and followed her in. After taking off my shoes, I looked around the house I'd grown up in. Nothing had changed. The smell of pickled cabbage and lemon Pledge hung thick in the air.

Finally, my father and Andrew came through the door. My dad had my two bags and Andrew's weighing him down.

"He wouldn't let me carry anything," Andrew whispered.

"Come help me with lunch." My mother grabbed my arm and pulled me toward the kitchen. Bewildered, I stood at the threshold between the hall and kitchen, keeping an eye over my shoulder. I didn't know how to cook. My mother had always thought school was more important than any domestic task. I wondered what she really wanted from me.

Andrew looked bewildered at the prospect of being alone with my dad. Part of me wanted to leave him to figure it out on his own. This was only the first of many days we'd all spend together over the next twenty years. As my soon-to-be husband and the grandfather of our unborn child stood awkwardly, I threw them a bone. "You guys could put the bags in my room." Men bonded over tasks, not talking. Maybe the hairy topic of who was sleeping where could be sorted out as well.

Entering my mother's domestic lair, I realized the longer I'd been away at college, the less this felt like home. I sat on a stool at the white tile counter, waiting for the impending interrogation.

Afternoons and evenings of doing homework from public and Korean school blurred into a solitary memory of my life in this house. I'd struggle through English and math, and Oma would help me with both while wearing plastic gloves and sorting rotten vegetables from fresh. Korean, though, I didn't get much help with. They were adamant that I struggle through those word endings on my own.

"Are you going to keep the baby?" My mother asked in Korean, not once making eye contact. Swish, plop went the sound of my mother's plastic gloves mixing the noodles and vegetables of the *chapchae*.

My head swam. I nearly fell off the stool. I wanted to blame morning sickness, but it was the feeling that I'd disappointed my parents that turned my stomach. I didn't know how I thought I would put this one past my mother. I was her only child and I'd always suspected she could read my mind.

"I'm not showing," stumbled off my lips.

"I'm your mother," she said in Korean. No further explanation was necessary.

"*Please* don't tell Apa," I said. One thing at a time. Andrew. Marriage. The baby. My daddy had big plans for his little girl and I'd be putting a wrench in the works. If I wanted their support, I needed to spoon-feed them my plans. It's how I'd gotten them to allow me to go to Owen. Other stuff they'd never approve, I learned to hide. But a baby wasn't something I could keep at a friend's house or hide between the mattress and box spring.

"You didn't answer my question," my mother said, stripping off her glove and pulling plastic wrapped bowls from the refrigerator. Walking to the other side of the kitchen, she stirred soup which smelled like *maeuntang*.

"I'm keeping it."

Even with her back to me, I could feel her disappointment radiating across the room.

"And I suppose that boy you brought home is the father."

"We've been together nearly three years, Oma. I introduced you to him during parents' weekend our freshman year."

"Is *he* giving up business school?"

"*I'm* not giving up medical school."

"Tell me how you're going to navigate medical school with a newborn."

"Daycare," I said. I had hoped my parents would be a big help but if not, I'd assumed that I could find childcare. I couldn't be the first mother to go to graduate school and raise a child.

"Naïve is what you are, Nari. I had a baby. For two years it was nearly twenty-four hours a day."

"But Apa was working. You were alone in New Jersey."

"That boy will be working. You'll be alone in Los Angeles."

"Anything I can help with?" Andrew said, bustling into the kitchen, my father bringing up the rear. They stood in stark contrast, the tall, thin boy just out of adolescence. His feet clad in sport socks and spare slippers. My father, shorter, stockier, had his hands shoved deep into his dark brown trousers. Apa's navy blue sweater vest stretched over the small belly he was developing. Probably from too many desserts. The local Korean bakery was a novelty of red bean cakes and green tea *boba*. It pulled my parents in after every church event like a magnet.

My mother's mouth closed tighter than a clam. Her permed curls didn't move as she set one serving bowl after another on a tray. She'd be skipping the low-to-the-ground kitchen table where I'd eaten nearly every meal in this house for the formality of the big western dining room she used to impress guests.

Andrew wandered to the dining room and sat on one of the armchairs. I rushed in and shooed him away from my dad's place, and seated him next to my own chair. Then I helped my mother bring in tray after tray of banchan, soup, and rice.

I hadn't believed in God after my first few months at Owen. Nevertheless, I sent up a silent prayer of thanks that two weeks of dining hall chopstick lessons made Andrew competent. We had forks and knives for guests. But I wanted them to treat Andrew like the family he'd soon become.

Only the sound of steel chopsticks filled the cavernous room. This was nothing like Andrew's house. His brother Simon would have been doing something inappropriate at the table while everyone tried not to laugh. His mother would be chastising the boys. When his father finally emerged from his study, halfway through the meal or right before dessert, the boys would quiet down and he'd lecture them on the importance of one aspect of business or another.

Kind of like Daisy's house with a tenth of the alcohol.

Andrew lay down his chopsticks exactly like I'd taught him then cleared his throat.

"Mr. Yoon, sir. I'd like to ask for your daughter's hand in marriage." Even though he'd already asked me, my heart melted a little bit more. Like his proposal to me, it was clearly rehearsed.

My parents had to be moved by his earnestness. But as I looked from one stony face to another, my heart froze a little bit at a time, until it felt like a block of dry ice in my chest. My body would freeze and shatter in a moment if they didn't at least thaw a little.

"Oma? Apa?"

For a long moment there was no sound in the room at all. The faint buzz of a distant lawnmower then the hum of a leaf blower filled the air.

My father's fist hit the table so hard it set the bowls to rattling. "I appreciate your manners, son. But my daughter is too young and uneducated to get married."

Three and a half years at Owen and he thought *I* was *uneducated.*

I said, "Apa, I love him." I hated the adolescent pleading note in my voice. But he had to understand I'd chosen Andrew. He was my future.

My father wouldn't even look at me. Instead, he turned to my mother, speaking in rapid Korean. I was too young, he said. What about me being a doctor, not some housewife? I saw my mother shrink a little. Why hadn't she raised me better? She'd only had one child and had been home all day, and look what I'd turned into. A woman willing to chase a man.

Deliberately, I stood and walked from the room. I grabbed my purse from the table and pulled the ring from the pocket where I shoved it. I pushed it onto my finger where it had been for the past two months and walked back with greater resolve. I thrust my hand in the middle of the table above the soup and steam. It caught the sunlight radiating through the patio door.

"Oma, Apa, I'm twenty-two years old, not twelve. I love him. We're going to get married after graduation. I'd love for you to be there. But I'll do it either way." I swayed a little after the speech. I'd never defied my parents on anything—big or small. I'd worn the clothes they'd picked, went to the schools they had approved, only chose my few friends from the preapproved church crowd.

But I'd learned a lot about myself, stretched my wings while in Olde Haven. Which is maybe why they'd wanted to me to go to college near home. Maybe they were afraid of just this thing happening. But it *had* happened. I'd fallen in love, found my soul mate, was going to have his baby. It could not be erased with silence or dark guilt-laden stares.

"No daughter of mine is going to throw her life away," Apa said, standing. His face was flushed like he'd drank a six-pack of *soju*. But a half empty pitcher of *bori cha* was the only beverage on the table.

"What are you going to do, Apa, Oma?" She looked between the two of them. "Disown me? That's so twentieth century," I yelled back, trembling with the force of my fury.

" *Ye*," Apa said, turning away toward the sliding glass doors.

"Andrew, I think we should go," I said.

He looked bewildered. Slowly it dawned on me, the exchange had been entirely in Korean. "We have to go now," I said softly.

"I don't—"

Of course he didn't understand. His family had had three hundred years to get used to the American way of life. My parents were barely at a quarter century. He brought the bags outside while I found the keys and backed my car out of the garage. My dad had done what he always did. He'd kept the little BMW running and in pristine condition while I was away at school. God forbid I didn't have transportation to get me to and from my hospital internships during the summers.

Once he loaded the bags in the hatchback, Andrew slid into the passenger seat. His left hand grasped mine for a long moment.

"Where to?" my fiancé had asked, ready to follow me anywhere.

"Where to?" Lucas asked. The similarity of the question was jarring. It pulled me from the past to the present. When I didn't answer right away, he followed up with, "Where were you?"

I blinked and looked around. On the 405 freeway headed south toward San Diego was the literal answer. For a long moment I wondered how I'd gotten here. I knew I'd woke up, taken a shower, gotten dressed. Stepped into Lucas' car. But *how* had I gotten entangled in his search for his mother is what I needed to know. On so many levels this was an excruciatingly bad idea. This man was not a way for me to work out my demons even though I was using him for just that both in and out of bed.

When I didn't say anything, Lucas smoothed his hand down my thigh. I looked down at his big hand and got all tingly thinking about ways I'd like him to touch me. The flood of guilt that followed squelched all good feeling.

"Daydreaming," I said flatly.

"What kind of things do you dream about, Nari?"

His deep voice vibrated across my chest. I sat on the fence half ready to lie. To do what I always did, make up something pretty, nice, socially acceptable. "I invited Andrew to my parent's house during Thanksgiving of my senior year."

Lucas flicked the signal bar, harder than I thought was necessary, switched lanes, then did it again to pass a slow moving tractor trailer that was parting the stream of traffic like a rock in the center of rapids. "How did that go?"

"Very badly," I said. "I thought I knew them. Thought they'd be happy for me." But I'd misjudged so badly that the weekend had me rethinking every decision I'd made since graduating from kindergarten. Feeling like I was on the verge of another maudlin woe-is-me moment, I changed the subject. "Do you want to talk about where we're going?"

Lucas glanced at a map he'd laid on the dashboard and moved over to the right lane. Ten minutes later, we were pulling up to a wide space in a tree-lined mini mall. Its beige stucco exterior was no different than the buildings across the six-lane expanse of roadway. "I need something," he said.

I followed him into the coffee shop. He stood and looked at the menu so long that the baristas moved away from the register and started polishing already gleaming surfaces.

"Sit. I'll order." I got him a cappuccino and myself one of those blended ice drinks I could nurse for half the day. Bittersweet confections weren't my thing, but I didn't like to make waves. Lucas didn't need to be worrying about my drink preferences right now.

I brought back the coffees and joined him at the table. "How did you contact this woman?"

Lucas looked down at the papers he'd gripped in his hand for much of the trip. "Laura Wallace." He took a long sip. "One of the adoption websites. Our dates and hospital match up."

"Did you get a picture?" I didn't say this time, but I'm sure Lucas got my implication.

"No." Lucas grasped and released the documents.

"Give those to me," I said. He handed me the papers he'd lifted from the passenger seat when he'd picked me up that morning.

While he sipped from the tall paper cup, I looked. Other than a map to the woman's house, he had a heavily redacted birth certificate and a print out of information from the adoption seeker website. Lucas didn't have anything else in his short stack. I'd have asked for family pictures, I think. Make sure it was the right tall curly haired blonde. But maybe all of that would come later. There wasn't a protocol, that I knew of, for finding your birth parents.

I tried not to let my breath accelerate as I imagined myself in Laura Wallace's shoes. Maybe I'd never have to face this. If she wasn't looking and I wasn't looking, one day I could forget.

Smoothing out the papers, I looked at the map. "What time are you supposed to be there?"

"I told her around eleven."

I stood. "Then..."

I took over navigation while Lucas drove to Imperial Avenue. The squat home was goldenrod. That was the only way to describe the intense yellowness of the stucco. Unlike many of the other homes surrounding it though, it was freshly painted.

With the engine off, the roar of the nearby 805 freeway almost drowned out the sound of our beating hearts. I knew why he was so nervous. My near panic, I couldn't explain.

The way I tamped down the panic was with action. So I didn't wait for Lucas. I got out of the car and strode to the door. Before I could find and push the bell a tall, blond woman answered. Relief for Lucas flooded my veins. If this woman didn't share his DNA, then I'd give back my medical license. It wasn't a mistake this time.

"I'm Nari." I extended my hand.

"Laura Wallace," she responded out of politeness. Her screwed up features told me she hadn't been expecting some Korean woman to wash up on her doorstep like driftwood from the nearby beach.

I moved out of her line of sight, tilted my head toward the curb. "That's Lucas."

"They kept your name," Laura whispered. Lucas walked toward her, each step as slow as if he were walking through ankle high wet sand.

Lucas hunched and leaned and looked like he wanted to hug this woman, but something censored him. Instead, he offered his hand. She grasped it instead of shaking. Turning it over, back and forth, examining every lifeline, every knuckle, every hair.

I looked from mother to son. There was a connection there that had never been severed. Damn. I spied a neighbor watching us curiously. I wanted this moment to be private for the both of them.

"Can we?" I gestured toward the open front door.

"Of course, I'm sorry, I..."

"No need to apologize," I said.

"Sit, sit." A puffy butter yellow leather sofa and loveseat filled the small living room. I took a seat on the edge of one. I had to pull Lucas down next to me. The woman excused herself and came back with a small three ring binder. She sat on the couch cattycorner to us and opened the cover. With shaking hands she pulled apart the binder's rings and pulled out a single plastic sheet. Within it was a single piece of paper.

Even upside down, I could see it was a Certificate of Live Birth from the state of Hawaii. Shifting forward, Lucas took the page and laid it on the coffee table. He pulled out his own redacted document and laid them side by side.

To my untrained forensic eye, they looked identical. For long minutes, we all looked at the papers. I took in the information like I was memorizing a medical history before presenting at rounds. If questioned I would certainly be able to give you his vitals: Pulse racing. Blood pressure elevated.

"William Coates?" he asked, glancing up at Laura. He looked away quickly as if having his mother within his sight was simply too much to take in.

"Your father."

"He was in the U.S. Navy?"

"Yes. Stationed in Kauai, Norfolk, Korea for a stint, then here last."

I knew where these questions were going. I wanted to get up and leave. Staying felt like foreshadowing. And this is a scene I didn't want to play out for the future. I looked around, but saw little ornamentation in the place. There was nothing for me to impolitely fiddle with. It was as if she'd only lived here for a few months, or was staying in corporate housing. It was that impersonal.

"Is he alive?"

Laura hesitated. "Yes."

"Why did you give me away?" I looked away when I heard his voice crack. It took all my will to bury my fight or flight response. Because I wanted to run.

16 LUCAS

Nari drove my car with the fluidity of a racecar driver. Her grip on the steering wheel was sure and her movements swift, darting around traffic with a confidence probably born of a lifetime of driving. I imagined California girls came into this world with a set of car keys in their hands instead of a rattle.

I still hadn't gotten used to the six to twelve lanes of traffic that were considered normal here. No tall pines or leafy deciduous trees lined the San Diego Freeway. It was nothing like Vermont with one driving lane and one passing lane that sometimes expanded to three around big towns. New England was pretty and utilitarian at the same time. This dusty desert was all utility.

Instead, big box stores and mini malls littered the exits. I tried not to feel maudlin about the distance, both physical and emotional, from my family. A single decision had changed my childhood from military brat to professor's son.

"I could have grown up here, maybe," I said. "Like you."

Most doctors learned to hide their emotions. The whole day Nari had been more clinical than off duty. When she took a hand from the wheel and released her hair from its confines, it was oddly sensual and made her more vulnerable, approachable. The silken strands cascaded down to her shoulder, obscuring much of her face. She never wore her hair out. I took the action as an opening.

"Were you born in California?"

Her eyes left the traffic and assessed me. I didn't know if I'd passed or failed her test, but she answered me nonetheless. "New Jersey."

I don't know why that surprised me. She seemed Southern California through and through. "When did you move out here?"

"I was two or three. I don't remember being back east."

"What's it like? California?" For the briefest moment, I was willing to indulge in my childhood fantasies of how my life could have been different. Of all the scenarios I'd considered, the child of a military officer had never crossed my mind. Lovers torn apart by war, a teenage mother hiding from her parents. But never this. This was too cold and calculating to have imagined.

Nari's "Nothing like television," interrupted my thought process.

"Didn't surf to school in the morning?" I asked, trying to sound lighthearted when I was anything but.

Her spontaneous laugh was low and delicious. I was suddenly very glad I'd brought her along. "Kind of hard to do in the IE."

Inland Empire, I translated in my head. Somewhere east toward the desert if not in it. No one here was from plain old Los Angeles. Everyone had something else to add—this valley or that one, the hills, the basin, the beach, the South Bay. Sometimes I felt like I needed to bring a map to every conversation. Maybe one day I'd get the geography, abbreviations and acronyms. Or maybe I wouldn't stay that long.

"What did you think of Laura?" I needed a clear-eyed opinion. Maybe I was being too harsh. I'd never been a woman faced with a choice.

"She was...nice." Nari pulled her diplomatic, dispassionate doctor's voice.

"Do you believe her?" Because I didn't. Because it couldn't be that simple. Her husband—my father—I corrected in my mind had said he didn't want a child. And just like that, I went from being a Coates to a Tucker. Nothing in Laura's, my biological mother's—my real mother's demeanor had cried agony or yearning.

She hesitated a long time. I realized I'd probably asked her to cross a minefield, blindfolded.

"I believe she thought what she was doing was absolutely necessary to save her marriage."

"She had parents, a sister. I think she could have taken care of me."

"Your father wasn't faithful. She was far from the mainland, on a base. I'm sure her choices seemed limited."

"But surely she could have gotten a plane ticket home to Minnesota." And chosen me. The first choice of my young life and she'd chosen her husband over me, her first born son.

"Are you going to look for your dad?"

"I don't know." Why would I seek out a man who hadn't wanted me before I'd been more than a glimmer in his eye? "He had a part in this. He knew Laura was pregnant but didn't give up the other women. Didn't do anything to assure her that he was going to be there for her and a baby."

"She followed him to Korea." Nari was so damned even handed. As if the choice between a man and a defenseless, helpless child weren't a false one.

"She made a single irreparable decision." I hated people who blamed the mother. I hated the branch of psychology that said everything was the mother's fault. But maybe the scale wasn't exactly even. A mother had greater responsibility. It probably wasn't fair, but it was unerringly true. "She changed my life forever," I said with finality. I was squarely in the maternal blame camp now, and I didn't give a damn about the rightness of it. About whether I was being a proper feminist ally. My mother had given me away like I was a purse or a pair of shoes she didn't like.

"I don't understand," Nari said, sounding genuinely perplexed. As if she hadn't just sat in the living room of the woman who'd tossed me away like a used tissue. "You love your mother and father right? The people who adopted you."

"I do." I did. I would be forever grateful to Joyce and Matthew Tucker for essentially saving my life. Making me their own. Loving me even though we shared no genetic material.

"You didn't have some tragic upbringing where you were beaten or starved or shoved into the basement, right?" Nari said, her plain tone indicative of her train of thought.

"No. Far from that." I'd had nothing but love, acceptance, and encouragement. I pushed the last few months of nearly stony silence from my mind.

"So maybe it turned out for the best. You had two stable parents who loved each other. You had a brother and sister who looked up to you."

"Christian and Brooke aren't exactly speaking to me right now."

"The Tuckers paid for you to go to Dartmouth?" She plowed on, arguing the case for adoption.

"At a discount, but yeah they helped with college and med school. No mortgage-size debt here." Staying local had put me in a much better financial position than many of my med school classmates, many of whom worked a second job doing overnights in needy hospitals or shifts on the county jail ward.

"That's a lot more than most kids get. I'm not saying you should be grateful, or you shouldn't wonder what might have been. But it probably turned out for the best. You heard what Laura said once you told her about your life. She said it was the best possible outcome she could have hoped for." Nari paused for a long moment, weaving between slow cars. "I'm sure she went to sleep every single night wondering what had happened to you. Were you safe? Were you warm? Were you happy? Had she delivered you into the arms of child molesters or abusers? She probably worried whether you were hungry or somehow locked in a closet like those awful true crime cable shows. Be happy or at least content. You had everything. You had love. A mother who gives up the child of their flesh would only want to know those things."

Nari's aptitude for empathy was unnerving. She sounded as if she knew of this particular agony firsthand. Her patients must love her ability to put herself in their shoes and understand their choices. Finally at my building, I pushed the overhead button and the gate opened. Hesitant for the first time, Nari inched forward until she found my spot, then deftly backed the car into the narrow space. After turning off the ignition, she pulled the keys and dropped them in my hand.

"You want to come up?"

Her hesitation was not great for my ego. But I didn't want to be alone right now. I didn't know why. But the thought of hours alone contemplating my mother's choice—or her sacrifice, depending on how I framed it—was as appealing as laying on a bed of nails.

Eventually she said, "Sure, I guess."

We rode the elevator in silence. I turned on the lights and she followed me in, leaving her shoes and purse by the door, perching precariously on the edge of the couch cushion. My mother, my adoptive mother that was, had always asked if my siblings and I wanted to stay for dinner when we were like this, unsettled in our own skin, looking as skittish as kittens. If I made her this nervous, then maybe her feelings for me were growing like mine were for her. I watched Nari, who was lost in thought. Unguarded, she was so beautiful, fragile. I could easily fall in love with her. She was everything I hadn't known I was looking for.

Not wanting to be caught watching her, I stepped away. I brought us both cool glasses of water and sat next to her. The skintight jeans and a purple blouse that looked like it would fall off with a flick of my finger left little to the imagination. I nudged her with my knee and heat stole up my leg. I wasn't usually someone who belabored a point, but I needed her to understand that something about Laura Wallace's story didn't ring true.

"I know you don't have any children. But could you imagine giving birth to a child and handing it off to someone taking him or her to parts unknown?"

17 NARI

The water I'd just drank, the lemonade Laura had served, and the overly sweet frou-frou coffee drink threatened to come up right then.

"Excuse me," I said and made for the master bedroom. I slammed the door and threw the lock on the en suite bathroom. I sat on the lowered toilet lid and swallowed profusely. I felt like my heart was going to come up out of my chest along with today's drink menu.

It was like he knew. But he couldn't know. He couldn't suspect that I'd put my own daughter up for adoption. He couldn't know I'd left her at the hospital like a stray dog at the pound. That I still to this day couldn't decide whether it was the best decision or worst decision of my life.

I stood, turned on the overly bright lights and looked in the mirror to see if my face was lined with guilt. Nothing but the same face I'd had my whole life stared back at me. A little pale, a few laugh lines, but no blood red letter bled from my forehead.

I lifted the hem of my shirt. Even in this light, as bright as an operating room, the *linea negra* no longer showed. There were faint stretch marks around my bikini line, but who but the most dogged observer would notice that or attributed it to anything but weight gain and loss? The other changes like my slightly broader hips wouldn't be noticeable either without a before and after photo.

Sitting back down, on the side of the tub this time, I put my head between my legs until the bout of nausea passed.

"Nari," Lucas called. Then his knuckles thudded on the wood door. "You okay in there?"

I looked at the big dial of my man-faced watch, but I had no idea how much time had passed since I'd come in.

"I'm fine," I said. I stood and opened the door. Lucas' hand was raised, poised to knock again.

"What happened?"

"Just a dizzy spell," I lied.

"Maybe it's because you haven't eaten anything all day."

"Neither have you," I said.

"Nerves. Let me make us something," he said, leading me back to the living area.

I sat at the small black granite island, nursing my self-involved guilt. Today had to have been one of the most nerve-wracking, heart-wrenching days of his life and here I was reliving my own pain and trauma. But I couldn't walk out now. This relationship thing required I be there for him. And I wanted to be. I really did, but I wondered if it wouldn't kill me first.

I watched while he pulled out an onion, cheese, and a couple of apples. A mandolin followed. Deftly he sliced apples, onions, then cheese. Twenty minutes later, he'd assembled some kind of pie. While we talked about work, the apartment filled with the most amazing odors. Nothing like the food I'd grown up with. Nevertheless it reminded me of dinner in Owen's dining rooms.

With a little fanfare, Lucas pulled the round pan from the oven.

"What is it?"

"My mom, Joyce's, apple cheddar and onion tart. She made it every fall when the roadside stands were overloaded with the fall harvest."

I nodded when he asked if I'd like a slice. Lucas took a seat next to me. He'd devoured one slice while I'd only taken a bite.

"Do you like it?" he asked.

"It's different," I said. The mix of sweet and salty was truly interesting, not that I'd eat it every day.

"You don't have to finish it," he said, pointing to my remaining slice.

"I don't have much of an appetite," I said. Not only had the world changed from Technicolor to sepia after everything happened, food had never been the same either. I ate to survive.

"It's better with hot apple cider," he said.

What was it about Lucas that brought back so many memories of New England? Was it his accent, the crisp northeast tones rolling off his tongue? Or was it his quest to fill in the blanks from his past that made me think about my own? Like now. I'd first tasted apple cider while driving to a county fair with Andrew. We'd pulled to a roadside stand and shared first a cider in his car, then a make out session not a mile down the road.

I needed to shake off the past like a dog sheds water, flinging droplets everywhere. I stood and walked to the living room. The light from the open kitchen had a steep fall off in here. Lucas, thankfully, took the hint and sat next to me on the couch. For not the first time in my life, I thanked God or whomever created testosterone, the hormone that gave men a single-track mind.

Pushing everything from my overactive brain, I leaned forward, tracing the sweep of his brow. I moved my fingers toward the hair that curled around his ears to his jaw. Lucas entwined his fingers in my hair and drew me to him. I closed my eyes and waited for the kiss that would devour me, that would send me to any place but here where ghosts were haunting me.

Instead of lips and tongue, Lucas' eyes locked with and held mine. I tried to keep from shifting on the couch, tried not to blink or look away. I think I failed miserably.

"Are you attracted to me, Nari?"

Of all the possible things he could have said or asked, that one threw me for a loop. Hesitating for only a fraction of a moment, I nodded in response. "I wouldn't have slept with you if I wasn't." I made my tone as glib as I could muster.

"I know you slept with me those first few times to forget." The contents of my stomach formed into a ball of lead. Fully clothed, I felt naked and raw in front of him. I was made of glass and he could see right through me. Right to the heart beating out of rhythm, to my brain, its electric impulses broadcasting all my secrets. "The next time we make love, I want it to be because you want to remember."

I leaned forward again, letting my eyelids flutter closed, offering up my lips, trying to get him to forget all that integrity. He cupped my shoulder, moving me back a fraction. "Did you hear what I said?"

"Yes, Lucas." I tried to fill my nod with solemnity. "But memory isn't all it's cracked up to be. Sometimes sex can be a good way to blow off steam, push away the hard stuff of the day." I concentrated my efforts in a different place this time, pulling the tongue of his leather belt from the buckle, disengaging the pin. I loved his little jolt at the soft clink of animal hide against metal. I pushed a finger under his shirt, tickling the whorl of hair surrounding his navel.

All his breath came out in a huff. Taking that as a sign of acquiescence, I popped the snap on his jeans, undid the zipper, and ran a single finger down the erection tenting his boxers. His chest expanded with a sharp intake of air. Taking the lead, I unbuttoned one shirt, easing it from his shoulder and pulled the knit one under it over his head.

Before Lucas, I'd never thought much about chest hair, but I have to admit that I liked the smell and feel of Lucas'. I got all shivery just thinking about him over and above me, the friction of that hair across my body, like a thousand downy feathers on my skin, while he thrust deep, burrowing toward my womb.

Deliberately, I pulled the faux wrap blouse over my head. The little bandeau bra I wore out of a sense of propriety more than need followed. Lucas' eyes dilated, his hands moving to my breasts as if they had a mind of their own.

Now we were getting somewhere. I slipped my hands into his boxers and pulled his taut little butt forward. Our bodies connected and it was like the Fourth of July all over again. He ducked his head and kissed me. It seemed like we went on like that forever, his hands roaming from my breasts, through my hair, down my sides, finally cupping my ass and grinding us together. A single human hair couldn't have found its way between us, we were so close.

"Can we move this party to the bedroom?" I said. Then I looked down. "Or the couch can do if you like."

Lucas pulled his undershirt from the couch. "Here. Put this on." He bunched up the shirt and pulled it over my head. Like a child reluctant to get dressed, I stuck my arms through the holes. He looked away toward the kitchen while zipping, snapping and buckling his pants and belt. "Damn, it's still like a wet t-shirt contest without the water."

At my look, which I can only assume was perplexed, he gestured for me to sit. This time he sat at least a foot away. I turned toward him, our knees touching, trying to keep us connected in any way I could.

"What?" I wanted to get back to the sex part. I hadn't bargained for a discussion. Talking was not my strong suit. Seduction was.

"Do you like *me* Nari?"

"What do you mean? I'm practically naked in your apartment. I would think the answer is obvious." Lucas shifted in his seat. He rose from the couch and paced out his frustration. "If you come here, I know a way I can show you." I grabbed for his hand, ready to pull him toward me, but he snatched it away like I was fire and he was about to get third degree burns.

"I'm serious. I need to know you like me, not the idea of me."

I nearly lost my breath, but for a different reason this time. He'd hit far too close to the truth. "I'm here," was all I could concede.

"I need more than that, Nari. Joyce and Matthew adopted me because of the idea of having children. Sometimes I feel like the reality of me has to compete with what they imagined a son would be."

"But they've had you in their lives for thirty plus years. Surely who you are has replaced any idea of who you'd be."

"I'd have said yes, absolutely until this finding my own parents thing came up. Now that I'm no longer the adopted son grateful for the Huxtable-like family upbringing, their carefully crafted reality has been shattered." He paused a long time. I could see his throat working, Adam's apple bobbing below the squared off jaw dotted with late day stubble.

I patted his arm, awkwardly. I had never been good with outward displays of emotion except in the examination room. It was easier to feel for complete strangers, hold their hand, wipe their tears. Real life wasn't clinical, but messy and difficult.

"Even Laura had an idea of me. I can only begin to imagine what she'd filled in during the last thirty five years. But whatever it was, I couldn't have been it."

"I don't have an idea of you, Lucas," I said. "I guess this is maybe the one advantage of having known you for only a couple of years. What I know about you is from what you've said, done, been in the office and with me."

"Do you promise that you don't see me as a replacement for Andrew? For what you lost? I don't want to be the stand-in for the husband you wish you'd had."

"I'm not...you're not...Andrew..." I protested as the possible truth of his words sunk in.

"You haven't had a single relationship in the last decade. I think that says something."

Anger fizzed in my veins. Why in the hell were we arguing and not fucking? I wrapped my arms across my breasts. "Since you seem to be the expert on non-verbal cues, what does this one say?"

"That you're using me to get past your grief. Maybe you need to figure that out first."

"I'm not grieving," I said, mentally scrabbling for purchase. "I'm trying to love you. Maybe you're the person grieving for something you can't have. I've made peace with my reality."

"Love me?" Lucas paused a long time. "What do you mean, love me?"

"I'm not sure what in the hell I mean." Escape plans formed in my mind. I pulled a tight knot in the right side of his shirt and walked straight to his front door. "I can't deal with this kind of passive/aggressive bullshit."

"Where are you going?"

"Home. Either you want me or you don't. But you have to figure that out. Maybe today is not the best day to be having this conversation." Even in my most bitchy moment, I had to acknowledge that meeting his birth mother had amped up the stress level far too much. He needed time just to process that.

"Is that how you deal with the hard stuff, Nari, by obliterating it? If you can't use sex as your drug of choice, you're going to hide out?"

"Maybe you're right, Lucas. Maybe I'm not ready for you, this, whatever there is between us." I didn't care how juvenile it looked or felt, I was taking my toys and going home. It was the best thing for both of us.

18 Lucas

"You forgot something," I said, making no move to physically stop Nari from leaving. She'd scooped up her shirt and jammed it in her purse.

She dropped her hand from the brass doorknob, turned and looked directly at me. Something in her eyes made me hesitate for a moment, but only a brief second. There was no way we could continue if we danced around her using sex as her drug of choice.

Nari glanced down at the sparkly purple top spilling from her stiff leather bag. "What did I forget?"

"Your courage," I said.

"What in the hell is that supposed to mean?"

"You're refusing to face your demons head on."

"How can you say that?"

"Because you think fucking me will somehow rid you of Andrew." Crude language wasn't my standby, but seemed necessary to scrape away the layers.

"That's really beneath you."

"Is it? Because nothing I'm seeing says you can make any kind of relationship with me until you resolve whatever's going on with your past. I don't know if you need to put it to rest or what...but do you seriously think you could love me, fall in love with me when your heart is elsewhere?"

"I will never be able to forget Andrew. I don't think it's fair that you would ask me to push aside my first husband. I may love him, but I'm not in love with him."

"When did you reach that little revelation? Because I distinctly remember you saying just the opposite to me."

"You'd kind of persuaded me to change my mind. To give you a chance. To try this—us. But I'm starting to think I was wrong."

"I don't believe you."

"Why?"

"If you've really changed your mind, what was that little performance over there by the couch earlier? You had that same single-minded determination to get my pants off that you did those nights at the bar."

"I'm not some shrinking violet, Lucas. I thought you knew that. So what, I wanted to have sex. I wanted to have it with *you*. Is that a crime?"

"It's not a crime if that's the truth. It's just that..." I didn't know what it was. Maybe she'd finally moved on from Andrew, but I hadn't. It wasn't that easy to stop loving someone.

"What?" Her voice had gone from shriek to whisper. She dropped her bag and padded toward me. The sexually aggressive panther look was back. My cock responded while my brain rebelled.

"That..." I closed my eyes for a second. A willing woman had a way of distracting me from logical thought. I knew she was doing it on purpose. I took a step back. "Let's get all of the stuff with Andrew on the table, then."

"I've told you all there is."

"I don't think so, Nari." Something flickered at the back of my mind. I hadn't had this feeling since I took boards exams. I hated knowledge that was just outside my grasp. "I wasn't a history major, racking up dates of wars and battles, but I did my fair share of memory tricks in school," I said, trying to pull a bunch of disparate facts together.

"What are you talking about? I don't like this push-pull. It's you who's throwing up the barriers now."

A light bulb flickered on—came to life. "What happened at the end of June, Nari?"

"Don't..."

"Don't what? Get at what you're holding back?"

She shook her head. Big movements. "I can't do this..."

"And there you go, running away again. We can't have any kind of relationship without the truth on the table, Nari. That's a rule I live by. Finding out you're adopted changes everything. Deception—even the most passive obfuscation of the truth hurts."

"Why do you need to know every little thing about me? Love shouldn't be a deposition."

"I'm not asking for every little thing. I'm asking about the big things." I swept my arms in huge arcs. "The elephant in the living room."

She was silent. She wasn't saying a thing. But she hadn't left either.

"There's something here. But we can't...I can't move forward without all the cards on the table. I've shared all my demons with you. I'm looking for a little reciprocation here."

Nari squatted on the floor and started pulling objects from her bag. First, her purple blouse floated to the floor, loose sequins pinging against the slate entryway tiles. Next came tubes and containers of different sizes. Then her phone skidded across the floor.

Finally finding what she was looking for, Nari removed her wallet, and unzipped an inner compartment. She pulled out a small square of paper. My heart dropped from my throat to my intestines. It looked like a photo. I didn't want to see a picture of her first love. What guy did? How would her showing me the picture prove she'd moved on? What did this have to do with late June?

When she extended her hand, I reluctantly met it with my own. Because I'd asked for this bare-naked honesty instead of a bare-naked Nari. The latter of which frankly seemed like a better idea right now. Me and my damned ethics and morals.

Clear to muddled went my brain. The tiny square was the picture of a newborn. The little pale face looked as exhausted and befuddled as I remembered babies looking during the six weeks of my obstetrics rotation.

I looked up and met Nari's unblinking gaze. "What does this baby have to do with Andrew?"

"That's our daughter."

"Daughter?" She'd said that girl in her apartment was her cousin, not her daughter.

"That's the little girl Andrew and I made. It's why we got married sooner rather than later."

But there was no baby or little girl or bigger girl in Nari's apartment. My normally agile brain felt like sludge. "Where is she?"

Nari's sigh was long. She stood, holding out her hand for the picture. I placed it back onto her outstretched palm. "I gave her up for adoption...eleven years ago." Nari looked at her watch. "Eleven years and two months ago."

"June..."

"Twenty-fourth is her birthday."

Vibration on the tile floor broke the tension.

"Are you on call?" I asked.

"I should probably answer it." On hands and knees she sought out her phone.

19 NARI

It wasn't work calling. The number on the phone was both familiar and unfamiliar at the same time. A shiver shook my arms and I nearly dropped the phone. Andrew's number. Not his, but his parents'. Wildly I did an sweep of Lucas' apartment as if it were possibly bugged.

On the fourth ring, I tapped the green phone shaped button.

"Nari?" The voice was Andrew's. I nearly fainted from the shock of it. Wild speculation filled my head. Had his death been some wild and crazy mistake? Had they collected the wrong body? I steeled myself against hyperventilation and panic. Was this a guilt-induced hallucination? I put my picture of Minnie back into the secret compartment of my wallet where it should have stayed.

I turned my back against Lucas' scrutiny and paced toward the kitchen, wishing the apartment had more distinct boundaries. The well laid out open plan wasn't pretty any more. Instead it exposed me, made me vulnerable. I opened my eyes and gathered my wits. The voice wasn't Andrew's. It was the same deep, northeastern self-assured voice of a Clarke brother.

"Simon? It's Nari."

"How are you?" he asked. This time I could hear the difference like night and day. Simon's voice had always been more confident, throatier than his brother's.

"Good. I guess. Haven't heard from you in a while."

"It's still hard." I heard his swift intake of breath through the three thousand mile space between us. "I'm coming to Los Angeles."

"When?" My question must have been loud or hopeful. Lucas stopped fiddling with his clothes and he looked at me, a question in his eyes. But it wasn't about who was on the phone, but about the baby. There were too many question marks from Lucas. I turned my attention to repacking my bag and to...Simon. "Did you say you're coming to L.A? Why? When?"

"I'm landing tomorrow morning. I was hoping we could go out for a late lunch."

"Give me your flight information. Hold on." To Lucas, I asked, "Can I have a pen and paper?"

"I'm sorry. I didn't mean to interrupt your evening." Simon's voice was full of hesitation and apology. That wasn't at all like him. Instantly, I regretted the distance

I'd put between me and the Clarke family when I'd gone away to have the baby.

"No worries. You would never an interruption. I'm so glad that you're coming to town. Are you working out here?" Simon had done what their dad wanted. Gotten one of those jobs that was about making money, not making anything. Last I'd heard, his company had bought up a bunch of small retail chains. He was probably coming out here to fire some unsuspecting hourly workers.

Mentally chastising myself, I stopped the direction of my thoughts. I was being terribly unfair. Andrew's youthful idealism may have worn off. I'd have still loved him if he had one of those jobs. My parents may have learned to adore him if he'd had one of those jobs.

"I actually have to go pack," Simon said, stopping the speeding train of judgment I'd let loose in my brain. "Let's meet tomorrow. Thanks for picking me up."

"Anytime," I said. I put the phone back in my purse in a daze, realizing I'd missed the Clarkes; Andrew and Simon's effusive mother, their taciturn father, the boys' antics.

"Who was that?"

"Andrew's brother, Simon. He's coming to town tomorrow. For lunch. I've got to go get ready."

20 Lucas

She ran out of my apartment like her hair was on fire. No explanation on this Simon character. No comment on the fact that she'd had a child. A little girl she'd given away. Nothing. Because despite what she kept saying, one way or another she was running back to Andrew.

I let her go this time. I didn't ask her back, call her on being a hypocrite or a liar. There was something very wrong in my judgment of women. Maybe because the first two women in my life hadn't been up front with me, my compass pointed in the wrong direction. There had to be women out there who didn't say one thing, but mean something entirely different.

Undressing, I left a trail of clothes in my wake. I'd never had much in the way of traditional faith. But maybe there was something to the idea of reincarnation. What in the hell had I done to have two women in my life who gave up babies without a second thought?

Regret. I'd wanted a lot more of it from Laura that afternoon. How could a mother let something as trivial as a crappy adult male-female relationship get between her and the child in her womb? I didn't have any children, but couldn't imagine a more unshakeable bond. But I'd watched two women talking about pushing a baby out and handing it away as if it were no more difficult than giving clothes to Goodwill. There wasn't a single sappy Lifetime Channel, Hallmark moment between them.

Naked, I stood before my open closet. Reaching into the back, I pulled out the gift Brooke had given me last Christmas. My sister's infectious laugh had filled the room when she'd handed over the box.

"For your new L.A. lifestyle," she'd said, barely keeping our mother's hazelnut coffee from snorting through her nose. If I'd been less jet-lagged, I'd have taken her outside for a snowball fight and shown her what's what. But I'd played the mature oldest brother and had taken the box without comment.

Inside was an outfit worthy of the upstairs neighbor Larry in old reruns of Three's Company—minus the gold chains. I'd laughed good-naturedly along with my brother and parents. On my return to L.A., I'd quickly stashed the outfit in the back of my closet, planning to donate it the next time the Mission called to let me know their truck was in the neighborhood. But I'd never let it go. Maybe I could put it to good use.

To hell with it. I was single, successful, reasonably attractive. I pulled the shiny midnight blue shirt from its hanger, snipping the tags with cuticle scissors from my dresser. The pants were skinnier than I was used to. But maybe that's what guys who went clubbing in Hollywood wore. Gossip magazine hound that Brook was, she'd know that better than me.

I pulled some tighty whities from the back of my drawer. I wasn't going to try to stuff my very comfortable, medically sound seersucker boxers into those pants. One shave and twenty minutes later, I practically had to wolf whistle at myself. Not bad at all.

I took the lime green Subaru—not going to get any cooler instantaneously—over to Sunset and drove down the electronic billboard-illuminated street under twenty miles per hour, studiously looking away from the no cruising signs. When I saw a club that looked loud enough and dark enough to chase my Nari blues away, I pulled over and gave The Green Machine to the reluctant valet who looked crestfallen that the other vest guy got to park the new Tesla. Despite the uncoolness factor of my car, he happily took twenty of my hard-earned dollars to park five feet away from the front door.

Though my clothes were better than the car, the bouncer wasn't keen on letting me in the club. I'd forgotten this part. The sacred velvet rope.

When I'd been with other medical residents letting off steam in SoHo or Tribeca, the wait had been part of the fun. Now I felt old and awkward. Five seconds from taking myself back downtown and chalking this up to the worst idea ever, a gaggle of three twenty-something girls grabbed me by the elbows.

"We're Heidi, Lori, and Marci," the blondest and toothiest of the group announced. "I got a part on *Two Broke Girls* and we're celebrating!"

On that exclamation point, I was swooped into the inner sanctum, past the velvet rope and to a tiny table for four. One of the "i" girls clicked her fingers and a waiter appeared at the table in an instant. I didn't hear a thing over the music, but Grey Goose and mixers arrived.

"Bottle service okay?" the actress asked.

I shrugged. What the hell? I was along for the ride.

They poured four shots, toasted to booking the role, and drank. Not to be left behind, I threw back the concoction they'd called the cranberry kamikaze.

By the time the girls got up to dance, I knew who was who. Heidi was the actress. Marci was a casting assistant, and Lori worked in the mailroom of some talent agency, if I'd heard the acronym right.

Eight years of college had well shielded me from dark rooms and pounding bass. But I'd also missed out on gyrating flesh on display, apparently. It was a sight to behold. Thousands of hot girls were within spitting distance of my apartment and I was twisting myself into knots over Nari.

When they came back, we all did something called Bomb Pops. It was red white and blue like those popsicles from my childhood and about as sweet. But when Marci parked herself on my lap, and leaned in for a little lip action, sweet was good.

They dipped the next round of glasses in cake sprinkles and we all toasted and downed something called a cake pop. There was a lot of vodka and little cake in the drink. Marci had straddled my hips by then and had turned the full force of her charms on me.

I put the empty glass on the ledge behind me and focused in on two of her charms. She looped her arms around my neck and leaned in for a kiss. Her friends hooted when she opened and our tongues met. I moved my hands from her shoulders to the huge breasts nearly spilling from her powder blue tank. Damn. She felt nice and soft and free of emotional baggage.

The other girls went back to the dance floor, and Marci pulled me upstairs to a private VIP booth. She yanked the curtain around the white leather couch and lifted her tank over her head. Whoa baby. Holy mother of God. Where in the hell had women like this been during my horny teens?

"Go ahead, touch me. I know you want to," Marci invited.

"I'm kind of involved with someone," I heard my truth serum-vodka filled self blurt out.

"She's not here. I am." Marci leaned close, her nipple nearly brushing my lips. "I won't tell."

"Excuse me. I gotta go," I said and shoved my way from the VIP area to the first men's room I could find. Those very sweet girly shots hadn't seemed all that potent, but my head was swimming.

I tried to piss away some of the alcohol, and got a glass of water from a sympathetic bartender before making my way back to the table we'd shared downstairs. The girls were nowhere to be seen, but the tab was there.

Eight hundred dollars plus gratuity was what this moment of stupidity was going to cost me.

"Your friends said thanks for the drinks. They headed out to celebrate."

Ouch. Made the fifty-dollar cover charge seem cheap. I handed over the plastic and signed away a chunk of my savings. I wasn't Nari. Trying to act like her wasn't my speed. I wasn't some douchy guy who had sex with girls in the back of nightclubs.

The staff eyed my table and all but said it was time for me to move on. They had more idiots willing to toss their money at overpriced vodka and blond twenty-somethings.

The valet handed me my keys, but I pocketed them. There was no way I should get in that car and drive downtown. I didn't want to add death to my night of irresponsibility and stupidity. So I walked further down Sunset and dialed the last number I'd called, Nari.

Thirty minutes later, she pulled up to the bank across the street from the club.

"Even your sweats are designer," I said into the cab of the Range Rover.

"Thanks for calling me," she said, her face as serious as if she were giving a cancer diagnosis. "No matter what happened between us, I wouldn't want to lose you to a drunk driver."

Just when I thought I couldn't feel any shittier. I pushed the button down, opening the window. I needed fresh air to ease the nausea in my stomach. Vomiting in Nari's very expensive looking chrome and leather and wood filled car would be the last straw.

When Nari pulled up to her building, I spoke up. "Why aren't you taking me home?"

"Look. I don't have time to drive you downtown, then pick you up in the morning to rescue your car from where in the hell ever it ends up." Nari looked pointedly at the car clock, twelve-thirty am pulsed from the LED readout searing my eyeballs. It was like I already had a hangover before the morning sun. "I have to go to the airport to-morrow."

Not able to argue with her reasoning, I followed her upstairs. "I'm going to bed. You can sleep off what in the hell ever you drank and figure it out in the morning."

I didn't hear anything else she had to say, because I had to run to her guest bathroom and puke up the rain-bow of alcohol shots I'd taken in. Probably should have eaten something more than a slice of apple cheddar tart before I went out. Probably shouldn't have thrown down all the silly colored alcohol.

Nari's bedroom door was firmly closed when I rinsed out my mouth and pulled myself together, so I pulled off my shiny club clothes, tossed them into her empty washer. The door to the second bedroom was locked tight as well, so I positioned myself on her couch. I was out cold before I could think about what a mess I'd made of the day.

21 NARI

I wasn't stupid enough to wake the beast on my couch. Mortified by what I'd shared yesterday, I tiptoed out of my apartment. Hopefully Lucas would have the good sense to find himself a cab and lock the door on his way out.

Putting off any conversation with him until we were safely in the confines of the clinic was at the top of my priority list.

Once out the door and down to the garage, I climbed into my big SUV and sat for a moment before starting the ignition.

Simon. It had been how many years since I'd seen him? I ticked back on my fingers. Maybe three, four. He'd headed up the liquidation and bankruptcy of a discount housewares chain with a zillion stores in California. We'd had an awkward dinner where we talked about everything *but* Andrew. Didn't make for a lot of conversation.

After starting the car, I pulled out of the garage. The roads to the airport were empty on Sunday morning. Los Angeles wasn't a city of churchgoers. All the club hopping people, like Lucas, were doing the same as him, probably, recovering on someone else's couch.

I pulled over to a coffee shop on Sepulveda when my phone dinged. Simon had texted. He had landed. I looked down at my clothes. Sleeveless off-white silk top, beige linen pants. I hoped this was okay, that the cashmere sweater wasn't overkill. There wasn't time to make an emergency trip to the mall.

Flipping down the mirror, I gave myself a final once over. Which fashion guru was it who'd said pick the accessory that stood out the most and ditch it? The pendant was too much, so I unclasped it and stuffed it far into the recesses of my bag. With pearl studs, I felt simple, understated, the kind of woman I'd have become if I'd stayed in the Clarke family.

The Indy 500-like roadway around the airline terminals kept my mind off the reason I'd never be in the bosom of the Clarke family. On my second go-round, I finally saw him waving like a demon. Simon's hair was shorter than the last time I'd seen him. I guess he'd outgrown the longish mane he and Andrew both sported during their late adolescence.

I popped the locks and swallowed the lump in my throat. In so many ways, he reminded me of Andrew. The same big knuckled hands. The same eyes. Blinking more rapidly than usual, I looked away. Needed to focus on getting out of the terminal's traffic spiral and on to Sepulveda.

"Where are you staying?" I asked. It was easier than hello.

"Checking into the Fairmont. Thought we could have Afternoon Tea. I remember you liked that."

I fiddled with the navigation, zooming in on the map, though I knew exactly where I was going. I changed the temperature to maximize Simon's comfort. I opened the sunroof.

"Weather's great today." It must have been the wind coming in that was making me tear up. I leaned closer to the wheel, cutting my brother-in-law out of my periphery and focused on getting us there in one piece.

While Simon checked in, I found us a table on the restaurant's outdoor deck. I shouldn't have been surprised he'd already made a reservation. The Clarkes had been amazingly thoughtful about formalities like that.

"They brought sandwiches, scones, and water. I hope that's okay...I didn't order tea yet. I didn't know what you'd want," I said when Simon wove his way to the table.

As if hearing what I'd said, the server materialized at the table.

"Nari?" Simon asked in a voice so much like Andrew's, I wanted to get up and walk away from the memories flooding through me. But I kept my butt firmly planted like the mature adult I'd grown to be. I wasn't a clueless twenty anymore.

"I'll have the chrysanthemum," I said. Maybe the tight bud blooming in the clear pot would keep me from staring too hard in the face of a man who embodied the past I was constantly trying to forget.

"Earl Grey."

The Clarke brothers were the only men I knew who could order tea or wine and make it appear utterly masculine. I'd never been attracted to Simon. Nevertheless, I wanted to lean forward and caress the hint of stubble on his cheek, or lean into the shoulder that I knew would fit my head like Andrew's had. Even the faint smell wafting across the table reminded me of my deceased husband. Though logically I knew it was only because they probably favored the same brand of soap, it still made every fiber of my being want to reach out to his.

"Are you seeing someone?" Simon asked, turning his whole body and attention toward me, eroding my resistance.

The sandwich I'd pulled from the tiered tray fell from my hand, making an indelicate salmon and cream cheese splat on the table cloth. Deftly, Simon rescued it and placed it on my plate.

"It's okay, you know. We're not expecting you to live like a nun." The gentle permissiveness in his demeanor only amplified the guilt.

"It's not really working out anyway. I think …"

"Why not?"

"It's stupid. It's a guy from work. A doctor. Lucas. He's in the middle of reuniting with his birth mom. That kind of thing doesn't leave much space for a relationship." I shook my head. I didn't want to talk about the bundle of bad decisions that was Lucas.

"I don't know if this particular guy is worth it, but I'd love to see you happy with someone."

"May not happen for me. Maybe I had my one chance." Because of the disaster that was Lucas, I couldn't see a future with anyone right now. After a very long hiatus, maybe I'd consider it.

"Don't say that, Nari."

"I met 'the one' early. If he'd died fifty years later, no one would expect me to pair up. I had my run early, that's all." I knew I sounded defeated, pathetic probably. But I couldn't help myself. Why did Daisy or even Lucas think I was whole enough to try this again?

"I think you'd make a wonderful wife to someone new, and a great mom." He held up his hands in supplication. "My opinion after knowing you a dozen years, is all."

I eyed the food although it didn't hold much appeal. The waitress poured some nearly clear tea into my cup. I braved the jolt of recognition and looked at him more closely. I saw it now. He had that look of someone smug, self-satisfied, in love. The look of someone so happy they want to pair up everyone around them. "You seeing someone?" I asked as if I didn't already know the answer.

There was a long pause. "Actually, yes. I think Pam and I are serious."

"I'm so glad," I gushed. The gushing was a bit of a put on, but I was glad, really glad. The Clarkes deserved some happiness. Maybe a marriage, grandchildren would put smiles on their faces. New life and all that.

Simon had no problem finishing the sandwiches and half of the scones. It was some time before he spoke again. "I'm actually thinking of asking her to marry me."

"That's so great," I said, trying to make my feelings match my voice.

"I want you to come to the wedding. Nari."

"I'd be happy to come," I said. Yeah, well. Whatever. Happy wasn't exactly what I'd be. But I would fly east and smile like my life depended on it. That or find a continuing education conference that "happened" to be the same week. But I'd figure that part out later. "So how'd you meet, Pam, was it?"

I sat back in the padded floral chair and let Simon's chatter wash over me. He seemed very much in love with the woman he was describing. I tried not to be jealous that one person could meet another and fall in love. That it seemed so easy and normal for him, for them. But so complicated for me.

"So I came to ask you a huge favor," Simon said, his face both earnest and serious.

I couldn't think of a single thing *I* could do for him. Unless she needed a physical and a specialist referral. "Anything," I said. That was true. Even if he didn't know it, he'd once been my brother-in-law, was still family.

"I don't have any idea how to ask for this." Simon uncharacteristically stumbled over his words.

"Just ask." I hated beating around the bush. I imagined the worst, that he would ask me to be a surrogate for his soon-to-be wife. But even I knew it wasn't likely there was something so far-fetched in his mind.

"I would like to give Pamela my grandmother Maude's ring."

I don't think I blacked out. I really don't. But when I put my hand on the china cup to steady my unsteady fingers, the tea was cold, and Simon's face was full of concern.

"Nari?"

"You want to take away the one remaining link I have to Andrew?"

"That's not the way I see it—"

"And give it to another woman?"

"Nari, our grandmother wanted it to stay in the family."

"What happened to Van Cleef and Arpels?" The question had no class. I didn't care.

"I know this is hard—"

"Didn't you just say that I was family? I'm not going to run out and hock the ring, or anything like that. It's safely put away."

"The tradition is for it to be passed on to the next generation of Clarkes. It's not like you got married. That would be a different matter altogether."

And the lies piled up. Secret marriage. Secret baby. This was worthy of the crappy soaps people used to watch during college and med school. Of course, as far as Simon knew, the buck stopped with me.

There would be no next generation. But even if I ever saw my daughter again, would I give Minnie the ring? I didn't even know who she was. Who she'd turned out to be. If she wanted to know her birth mother.

I cleared my head. My mind was going down a forbidden road. I needed to give Simon what he'd came for. That ring came with a promise of forever after. That promise had been revoked by the drunk driver that killed Andrew. "Do you want to get it now?"

"I thought we'd finish tea. Maybe you could show me a bit of the city."

He wasn't a tourist. But he wasn't a native either, so I could probably show him something new. This wasn't his first or last trip to the City of Angels. "Did you have business in town?" I'm sure his colleagues would be eager to take him out for a night on the town, especially if it meant prolonging their jobs.

Simon's signing for the tea, and making work of the tip calculation was the worst deflection I'd ever seen.

"I thought we could spend some time together," he said, too cheerfully for my taste.

"You came here only for the ring, right?"

Long silence. "It's just that Mom and Dad and I thought it was time to bring it home."

Her house wasn't home for the Clarke family heirloom. It stung more than it should. "Let's go now," I said. Because if we talked about it one single minute further, I'd never be able to give it up.

"I like what you've done with the windows," Simon said when we got to my place.

I hated that. I hated that he was trying to be nice. "Silk and Belgian linen," I found myself answering as if interior decorating were important. "Do you want water?" Now I was auditioning for hostess of the year. "Wine, soju, tea?" I asked, ticking off the contents of my cabinets.

Simon's laugh felt forced. "I think I've had enough liquid. Can I use your bathroom?"

I pointed the way to the powder room. The path to my bedroom was like a slow walk to the gallows. My reflection in the mirrored closet doors pained me, so I pushed one open quickly, watching my pinched face disappear. The cardboard box was where it always was. It would be in a navy velvet box under the albums and ticket stubs. I was lifting carefully when shouting pierced the fog of my brain.

Laying the box gently on my duvet, I got back to the living room in a second.

"What in the hell is going on?" My question was moot. Because I quickly figured out what in the hell was going on. Simon was standing in the living room looking at a very stunned Lucas—dripping wet, bath towel wrapped around his waist. The expression was mirrored on Simon's face. Probably mine as well.

Where was life's rewind button? I'd happily go back thirty seconds, two days—twelve years.

"I thought you'd left," I said to Lucas. Because that's what drunken lovers did. They tucked their tails and went home to sleep off their hangovers. They did not stick around and take showers.

"I...needed to shower before I got in a cab," he said. "I didn't think I'd cross paths with—" He cocked his head toward Simon.

Seriously? He thought I was that girl. Getting one guy in bed before getting the other one out. Mortification heated my cheeks. Maybe I'd done more than a thing or two to give him that impression. Fortunately, embarrassment didn't tie my tongue. "This is Simon Clarke. Simon, meet Lucas Tucker. He's the doctor in my office I mentioned this morning." Perplexed replaced shocked. "Simon is Andrew's brother."

Ever polite, Simon held out his hand. "Nice to meet you. I've heard great things. Hope you're treating Nari well. She deserves happiness."

Holding the bath towel tight with one hand, he gripped Simon's—hard.

Men.

"Same here. What brings you to L.A.?"

"Came to see my almost sister-in-law," Simon said. Well that big lie of omission was out. I'd never told Lucas how big the secret was, or that it was a secret.

"Did you bring your wife? Girlfriend?"

When had Lucas gone all caveman? I let it pass. I'd take any distraction from him mentioning that he'd thought there was a marriage, while Simon clearly hadn't been privy to the whole truth.

"Pamela had family obligations this weekend," Simon answered diplomatically.

"How long have you been seeing Pamela?" Who in the hell cared about Pamela with a ring-retrieving man on one hand and a wet naked one on the other?

"Do you want to get dressed?" I asked, reminding him he was naked and wet, in a living room. I hadn't seen anyone naked and wet in a living room since college.

"My clothes are in the dryer," Lucas said, lifting his hand and pointing, nearly losing half the bath sheet. I was never happier that I hadn't skimped on towels. Daisy had made fun of my spa-size linens when she'd lived here. She'd praise me now if she could see this.

After losing one hell of an expensive duvet when Daisy had left it in the communal laundry a while back, I'd sprung for my own stacking unit. For a long moment, the rhythmic drumbeat was the only sound in the too crowded apartment.

"Not to be rude, but don't you have a washer-dryer?" My pointed question was for Lucas. "After last night—"

"Maybe I should come back later," Simon said with impeccable manners. Like he hadn't walked in on the most fucked up domestic scene ever.

"No, let me get it for you." It was now or never. I knew that.

"Get what?" Lucas butted his stubbed nose where it didn't belong, again. It didn't look like he was going to get clothes anytime soon. Maybe I had a bathrobe that would fit. "Get what, Nari?" Lucas's pointed question took me away from the speculation on ways he should cover up.

"Great grandmother Maude's ring."

Lucas' eyes pierced straight through to my heart. "Your engagement ring?"

"It's been in the Clarke family since the Mayflower or something like that. The first son to marry can give it to his wife. Then on the tenth anniversary, we'd have gotten our own, and given this one back, but—"

"But—" Lucas looked like he wanted to say something. I pleaded with my eyes for him to exercise his right remain silent.

"Nari told you what happened right?" Simon said, his eyes drilled on Lucas'. "They never got married."

"Do you think you should—"

I interrupted. There was no reason for Simon to know. Some truths were taken to the grave. "But I'd probably be giving it back anyway right about now. So you're actually on schedule. Let me..." I left them alone in the living room for only as long as it took to retrieve what was no longer mine.

There was no time to skip down memory lane. I pulled open the keepsake box, and fitted my hand around the velvet. I resisted the urge to open it, reminisce, remember. The smaller velvet box underneath remained in its resting place. The wedding ring would remain mine, at least. It wasn't an heirloom, pretty, or even all that expensive. But the simple platinum band with its single miniature diamond was all I had now.

Deliberately, I marched back out and put the box in Simon's outstretched palm.

"He went to find his clothes, I think," Simon said, closing his hand around the box and depositing it in his sport coat's inside pocket.

"Let me drive you back to Santa Monica."

"Do you want to have dinner? I don't know if I'll have a chance to come back to town before the wedding."

"You haven't popped the question?" Didn't asking for the ring seem a bit premature, is what I wanted to say. What if she said no? I could have held on to this little piece of Andrew a little longer.

Simon gave me a funny look. "We've talked about it." I guess I was still in the land of the immature. The last time I'd gotten engaged it had been a surprise. Mature adults over the age of thirty talked about these kinds of things. They probably had to plan weddings and honeymoons around careers and vacations, not when there were a few days off from school. "She wants a short engagement," he was saying. "We want to start a family right away. Neither one of us is getting any younger. I want our kids to enjoy their grandparents as long as they can."

I wondered, not for the first time, if Minnie would have enjoyed them. If the Clarkes would have loved her. Would she have reminded them too much of Andrew? Or not enough of Andrew and too much of me?

"I have to get to work early in the morning, so I don't think I can do dinner tonight." I knew my limits and I'd about reached them. Sitting stoically while Simon reminisced was a form of Chinese water torture I'd barely survived the last two or three times we'd done it.

"Yep, there's a seven-thirty meeting," Lucas said, coming back into the room. Fortunately, he was fully dressed this time around.

"Will you ride with us?" I asked Lucas. For a moment, at least, I needed a buffer between myself and both of them.

The goodbye at Simon's hotel was awkward. I hugged him hard. This would be the last time we were together like this. The next time I saw him, he'd probably be married, have a baby in tow. I don't know why there was such a sense of finality in our parting. But it was there. Maybe because I'd given up the last bit of Andrew.

I held up my hand and shaded my eyes against the sun as another Clarke left my life.

22 LUCAS

Nari hopped back up onto her seat and slammed the door—hard.

"Where's your car?"

Having ditched one guy, she seemed eager to cut me loose as well. But I didn't want to be gone that easily. I wanted to know why Simon didn't know about her marriage. Why she chose to tell *me* about the baby. I bounced my phone on my knee. "Can we swing by Sunset? I have the keys, so it should still be there unless the city towed it."

"Fine," Nari said, pulling saucer-sized sunglasses down over her eyes. She shot north on the ramp to the Pacific Coast Highway. The Range Rover moved fast for something that had to have the curb weight of an Asian elephant.

"Ocean's different out here," I said. Nari didn't turn her head. I looked around at all the gadgets, hoping I was doing a good job of keeping up a conversation with the car's interior.

We came to a five-way intersection with the Pacific on one side and cliffs on another. She swung a hard right. Even with a seatbelt on, I held on to the grab bar for dear life. With the SUV's high center of gravity, every twist and turn sent me sliding across the leather.

Nari slammed on the brakes to avoid a collision with the Mini in front of her. The sign said we were at Capri road. From my Sierra club Saturdays, I knew we were a long way from Hollywood.

"Are we going to talk about it?" I said.

Alchemy must have turned her foot to lead, because we zoomed past several canyons faster than I could read the signs.

"Talk about *what*, Lucas?" Her voice was flat. "There's nothing *to* talk about."

"How could you give your daughter away?"

Though we nearly clipped a man on a three-legged stool squatting next to a homemade "Map of The Stars" sign, he didn't move a muscle. As we took the corner on to a residential street far too fast, I imagined he'd had too many brushes with barreling luxury trucks to be fazed.

The Range Rover's brakes were pretty good. Nari screeched to a halt on a tiny street in what I think was

Brentwood. Tall fences with even taller trees behind them shaded the roadway.

She turned on me, whipping off her sunglasses. "You think it was easy?"

"You get up, get dressed, and walk through the day."

"This is so unfair and judgmental. You know what I go through every year."

"Does the sexual healing work?" I couldn't keep sarcasm from my voice. "I couldn't find it last night."

In a flurry of movement, Nari unbuckled herself, jumped from the car, and stalked down the street.

My head pounded with the door slam. But I sobered up quick enough to get myself out of the car. She couldn't move that fast in her strappy sandal things, and I was able to easily overtake her.

"I'm sorry," I said, laying a hand on her bare upper arm.

"Are you?"

"It was uncalled for, what I said back there." I wanted her to know that I wasn't a mean spirited person. I was confused, though. So very confused how a normally compassionate woman—a woman who worried more about her patients than most doctors—could do something so cold.

"I thought it would be easier than it is," Nari started. Her eyes closed. I could see that she had been transported to the past. "The woman at the agency said it would be difficult initially. The physical pain of my milk coming in, the episiotomy stitches. But that, that was the easy part. A hormone shot and pain pills cured me in a few days."

"But..."

She blinked rapidly a few times, pulled her sunglasses down, turned away from me.

"But what, Lucas? Do you want to hear that everyday my heart aches a little? That I avoid playgrounds, pediatrics, and parties. That Minnie is eleven years old—"

I brushed a hank of hair that had escaped her bun, over her shaking shoulder. "You named her?"

"Your mother named you. Babies are little people. They're just people we can't keep."

"But you could have kept her. You didn't have a crazy husband or overbearing religious parents." I paused. Maybe that was it. I'd met kids in school with fundamentalist parents. Parents they hid every non-conforming aspect of their lives from. "Was it your mom and dad?" I asked, ready to lay blame.

"Threatened to disown me," she said with such finality I almost believed her—almost.

"But wouldn't they have changed when you had the baby?" Didn't all parents come around when their wayward children brought cherubic little ones around?

She shook her head like her parents were immune to the charm of babies. "Plus, my husband had died."

"What about his parents? Surely—"

"At the funeral, I didn't get to sit where the spouse sits. Everyone assumed he had no spouse because he was a college student and it wasn't the 1950s. Are you suggesting I should have told them then, graveside? Hey, I know you lost a son, but you've gained a daughter in law."

"They might have—"

"There was no reason to ruin the picture they had of their son. He hadn't told them yet. He was supposed to have told them that night, but he didn't. Maybe they said something that changed his mind. I had to stop wondering about what could have been. I had to make a decision about the baby rapidly growing inside of me."

"You had options—"

She shook her head vehemently. Nari said, "How would I have had a baby as a single mom and gone to medical school?"

"Your parents would have come around...eventually."

"Maybe yes. Maybe no. But I didn't have a crystal ball. What I could see of the future looked pretty bleak."

"You couldn't figure out something?"

"I didn't see it that way. What I had was little time to make a very hard decision. What I saw was that I had no means of support. My mother promised her and Apa's unconditional support for a good number of years if I went to Korea during the pregnancy."

"You had the baby there?"

"No."

"So you went away? Like to a home for unwed mothers." I had a hard time seeing her in a rocking chair on some porch of a southern clapboard house.

"It was my uncle's house. My parents live in a very tight-knit community. I didn't want to make it any harder than it had to be for them. I didn't want to be a lightning rod for church gossip."

"It was the new millennium, not the fifties."

"Tell my parents that. They're still stuck in nineteen seventies South Korea."

I had been that helpless baby. I had been the unwanted one. "Didn't you want her?"

"Yes, I wanted her. But I also wanted a life. A future."

"She could have been part of that." It wasn't as if Nari were without resources. Nothing like one of the poor women I'd treated during my residency not able to heat their houses and put food on the table at the same time.

"Don't you think I've been down this road —second guessing myself—a hundred, if not a thousand times, Lucas?"

"I'm just trying to understand. Adoption is for teenage mothers, women on the edge of destitution, rape victims. Not middle class girls from Ivy League Schools."

"What do you know about women's lives? I made a decision. A past-eighteen, adult decision about what would be best for my little girl. I'm sad. Sometimes very sad. But I don't have an ounce of regret. She's somewhere out here with parents who love her. *Two* parents. Probably has everything money can buy. I couldn't give her that. Not one ounce of that. If she'd stayed with me, she'd have had one very sad homeless single parent with a degree in biology but no roof over her head. That's not a great start for any child.

"I made the best decision I could given the options I had. And I'm sorry if that's not acceptable to you. I—" she jabbed her hands at her chest. "I bear that burden.

Every day and every year. I'll take it to my grave. But I don't need you standing here in judgment."

"I'm not judging you," I said. But I wasn't convincing even to my own ears.

"You've been judging me since we had Mai Tais in Hawaii."

I held her small hands in mine. "It just that I really liked you, Nari, but—"

"But what, Lucas?"

"I don't know if I could be with someone who gave up her own child."

She looked like I'd slapped her. I watched her back away slowly; then she turned and strode toward her truck. As if in slow motion, Nari pulled open the door, hopped into the Range Rover, and smoothly executed a three-point turn on the narrow street.

I waited for her to back up and pick me up. That wait was in vain. The hulking SUV got smaller and smaller. The right blinker pulsed. Then the car disappeared around the curve onto Sunset.

The thump thump of feet sounded behind me. A jogger, fully suited up in what looked like a thousand dollars of exercise gear, pulled an ear bud out and jogged in place around me. "Nice shoes."

I looked down at my Red Wing chukkas. "Thanks." I nodded and he ran off. Hopefully the shoes would last on the long walk to Hollywood.

23 NARI

The intense gut-churning guilt of leaving Lucas stranded lasted for all of ten seconds. Pressing the trip meter to zero, I watched the numbers tick upward as I drove through Brentwood, past the 405, UCLA, into Bel Air, then Beverly Hills and West Hollywood. It was eight plus miles before I spotted his car, ticketed, but intact.

Hell, Mr. Judgmental Ass Sierra Hiker could make the walk or he could call a taxi.

Ten minutes later, the sound of computerized music filled the cab. I looked around. Sounded nothing like my iPhone notifications. I braked, pressing the button for my building gate. Something slid from under the passenger seat onto the floor mat. Easing into my assigned parking space, I turned on the dome light. It was a phone. The display had a 802 number. Woodstock, Vermont. Had to be Lucas' phone. Shit.

Before I could decide how many kinds of asshole I'd been, my own phone rang. For a hot second, I considered chucking both through the sunroof, cloistering myself in my place, and calling it a day. As shitty as Mondays were, they had to be better than this weekend.

"Simon," I said in greeting.

"We...Nari...I came here like a...I don't know what. Bull in a china shop isn't right. I was insensitive. Please have dinner with me. I don't want to leave things like this."

"I don't know if that's a good idea. Maybe we've said all that needs to be said."

"Please."

"Simon—"

"You're kind of my last link to Andrew as an adult. Mom and Dad can't talk about him except as a little boy. They've packed away the memory of those last few years. But I need to remember my brother, and you were a big part of that. He wanted to marry you. You were his future."

I held in a sigh. I'd do this for him. "I'll pick you up at six," I said. This maybe had to be the last time I talked to Simon. There were a bunch of reasons he shouldn't forget his brother. But maybe *I* needed to bury the memory. Maybe we'd reach a truce on that later.

That left me three hours to decide whether to rescue Lucas. The dome light winked out and I sat in the darkened cab going back and forth. Wouldn't he get to Kenter and make his way down to the shops on Bundy? Or maybe walk into a coffee shop on Barrington. One of those places would have a pay phone, or someone would let him borrow a cell to call a cab, surely.

Guilt started gnawing at my belly. Or it was hunger. Either way I couldn't remember the last time I'd seen a payphone in Los Angeles.

"Ummmm," I moaned out loud, then pressed the Homelink button to open the gate.

Two hours later, I was no closer to finding Lucas. I'd gone from the beach to Hollywood and back twice before I gave up. When I arrived at the hotel to pick up Simon, I was sure I looked the worse for wear.

"You have anything in mind for dinner?" I asked as he buckled himself into the seat.

"I thought we could go to the Santa Monica Promenade. I'm not picky."

I drove a couple of blocks and found a spot in one of the many utilitarian municipal lots that dotted the city.

We walked the four blocks up and back before deciding on a bistro with great al fresco ambiance.

"I thought you'd bring your guy friend," Simon said, snapping open the crisp white napkin and placing it precisely on his lap.

"I don't exactly know where he is." I pulled Lucas' phone from my pocket and placed it on the table. "We had an argument and he lost his phone."

Simon's look said he wasn't convinced by my explanation. "He lost it?"

"Look, he pissed me off big-time. So I did something not all that mature. I ditched him in Brentwood." I made my tone as blasé as I could. "I figure he'll call his phone. Or I can drop it off at work on Monday. No biggie."

"That's pretty low," Simon said just as the server slipped truffle and shaved parmesan salads in front of us. The way he'd said that had to rival the "we're very disappointed in you" talk parents give when they don't think punishment works any longer. I nearly jumped from my seat and made for my car to take a fourth trip up and down Sunset.

"He hikes with the Sierra Club." I said, pouring on too much vinaigrette and trying to still maintain breezy. "He's a pretty in-shape guy. He can handle a few miles."

"He was in clubbing shoes, not Timberlands."

"What do you want me to say, Simon?"

"What could he have said that would push you that far?"

For so many years I'd kept so many secrets. How had they all come to the surface in such a quick time? Everyone had a piece of the story. Daisy, the marriage. My mom and my uncle, the baby. Lucas, both.

"He said that in no uncertain terms, he couldn't see having a relationship with me."

"I'm sorry. That's pretty harsh coming from a guy who was naked in your apartment not too long ago."

I laid down my fork and fanned my face with my hands, trying to keep the heat from rising up my cheeks.

"He got the free milk," I said. "Guess he doesn't want the cow now."

"Nari, in no way do you resemble a cow."

I mashed my cheeks with my hands. "Yeah, well. Mooo."

"Sorry about all this." Simon held his hands in supplication. "I came at a bad time."

"How could you have known a guy I've been seeing for half a minute would find me morally reprehensible?"

"I don't want to pry, but those are big words." His chair scraped a little as he leaned forward. "Did you disagree over work?"

"No, it's nothing as simple as me being a Kevorkian fan and him not believing in DNRs."

"What then? Maybe I can help. I am a man, after all."

A man who looked a lot like my deceased husband. A man I suddenly wanted to confide in with every bone in my body. I was tired of hiding, concealing, pretending to be someone I wasn't. It was getting to be too much of a burden.

"He said he couldn't be with a woman who gave up her baby for adoption."

"But how does that apply to you? You never had a baby." Simon's face was so earnest. His look so matter-of-fact that I instantly regretted my honesty. I was about to ruin the picture he had of me as the sad, lonely widow. I didn't say a word. Fiddled around with the salad, letting reality sink in. Simon was a smart man who could compute a target company's profitability at a glance. Surely fitting together these puzzle pieces wasn't rocket science.

Finally he spoke. "You were pregnant?"

I nodded. "Very much pregnant."

"That's why Andrew proposed so early? He said that he was going to wait until graduation, but suddenly he needed the ring very badly. Mom had to make a special trip to the safe deposit box."

"We eloped."

"Jumbo Mexican shrimp with saffron rice," a waiter prompted. I pointed at Simon. "Curried Squash Soup with Red Lentils, Coconut Milk and Clams." I accepted the plate. Prolonging contact with the server, I asked for water, an extra napkin, and bread. It took three separate trips from three separate people to fulfill my requests. Only when the table was quiet again could I peek at Simon under my lashes. His face was business-like, stern. I steeled myself for the interrogation that was surely coming.

"You had the baby?"

"Yes."

"Where is he or she?"

"She. I don't know."

"Aren't adoptions open these days?"

"Not in California."

"And you're okay with that."

"Very much so."

"Why didn't you tell us you were married?"

"We eloped during Christmas break. I had tried telling my parents. That was an unmitigated disaster. The weekend he...the last weekend in Philadelphia, he was supposed to tell all of you."

"You were supposed to have come with him."

"It was the biggest mistake of my life. I wish I'd been there. But I had a big Physics exam on Tuesday. We were going to our first pre-natal appointment on Monday and I wanted the extra time to study." I pounded a fist against my temple. "This all sounds so damned stupid now. What exam could have been this important?"

"Don't beat yourself up. You didn't know," Andrew said.

"I don't know why he didn't tell them. But the way the funeral was planned, it was obvious they didn't know."

"But...later."

"Why, Simon? What would I have gained? I was pregnant. My mother was pressuring me to make a decision."

"What did she want you to do?"

"Give the baby up. Go to medical school. Finish what I'd started. What they'd really been paying for all along."

"I'm so sorry," he said, reaching across the table. Those big hands, nearly carbon copies of Andrew's, covered mine.

"Are you angry?" I tried not to flinch. "You can tell me the truth."

"Not mad, but mystified."

To my horror, tears leaked out. "I was a widow, pregnant, and needed to finish my last semester in college. I was probably too hormonal to be rational. But I just wanted to get better, go back to normal. My parents promised me that would happen if I let them take care of everything."

"I'm so, so sorry about the ring. Even if you hadn't been married I was being selfish to come out here and ask you for it."

"Your mom is right. It should be back in the family. Some living, breathing person should be able to enjoy it. Keeping it in a box is stupid."

Simon sat back, put his elbows on the table and rested his chin on his folded hands. His mother was probably having a heart attack somewhere. She had been lax about a lot of things, but manners hadn't been one of them. "Well, I feel like a colossal shit," Simon said.

"Don't. I can't take the guilt right now."

"Well that Lucas sounds like a colossal shit."

I laughed long and heartily at Simon's words. They were so unlike him, and so true at the same time.

24 LUCAS

"That was a really crappy thing you did," I said to Nari. We were standing in the clinic's empty waiting room. She'd had her hand on the door when I spoke. We'd ignored each other most of the day, but I wasn't ready to leave it—us—just yet.

"That was a seriously crappy thing you *said*," she shot back, not sounding the least bit guilt-ridden.

"I was stranded in L.A," I said, ignoring the meat of her response.

The walk down Sunset hadn't been too bad, actually. Once I'd gotten to Brentwood Village, I convinced the guy behind the counter of the Belwood bakery to let me use the phone. I might have said I was a doctor and that there was a dire emergency at UCLA. Fortunately, one of the

Sierra Club guys lived in West L.A., was listed by 411, and picked me up. But I wasn't going to tell her any of that. I wanted Nari to care that she'd left me marooned in the big city.

"Jesus. It was Brentwood. The worst that could happen is that you get run over by a van of gawking tourists."

"So that's it?" I said, snapping the jaws of the clipboard on the receptionist's desk. The loud crack of metal on wood bounced off the mostly empty walls.

Nari suddenly looked world-weary. My heart felt like a fist had clenched and squeezed the vulnerable muscle. I'd put that look on her face, no one else. "You have a deal breaker. I broke it. I don't think there's any reason to drag this—"

The door opened. I looked up the same time Nari did. "Can I help you?" I asked. The receptionist and nurses had gone home at six on the dot. We weren't equipped for emergencies, but I gave mean directions to the closest hospital.

"Are you Lucas' father?" Nari asked, staring at the guy in wonderment. "William Coates, right?"

I don't know how I hadn't seen it at first. But there in front of me was the other half of my biological parents. The tall curly-haired half. The square jawed half. The detached earlobe half. A puzzle came together. Standing before me was the secret to the universe—my universe at least. I had no idea what to do with that knowledge. It was like standing in a planetarium where all the answers were visible, but none obvious.

"You're Nari?" He shook her hand. "Laura said you'd come with Lucas."

"Laura didn't mention that you were local," Nari said.

"I'm not much anymore. Drove here straight from Tahoe." He removed what could only be described as a trucker hat, curling the brim in his hands. This was not a ninety-dollar fashion statement, but something he wore to protect his head from the elements.

"That's a long drive," I heard Nari say. "Why don't you have a seat? I'll get you a coffee?"

"That would be fine. Thanks," my...father...said. Nari disappeared into the back, and he sat. I stood.

"How did you find me?" I asked. I'd given Laura my phone number, but not much else.

"My...I...Medical Board."

Public license, public disclosure. I felt unaccountably nervous. Nari came back in with a coffee in one hand, a doughnut from this morning's Krispy Kreme run in the other. Seemingly grateful for both, William took a huge bite of the fried dough. "The good doughnut place in South Lake Tahoe closed about a year ago."

"So...let me get out of your hair. I'm sure you two have a lot to catch up on." The wind from Nari opening and closing the door was cool on my face.

After yesterday, I guess Nari didn't have any reason to stick around. I'd nailed that door shut but good. I stuffed down the regret that had risen up the minute her taillights had disappeared.

The green and gold striped chairs made an L shape around the room. I took a seat a few down and across. Hung my hands between my knees. It took a long moment to realize he'd finished the snack and had taken on the same pose. I recognized my own posture in the man on the other side of the room. That we shared this fundamental similarity made me ache down to my very bones.

Nari had made all the conversation when I'd met my birth mother, bridged the gaps. Here I was, alone with the very person I'd been searching for, and I was mute.

"Can I buy you dinner?" I finally asked.

"Sure thing." His laugh was full and deep. "Guess this doughnut ain't gonna cut it."

"Why don't you follow me?" I asked, leading the way to the parking lot. Once in the safety of the green machine, I blew out a breath that sounded more like a shout. I took another few breaths, reminding myself that this is what I'd asked for. I'd sought this out. I'd had questions and these two people had answers my adoptive parents didn't. If I wanted those answers, I needed to put the key in the ignition and get on with dinner. It took two tries to get the car started.

Signaling early, I took a wide turn out of the clinic parking lot. The gleaming sheep in the center of his grill stayed steady in my rearview mirror. I racked my brain for something that wasn't Japanese, vegan, or new-agey to eat. I signaled left and pulled into a little neighborhood bistro I'd been to with the clinic's director when I'd started.

We stood together in the vestibule awkwardly. Minutes that dragged like hours passed while we waited for a host.

A slim woman weighed down with menus finally approached. "Seems like father-son night. You're our third." She gestured toward two other tables with older and younger men. I wanted to lean forward and correct her. Tell her about Matthew Tucker the Dartmouth professor who raised me, who'd dropped the phone, his hand unsteady with nerves, the last time I'd called home. But I didn't say anything to stand up for my dad. I followed her and William to the next available table for two.

Nari might frown upon it, but I asked for a glass of wine anyway. This was a lot to handle stone cold sober.

I watched William study the menu with a frown. "Sorry about the food," I said with a shrug meant to apologize for Los Angeles' pretentiousness.

"I've been in and out of California for thirty years. Same shit—excuse my French—different day."

He ordered the burger without the arugula and I got a Kurobuta pork chop.

With no menus to shield us, I looked into his eyes. They were mine. The same ones I'd looked at for more than three decades. I was so used to looking at the keen eyes of Matthew and the mommy eyes of Joyce, that this kind of freaked me out.

I guess if I'd had a chance to get used to it, like thirty years…. But ten minutes wasn't enough.

"Did you agree with Laura? That the two of you couldn't raise me?"

"You don't beat around the bush," he said before taking a big gulp of water. "I went along with what she wanted, because I wanted her."

"That's not exactly how she tells it."

"We were young when we got together. I guess I wasn't quite done sowing my oats." He paused when the server brought our food. He asked for ketchup and a beer. I wasn't the only one having a hard time.

"How does an affair lead to adoption?"

"When your pregnant wife walks in on you."

"Oh," I sat back. Placed my knife and fork on the table.

"I was twenty-five. I thought the grass was greener."

"Was it?"

"No. That woman didn't want me. She wanted revenge on her own husband, my Laura, something. But she didn't want me. Time and again I put my marriage on the line for immediate gratification."

"You guys stayed together, though?" I was looking for where I fit in. Up until this point in the story, my very existence was a footnote in their drama.

"It was off and on for years. Rocky. I was deployed more often than not and liked it that way. Wasn't until a few years ago that I started to settle down. My buddies were my family, my best friends."

"Laura wasn't that for you?" It made me sad. Matthew and Joyce were that for each other. I hoped for—no expected—a true friend and partner for my own long-term relationships.

"She wasn't the port in a storm. Took too long to realize that, I think. She didn't ever get remarried."

"You did?"

He nodded. "Met a nice lady in Carson City. We moved to be near her family."

"Did you have any other kids?"

"Not that I know of. We didn't last either." His laugh was forced. "You? Laura said you'd come with your girlfriend. Was that her at the doctor's office?"

"Yes. No."

This time his laugh was genuine, unrestrained. "Which is it, son?"

The term of endearment knocked me for a loop. But I think he meant it in the old-guy-young-guy way and not in the biological way.

"We broke up yesterday."

He briefly shook his head. "Why?"

"Irreconcilable differences."

"What couldn't the two of you reconcile? She was real pretty."

I hesitated a long time before telling her secret. But I couldn't see the harm in sharing it with him. He'd never see Nari again. "I found out she gave a baby up for adoption when she was in college."

William Coates sat back in his chair with that one. I'd felt that shock myself, and knew what he was thinking. "Did she say why?"

"The baby's father had died. Nari didn't think she was in a position to raise her."

"It was a little girl."

"Did you know what I was?"

"Of course. Laura had named you. When we signed the papers, you were Lucas Coates. Baby Boy Coates," he murmured as if reliving a long ago memory.

"Nari didn't tell me about the baby she'd given up until long after she knew my feelings on adoption."

"Are you angry with us?" he asked.

"Not so much angry as bewildered. I can't fathom fathering a child, then letting him go."

"I couldn't either," he said. "Until I did it."

"Did you want to do it?"

"Laura and I were in a bad place. She didn't want to add a child to that mix."

"Why didn't you take me and raise me on your own?"

"Lucas," he said with a heavy sigh. "This was long before the father's rights era. I was on active duty. Central and South America were a mess. This was before all the base closures. Who knew where I'd be next? My brothers were all older. I'd never been around babies. Didn't have the first clue about how I could go about it."

"And what about Laura?"

His sigh was longer then. "It wasn't only the issue. She was more...how do you say it now...fragile. This was before everyone and their brother had anti-anxiety meds and Zoloft ads on the TV. She'd spend days at a time in the bedroom. Not eating or taking a shower. Me being gone, being with other women. None of that helped, I don't think."

"Was she institutionalized?"

"Nothing as serious as that. She found someone she could talk to. She quit drinking. But I had a hard time forgiving her."

"You blamed her?"

"She made me choose between you and her. In the end, I lost both of you."

I put down my fork. There was no way I could force anything past my clogged throat. My right leg bounced under the table. I laid my forearm on it to stop it. I looked across to see if he'd noticed I was holding back tears. Out of the corner of my eye, I saw that his leg was jiggling as well. Great. Suppressing emotion in your leg was an inherited trait.

"So you got any other prospects on the horizon?" he asked.

"Prospects?"

"Other girls you're seeing," he explained.

I was taken aback by the question. It was a perfectly normal thing for someone to ask a single guy. But I didn't feel single. I shook my head. "No. Tried the bar scene, ended up with an eight hundred dollar bar tab."

"What?" William Coates laughed. I joined him, then told him the story of the club and the "i" girls.

"Why were you in one of those places? I haven't known you but a minute, but you don't seem like a Hollywood scene kind of guy. Maybe Portland or Seattle, or even Brooklyn, but not L.A."

"I applied in the Pacific Northwest, but this offer came through first. I thought it would be a kind of adventure. Those other cities were a little too much like Vermont."

William eyed a busty waitress. "L.A. is easy on the eyes. I'll have to admit at least that."

"There are a lot of beautiful people."

"You've gotta get out there. Forget this girl. She's got to live with her demons, but you don't."

Part of me thought he was right. The other part wanted to run back to Nari. But I wasn't a big enough pussy to talk about my lingering feelings for her.

25 NARI

Daisy nearly tripped over the bags in the doorway, but she caught herself. For a woman who wore mostly flats, she never appeared quite solid on her feet. I'd read about a study from a few years ago, that said clumsy people could be "cured" with eight to ten weeks of physical therapy. But my best friend probably wasn't up for a discussion on spatial awareness.

"Did you have to put those bags right by the door?" Daisy asked after she righted herself.

"I need your help," I said, beckoning her in.

But she didn't come. Instead she knelt, her khaki covered knees not quite touching the floor and peered in the bags.

"'Cause you needed a Coach bag, a bomber jacket, and a yellow silk dress. Well...the dress is nice."

"I'm buying a few new pieces that I was missing."

Daisy pointedly looked at the purse shelves along one wall. She stood and walked to the bags, fingering their little dust bags. "And you were missing a purse?"

"I'm looking for something that will hold my eleven-inch MacBook and my wallet comfortably without being a laptop tote."

Daisy pushed her lips together and sideways. When she'd shot a porno flick at my apartment last year, she'd been so sorry that I was spared months of nagging and nitpicking from her. But I could see now that she was solidly out of the sex business, and totally legit, that she was ready with the unsolicited advice.

"I know I haven't mentioned it in a while...but maybe you should cut back on the shopping. I think having an entire bedroom as a closet is a bit, I don't know, much."

"You're just mad because I got rid of your bedroom," I threw back. "You're like that kid who came back from college and found a sewing room instead of a canopy bed and pop star posters."

"Cut the bullshit, Nari," she said, turning away from the bags and facing me. "I know you shop to fill that bottomless hole. What happened now?" She made a sweeping gesture. "Everything seems fine as far as I can see."

"Do they?" I asked, looking hard at her.

"Don't they? You made me realize that *I* wasn't teetering on the brink. I have a good job and a great boyfriend now."

I put down the blue jeans I was sorting. Skinny, straight, and flared fell back into a jumbled heap. "Well I don't."

"Have what? Were you fired?"

I wanted to thank her for that vote of confidence. "No. Lucas dumped me."

"Why?" she asked.

Her question was expected. But I didn't have a ready lie at my fingertips. I picked up the jeans again. Were Joe's Jeans out? I threw them on the discard pile. True Religion was so 2007, they joined Joe's on the floor.

"Did you hear me? You seemed so serious about trying out a relationship with him. If he pursued you, why did he do a complete about face?"

I debated the 7 For All Mankind. I could probably make the boot cut work at night. Tossed them on the keep pile. My upturned palms were blue. Damn, one of these was bleeding. A definite return reason. Poor dye lot, no doubt.

The touch on my arm made me want to jump a mile high, flinch, shrink back. Daisy was not a touchy feely woman. It's what I liked about her. Neither one of us had grown up in families you'd call affectionate. I wasn't used to the feel of someone brushing against my skin. I craved it. It repelled me. It made me want to cry.

"I did something he found unforgiveable," I said.

Her hand stayed firm on my arm. The other moved around my shoulders and guided me to the double bed in the center of the room.

"What, he hates Burberry?" Daisy asked. Her attempt at levity fell flat.

"Do you really want to know?"

"Of course," Daisy said innocently.

"He said he couldn't be with anyone who gave a child up for adoption," I said, then stood, stalked across the room as fast as I could around the clothes and shoes and bags. Secrets I'd kept so long spilled out of me lately. I don't know why but I couldn't hold it all in any longer.

"But what does that have to do with you?"

My head started throbbing, my nose itching. Damn it. I was going to cry. I bit my bottom lip as hard as I could. The tears receded.

"I can't believe you call yourself my best friend," I said, lashing out.

"Whoa. I'm here. I'm always here. What am I missing, Nari?"

"I was pregnant."

"When?"

"Our senior year."

"Oh…. Oh!"

Then, silence as she worked it out in her head. Daisy had always been like that. Silent when she was thinking. She'd have made a horrible doctor. Every patient would have been wondering if she were looking for an easy way to tell them they had five days to live.

"All the time you were sick, tired. I thought you were grieving Andrew."

"I was sad. My husband had died. And I was pregnant too."

"Why didn't you tell me?" she was trying to cover her hurt, muffle the whine in her voice. She was failing miserably at both.

"Because I couldn't decide what to do. Then doing nothing made the decision for me."

"That's why you went to Korea?"

I nodded.

"Why?"

"Because my mom thought it was the 1950s. She didn't want anyone to know. I agreed with her. I kept it a secret."

"You gave the baby up for adoption?"

I nodded again. Speaking was becoming increasingly difficult.

"Where is he or she now?"

"I don't know," I swallowed. Pushed past the golf ball-sized lump. "That's not true. She's probably in California."

"What did Andrew's family think?"

"I never told them. Well, I told Simon when he came to pick up the ring."

"I don't know what to say."

"What can you say? Giving up Minnie makes me unfit to be a girlfriend."

"Fuck Lucas. He's caught up in his own bullshit."

"But…" *I really, really like him*, I wanted to whine.

"What? You still like him." After all these years to-gether she could practically read my mind when I let her. "After he said that he can't see you because you did this one thing. Made a decision when you were what— twenty—that he's going to judge you for more than a dec-ade later? If he can't empathize, then he'd make a shitty boyfriend, and an even shittier doctor."

"He's a great doctor," I said.

"Fine, Nari. Maybe he's the greatest guy ever. But you're in his blind spot."

"Maybe if I'd told him in the beginning," I said. My friend was eyeing me like she'd never really known me. The guy I liked treated me like kryptonite. I was quickly making every single person around me miserable.

"Beginning of what? Welcome to the Westside Clinic, here's your office and crappy pressboard furniture, and oh, I gave a baby up for adoption. If that's going to be an issue…."

She had a point about the past. "So what do I do?" I asked about the future.

"Get out there. Now that you know you can."

I'd been out there time and again over the last decade. I didn't want out there. I wanted Lucas. But Daisy was right about one thing. That ship had sailed. I pushed up from the bed and added my new purse to the rack. In with new and out with the old.

26 LUCAS

Nari was turning some papers over, looking...lost. The self-assured, almost cocky woman that I'd known had disappeared overnight. The one in flawless clothes, who never had a hair out of place, who handled her truck with the confidence of a commercial driver. That woman had cracked open, revealing this quieter, more contemplative one. She glanced up and gave a brief nod of acknowledgment.

I held the multi-stickered color-coded manila file in front of me in lieu of a greeting.

"This patient wants a woman doctor," I said.

"Drop it there," she said, pointing one of the baskets on her desk.

"Do you want to know why?" I asked, trying to prolong the conversation.

"I'll look at your notes." Nari went back to her papers. I was dismissed, I guessed. But I didn't want to be gone. Even I knew I was being a contrarian as I patted my palm with the file a couple of times, then put it where she'd indicated.

"What's that you've got there?" I asked. Nosey and intrusive weren't sufficient to cover the impoliteness of the question.

"Are we seriously going to do this?" she asked, laying a hand on top of the non-work looking papers. Guess she was handling something personal.

I was bewildered by... everything. "Do what?"

"Pretend to be friends." She tilted her head in such a way that I was feeling pretty dense.

"Aren't we...friends at least?" I asked. Because I still wanted to be her friend. She was a woman who cared deeply. Who wouldn't want a friend like that?

"We may have been friend with benefits," she air-quoted me. "But that part is done. Now we're colleagues. Thanks for the file. I'll follow up with..." she picked it up and squinted at it "...Sarah Harrison."

"I like you—a lot. It's your choices I don't like. Your judgment I don't trust," I blurted out.

"Don't skimp on the honesty, Lucas."

I pushed the door closed behind me. This was not the time or the place. But I went ahead anyway. "I'm not the bad guy here. I'm sure there's someone great out there for

you. I'm sure there's someone great out there for me too—
"

She stood, moving files from her desk to a box behind her. "I don't need the pep talk, Lucas. Thanks for the referral." Her tone was dismissive. Her back faced me. She sorted through some stuff in the back of her office.

I pushed aside the few items between her and me. Then I did absolutely the wrong thing. I took three quick strides around the desk, stepped over the hazmat bin, and pulled her to me. Her resistance melted away in an instant, stiffness yielding to softness.

"I'm so sorry," I said into her hair. She pulled back to look at me. Her eyes telegraphed heartbreak. Then I did another wrong thing, I brought my mouth down upon hers.

Nari's gasp of surprise was an invitation. She tasted sweet and tart. In that moment it didn't matter who was adopted, I wanted her with a fierceness I'd never experienced before. I pulled the elastic from her hair, letting the thick curtain spill across my hand before I cupped the back of her head and pulled her infinitesimally closer.

My other hand slipped past the white coat, under her embroidered name, and zeroed in on her breast. The beaded nipple that poked at my palm made me groan aloud. This need, this urgency didn't have judgment. Didn't care about Nari's past. Wanted this woman—now.

The rap on the door threw a bucket of cold water on us very quickly. We jumped apart like teenagers discovered making out on a basement couch.

"Dr. Yoon?" a nurse practitioner inquired, poking her head in.

"Margie. How can I help you?" Nari sounded breathless to my ears.

Margie walked farther into the room. "Oh, Dr. Tucker, I didn't know you were in here as well." She looked back and forth between us. "I didn't mean to interrupt—"

Margie started backing slowly from the small office.

"I was just leaving," I said. "A patient wanted a woman physician. Dr. Yoon and I were discussing the matter. Patient confidentiality and all that." I waved toward the partially closed door.

"Oh, okay. Nari, these were the results you'd requested from the lab. They were able to rush." Margie dropped the paper in her hand like it was on fire and backed out of the room.

"I need to look at these before I go home," Nari said, taking her chair again and pulling the papers before her. A list of numbers engrossed her, shutting me out of her head.

I wanted to push her to talk, to finish what we'd started there. But the time and place were wrong. If Margie had come in five seconds later...we might have been having a whole different discussion—with the clinic's director about rules and decorum and ethics and professionalism.

There was no way I wanted to start my career out that way or jeopardize Nari's. I did the right thing this time and walked out the door.

I might have walked away, but I waited in my car. I stepped out the minute I saw her reflection in my rearview mirror.

"Can we talk?"

I waited a beat. Two. She nodded. "Where?"

Of course like an idiot I hadn't thought that far. Hadn't thought she'd agree. Nari was more decisive than I would have been in her shoes. "I'm going home. You can come to my place if you like. No obligation." Her clogs thumped to the monster truck she kept in the back corner of the lot.

I followed close, but not too. Down Olympic, winding up to her street. Every single stop light, I nearly turned a hard left or right or any direction different than Nari. There was no reasonable explanation for what I was doing. Nevertheless, I found myself sharing an elevator and holding her apartment door behind her. All in silence.

I pushed the door closed a little too hard. It slammed into the latch. The chain rattled against the wood.

She spun on me. "What you did back there at work was totally inappropriate."

I nodded. "I know. I'm really sorry." For a moment there, I'd nearly lost my mind. I wasn't completely sure my dick wasn't doing all the thinking now.

"You gave me the ultimate kiss off yesterday. I got it, Lucas." She was quiet a long moment. "Why are you here?"

We stood like gunslingers at five paces. Like a moth to flame, I closed the distance. I cupped her head in my hands. "This," I whispered against her lips. I'd never seen myself as one of those endlessly macho guys. But standing within fifty feet of Nari, I wanted to pound my chest, roar, then lock her somewhere tight where she could never be hurt. Keep her away from all the other guys who thought they wanted her but didn't really know her. "This is why I'm here," I said. Then kissed her. Hard.

Despite all her cool bravado and talk, Nari didn't resist. Didn't push me away. Accepted what I was offering. Even if that was only for this moment.

I walked her back two steps, shrugged off my jacket. She kicked off one clog, then the other. Like a flame to tinder, I was suddenly on fire. I couldn't get to her bedroom fast enough. Couldn't push her V-neck sweater off fast enough. Couldn't unbuckle my belt with enough speed. Like a bolt of lightning hit me, I suddenly understood her yearly need to lose herself with someone else. I wanted the combustion of our two bodies coming together to make me forget all that was wrong with what we were doing.

I knelt, pulling down her pants and underwear. I laid her down on the cloud of white bedcovers. She looked like the Greek goddesses we'd talked about so often in high school. Her golden skin stood in stark contrast to the snowy white duvet. Dark brown hair, brown eyes, brown pointed nipples begged for my touch.

I shoved off everything and knelt at the end of the bed. I picked up her hands in mine and drew her to me. When I sat back on my haunches, I lifted her slight weight onto my thighs. "Jesus effing Christ," I breathed, breaking commandment number three.

She was the aggressor this time, leaning forward and opening my mouth with hers. Surrounded by her hair, her scent made me crazy. I untwined my fingers from hers and smoothed them down the arch of her back. In response, she curved toward me, thrusting her hard-tipped breasts against me. Our mouths broke apart. She lay her head in the crook of my shoulder, breathing heavily. I palmed her ass, sliding up her ribs, then around front, finally landing where my thumb and forefingers wanted to be. I pinched and pulled until Nari sunk her teeth into my shoulder.

I don't know if it was pain or pleasure or both, but my cock got that much harder. My throbbing penis didn't escape her notice. At once, she had one hand on me, gripping hard, slowly pulling up and down. We both watched as the tip disappeared and reappeared from the foreskin.

"I've never...this is really hot," she said, sliding away. Then her mouth was on me. Pleasure more intense than I ever remembered experiencing blurred my vision, scrambled my brain. Enough of the fog lifted that I lifted her mouth from me and crushed it with mine. We rolled around. I was trying in any way possible to possess her. Her mouth, her nipples, all of her. Pinning her down, I knelt again, this time between her thighs. Using my mouth on her clit and two fingers inside her, I brought her to the edge.

"Let go," I said, my voice vibrating against her. Like that, spasms quaked against my fingers. Nari's thighs closed like a vice against my ears.

When her legs relaxed falling open, I lifted my head. The afternoon sun blazed through the window, highlighting the sheen of perspiration. My need to possess her nearly overwhelmed me. "Do you have—"

"Drawer."

I pulled open the bedside table drawer, fisted the purple packages I found there and tore one off. I had to grit my teeth to get the latex near the tip of me.

"I'll do it," Nari said, rolling it down unnervingly slow. Once I was sheathed, she pumped me a few times for good measure. Like a caveman, I pushed her back and plunged into her without preamble, without my usual polite introduction.

She was along for the ride though. I don't think I'd ever known a woman who enjoyed sex with as much abandon as Nari. She made me want to rock her world for a second time. But it never got that far. She pulled me down for a kiss and in a few moments, rocked mine instead.

I couldn't help but collapse on her. For a few long minutes, we remained joined. Deep breaths slowed my heartbeat, returned my lung function to normal, allowed me to take in the unique coconut and citrus smell that was the woman under me. I grabbed myself, easing from her. Limped to the bathroom like a wounded warrior.

She hadn't moved when I came back. Her eyes were closed, her chest rising and falling evenly. But I knew she wasn't asleep. I don't think I'd ever seen her that vulnerable. I lowered myself to the bed. The covers rustled as I turned to look at the woman next to me. A pointy elbow jutted toward me. "What now?" Nari asked, her forearm obscuring her eyes.

It wasn't a stupid question. I wished I had an answer.

27 Nari

"You should find Minnie," he said. If the syrupy weight of my lethargic bones hadn't held me down, I might have slapped him. There was probably a self-help book for this. It would be called: What to do when you have great sex with a great guy who says shitty things.

"She's eleven," I responded. Pulling out my clinical voice, I continued, "That's a hard age. Hormones are starting to surge. Separation's beginning from the parents. Not to mention that she's not a legal adult." We didn't treat children without their parent's consent. It was a huge no-no in our field. We left that to those clinics that were lightning rods for controversy.

"You could approach her parents," he reasoned.

"Why, Lucas? There's no good reason I can think of to do what you're suggesting."

"Can you really believe that after you've seen what I've gone through these last few weeks?"

In an instant I realized this conversation was not at all about me. It was about him. So I turned the tables where they needed to be. "When did you find out you were adopted?"

"I always knew. Maybe when I was three or five, I got it. Babies came from their mommies' bellies. My mom didn't have the pictures holding her stomach."

"My mom doesn't have those either, Lucas. I think she's way too modest or practical to do that sort of thing. Belly bump pictures do not make anyone more of a mother." I lifted my head an inch, sneaking a peek over at the naked man next to me. His face looked pained. I wanted to physically shake him and tell him to get over it already. He had a living, breathing family who loved him. "Being pregnant did not make me a parent, Lucas. Do you think gay parents who adopt are any less parents because the child doesn't share their DNA?"

Like I anticipated, his liberal Vermont guilt rushed to the surface. "No...no I believe people can choose their family or make one."

"Then how is it your parents are exempted from this license you grant everyone else?" I asked. When he didn't respond, I asked more quietly. "Why aren't I?"

I wanted to disappear into the silence that followed my question.

"William Coates is still upset with Laura."

I'd wondered what had happened at that dinner. Had it been awkward? Affirming? "Why?"

"He said it wasn't his idea to give me up," he said. If I wasn't listening for it I wouldn't have heard the slight yearning in his voice. I knew that feeling. The desire to turn back time. To have different choices made. He wanted his parents to want him. I wanted to have driven up to Philadelphia. Either I would have saved Andrew or we would have died together.

Skipping the emotional, I turned to the rational. "To hear her tell it, it was his idea to step out on her."

"Sounds like two sides of a bad situation."

"You can't blame them for not wanting to bring a baby into that. Daisy's parents probably should have divorced a long time ago. Instead her dad enables her mom's drinking. It's not a pleasant situation."

"Are you saying they shouldn't have had her?"

"Not in her case, no. They had a lot of money to smooth that over. And I love her. She's my best friend. But she is not without huge issues that she's still dealing with. If you add financial and marital instability, not to mention being out in the far reaches of the Pacific Ocean with no support system, I can understand Laura's decision."

Lucas' hand rubbed my arm. His eyes left mine and strayed down to my breasts. I reached out, cupped his jaw, and titled his head back up. I needed him to hear me before the other thing between us distracted him. The other thing pulling us together like magnets. The other thing that we weren't the least bit ready to talk about.

When he looked like he was done with talking and thinking about kissing, I sat up abruptly.

"I want the real you, Lucas," I said. "But you don't want the real me. It was never the other way around." When he didn't say anything I poked him—hard. I pulled at the flesh of my abdomen. "These are stretch marks, Lucas. I got them when I was twenty-one and carried a baby to term. A baby I don't have. A baby I'm not looking for. I've accepted who you were from the beginning. But you're the one who can't accept me."

He shook his head slowly, deliberately. "I'm sorry."

"Don't be *sorry*, Lucas. I am Nari Yoon and that's never going to change. My past is fixed. My future is full of possibilities. Whether you're a part of that is up to you."

The landline rang, shattering the downbeat mood.

"Is that your telephone?"

"It's my buzzer."

"Who's visiting you on a Thursday night?" he asked, a proprietary tone in his voice. A tone he wasn't entitled to have.

I had two guesses. I crossed my fingers while blindly seeking out my white silk robe. I could only hope it was Daisy.

But before I could answer the phone, press the button unlocking the downstairs door, there was a knock at my own.

Lucas stood on the bedroom threshold at least partially covered by boxer shorts this time. I wanted to usher him back in, but the key scraped in the lock and the door pushed open before I could even do that little bit of damage control.

The last time my parents had been in this apartment, Daisy had been filming sex on the couch. I'd done my best to usher them out, hide their eyes, and make excuses. But this time I didn't do that. I didn't make a fuss, or pretend what they were seeing wasn't what it was. If I was ever grateful to Lucas for one thing it would be that. He'd taught me to stop pretending.

"*Oma, Apa.* This is Lucas Tucker," I said to my wide-eyed parents. "He's a doctor in my office. Lucas, this is my mom and dad."

28 LUCAS

I did what any decent man would do. I stuck out my hand and shook first her father's, then her mother's. "Nice to meet you," I said. "I didn't get your names."

Before her dad could say anything, Nari took over. "My dad Soon-Bok Yoon. My mom Sun-Hee Ahn."

They bowed slightly. I nodded in response. I had no idea what the custom was here. I was hoping they wouldn't expect anything from me—the big American. A draft stole through the room, lifting the hair on my almost nude body. "I'm going to get dressed," I said, feeling way more naked than I'd felt with Simon there. Their silent scrutiny was unnerving.

That quiet abated the moment I closed the bedroom door. There was a lot of talking, some raised voices.

Thank God I'd waited until I got in here to get undressed. My clothes were everywhere in the bedroom, but at least they weren't on the couch, or hanging off the proverbial chandelier.

I slipped the button down shirt over my undershirt rescued from the floor. I sat a moment, scanning the room for socks. I found one, then the other, slipped them on my feet. Pulled up my dress pants, buckled my belt. Despite the attention to my wardrobe there was little break in the discussion outside the door. I heard a door slam, not once but twice.

I took a deep breath and manned up. Being a coward wasn't called for. All they knew about me was that I was nearly naked in their daughter's apartment. Not a great start for anyone meeting their lover's parents for the first time.

Nari's mom was setting her dining table, pulling food from a bag. Her father was sitting on the couch like he owned the place. The vibe was weird. I wondered if there was something about their culture that didn't follow the same boundaries I had with my parents. That any adult did. I tried to imagine my mother waltzing into my apartment without an invitation. Maybe stoic New England politeness made us different from people in ever-casual California.

Nari and her mother gripped the same bowl for a long moment. Words passed between them and they continued to set the table. "Do you want to join us for dinner?" Nari asked. They were the first English words I'd heard in several minutes. Her voice was tense while her face was deceptively placid. I wasn't sure if she wanted me to say yes or no.

I went back and forth for what was probably too long a time to be socially polite. "Sure, point me to my seat," I said like we were having a casual dinner and not enacting a scene from an Edward Albee play.

Nari pointed to a chair opposite. "You need me to get anything?" I asked. A quick shake of her head made me drop the subject and pull out a chair.

Nari's mom brought in plates, bowls, chopsticks. She worked in the kitchen without getting Nari's permission to open drawers or take out dishes. My mom would have asked first. Everyone sat, but I had no idea what to do with the little bowls of vegetables in front of me. There wasn't a fork and I certainly didn't want to ask for one.

I nearly panicked when Nari's dad sat down. I couldn't for the life of me remember his first name. I tried to make my glance in his direction furtive. His face was stern and closed. The guy looked like he never smiled, and he definitely didn't look like a first name basis kind of dad.

Sun-Hee hovered around the table without actually sitting. Nari's breath was a huff of annoyance. Amazing how a person morphed into their teenaged self in front of their parents. "Would you like some soup, Lucas?" she asked me.

I nodded, grateful I didn't have any food allergies. She filled my bowl. I recognized tofu, potatoes and scallions. I definitely wasn't going to ask what it was. I preemptively picked up the pitcher from the table, ready to fill my glass to the brim in case there was some kind of hidden spice like in Nari's lunch. Nari, her mom and dad reached to take it from my hands. I nearly dropped it on the table. How had I made a social faux pas so early, other than storming out of the bedroom naked? Drinking had seemed a safe bet.

"It's considered impolite to let someone fill their own drink," Nari explained. She picked up the pitcher from across the table and poured me a glass of light brown liquid. Okay, not water. I'd roll with it.

After they'd all started in on the food, I sipped at the soup carefully. It was kind of salty, I guess. Only a little bit spicy, I thought until I bit into something green. Turned out to be a hot-as-blazes pepper. I tried to sip at the not-water to hide the cough that nearly exploded from my lungs. After I had it under control and my face no doubt was sufficiently red, I shifted in my seat, looking between her parents.

"I'm sorry for barging in like I did," I said. "I didn't know you were coming for dinner. Otherwise..." Crap. I should have thought that through before I spoke. Otherwise—what—I wouldn't have banged your daughter before the soup course.

"We didn't tell Nari we were coming," her dad said. "We usually don't have to."

Family dynamics minefield. I was afraid to put my foot anywhere. So I shut up and sipped my soup.

"Actually, Oma, Apa, I wanted to talk to you about that," Nari started. "I was thinking of buying you guys out."

I watched Sun-Hee add rice to her soup. Now that was a good idea. I scooped some rice into the broth while I watched the exchange. Buy them out?

"Why?" was the only question from her taciturn father.

"I'm an adult," was Nari's terse reply.

"You're our only daughter. You'll get it when we die," Mr. Yoon said.

Curiouser. I violated my recently prescribed rule. "Did your parents buy this place for you?"

"They made the initial down payment and the mortgage payments while I was in medical school and during residency. I've been making the payments since," Nari explained slowly, like I was a patient and she was explaining aftercare.

My unfinished soup was whisked away and replaced with a plate. Sun-Hee offered me meat, fish and some kind of noodles. I took a bit of everything offered. I looked at the placemat. The soup spoon was gone. Only slim silver chopsticks remained. Great. I'd get to embarrass myself twice.

"I need you to treat me this like my home. Not come whenever you feel like it. Tonight is case in point," Nari said. I nearly dropped the slim metal sticks I'd only lifted from the table a moment ago. Curiosity or no, I was wishing I'd walked out the door when her parents arrived. I remember my dad when Brooke had her first boyfriend. The thought that some boy/man wanted to have sex with my sister nearly sent him over the edge. And he was a self-described sex-positive liberal. All that went out the door when a tall, deep-voiced boy showed up with facial hair, tattoos and his own car. It took some fast-talking from Mom to keep Dad quiet and then usher Brooke out the door. My conspicuous presence would only make them want to tighten the leash they had on Nari.

Nari's parents didn't look like they were ready to think about their adult daughter in that way. And she had more than a decade on Brooke.

"How do you know my daughter?" Mr. Yoon turned to me. I hadn't expected the first words out of her father to sound like an inquisition.

"We work together at the clinic," I answered. From the frown on Mr. Yoon's face, that was probably the wrong answer.

"You're a doctor, like Nari," Mrs. Ahn said. At least she seemed pleased about that.

"Can you get fired from this..." Mr. Yoon waved a hand between us.

"Don't worry. My job is safe, Apa," Nari said.

I needn't have worried about the chopsticks. I didn't get the chance to stick anything in my mouth, there were so many answers coming out about where I was from, my education, what my parents did, how old I was. Mr. Yoon all but asked what my intentions were toward his daughter. I was very glad the actual question didn't come up because that was the one thing I couldn't have answered if my life depended on it.

"Should we save something for Eun-ji?" Mrs. Ahn asked. "Is she studying late at the library?"

I ate the big pear slices from the center of the table and tried to remember why that name sounded familiar. "Oh, your cousin who stopped by," I said.

Nari's face froze. Her leg swung back and forth in wild motion. I think she would have kicked me if she could have reached me. I'd stuck my foot in my mouth, but I had no idea why. My hazy memory came into focus. She'd been giving the girl a fat envelope. I'd thought it money. "She's probably in her dorm at USC, wasn't it?" I said, trying to be helpful. The leg swung harder.

"Dorm?" Mr. Yoon asked. Then the rest of the conversation was lost on me as a spate of Korean flew my way from mother, father, and daughter. It ended when first Nari's father, then mother, and finally Nari stomped toward the second bedroom. The door was opened and all went in. More yelling in Korean.

My foreign language skills were shit, but even I could tell that Eun-ji was supposed to be in the room but wasn't. She surely didn't live here. She wasn't here the night I slept off that vodka drunk. I wouldn't have stripped Nari naked and done what we did with some girl barely out of her teens around.

Nari came back, leaving her parents in the room, still arguing.

"Cat out of bag. Thanks." she said.

"I have no idea what's going on." I threw up my hands. That applied to more than her parents, her cousin, or that extra room.

"Eun-ji is supposed to be living with me."

"You volunteered to have a college freshman live in your apartment."

"Sophomore. She lived with me for several months before we reached a mutual agreement that it wasn't working."

"But you didn't tell your parents."

"Or hers. Her dad was the uncle I stayed with," her eyes flickered around, "back then."

It all came into sharp focus. "They didn't want her in a dorm full of penises. Why not stay with the sexless aunt? She catches on that you have a life or you figure out she does, and you go your separate ways."

"A little money greased that wheel—but you've got the basics."

"Why didn't you say no? Did you want her here?"

"No. Who in the hell wants to live with a college student when you're not in college? My parents waved around their two-thirds ownership. My mother worried her brother-in-law would share with the world or Korea that I had a baby out of wedlock. And voilà, instant roomies."

"Now what?" I asked, gesturing toward that other room.

"As soon as they leave, I'll call Eun-ji and we'll figure something out."

"I'm sorry," I said. Didn't seem like I was good for her in any way, shape, or form.

"It would have come out eventually. I was just hoping to kick that can down the road."

"Should I go?"

Nari stood there a long moment, pondering the ten thousand dollar question. "Do you want to stay?"

"Very much," I said and meant it. I really wanted to stand by Nari, sleep by her side.

"Then I think I need to get them on their way," she said.

29 NARI

"Why do you think this is a good idea?" I was passing Lucas cutlery from his kitchen drawer. He'd set four places at the table. Two for us. One for Laura, the other for William. He was reuniting his parents after twenty-plus years apart. I figured if they'd gotten divorced, it was for a reason. I didn't think we should be playing God.

"They agreed. I want to get the whole story once and for all."

Agreed wouldn't have been the word I'd have used. They were guilted, cajoled, coaxed. They could have said no, I guess. "Will you stop, then?" I asked. Madness was what I considered Lucas' search for truth.

"Yes." He nodded.

Wow. There was an end. I wondered if that meant he'd stop pestering me as well. Our last few weeks had been in a tenuous truce of sorts. He didn't mention Minnie and I laid off his relentless pursuit of the truth. Instead we had great sex and even better conversation. This craziness aside, I really liked him—for me. How I ever thought he could have been a good match for Daisy, I don't know. If this were anything like normal, I'd be thinking about the long term, maybe the future. But in our reality I was living day-to-day.

The doorbell rang, pushing aside my thoughts. Lucas shifted on his feet, but wasn't moving forward. So I took the few steps and pulled open the door. Laura stood there, wilted flowers in hand. She wore a dress, heels, lipstick. I don't know why, but her appearance made me sad. Like she was going on a date with her son, dressing to impress. It was the opposite of what I thought a mother should do.

"I'll take these," I said, grabbing for the flowers. Daisies, mums, and some pink–and–white flower graced the bouquet. I pulled an empty peanut butter jar from Lucas' cabinet and jammed the flowers in. My mom would have cut them and dug up some sugar to add to the water. My domestic skills didn't go that far.

"Why don't you have a seat in the living room?" I said, stretching myself to the limit of my domestic skills.

Unsure of herself, Laura sat primly on the edge of the couch as if she were afraid of soiling the fabric.

I brought her a glass of iced tea. "Thanks," she said. Then she drank like a camel in the desert. Before I could

JOLIE MOORE

get back to the kitchen to help Lucas, she grabbed my arm. "I'm glad you're here. I'm not quite ready for dinner with just us and Lucas."

I nodded in understanding of his single-minded intensity. Finding a coaster, I put it under her drink, trying to keep my swipe of the condensation beaded on the wood low-key. "There will be four of us. I'm sure it'll be a nice meal," I said. "Let me get back to setting the table, okay?" I felt bad leaving her there by herself to stare out the windows, but I didn't want to be alone with his mother. With this woman who'd made the same choice I had. I was sure five minutes in, she'd sense my secret or I'd spill my soul. All of this time with Lucas had brought my secrets too close to the surface. It was getting more and more difficult to lie with a straight and happy face like I'd done for more than ten years. To pretend I was like everyone else—a serious professional. No marriage, no kids out of choice.

Before I could school my face and join Lucas in the kitchen, the doorbell rang again. I pulled it open and William Coates was standing there like I'd expected, but he'd come with an uninvited guest. A woman with long graying hair tucked earnestly behind her ears was standing by his side.

I extended my hand. "I'm Nari. Lucas'...friend."

"Nicolette Pennington," she said, then thrust another bouquet my way. Didn't anyone bring wine these days? Graciously, I accepted the flowers.

"William." I shook his hand again. No one had said a thing about five for dinner. "Please have a seat in the living room. Laura's already there. I need to help with dinner, set the table," *for an extra place*, I didn't say.

"Go say hi," I said, pushing Lucas from the kitchen.

I heard the murmur of voices as I pulled out an extra fork, knife and spoon and dragged over another dining room chair. I glanced at the pan on the stove. Lasagna looked ready to serve. I set up a trivet and moved it to the middle of the table along with garlic bread and salad.

"Dinner's on the table," I called. Sounding like a TV sit-com mother slightly horrified me. Briefly, they continued their discussion of the perils living downtown so close to Los Angels' famed Skid Row. Like a great hostess, I steered them to their seats. I put Lucas at the head of the table, his mother on his right, his father on his left. I positioned myself across from party crasher Nicolette.

The girlfriend lay the napkin in her lap. As I was about to stand and offer serving spoons and forks to Laura and William, Nicolette clasped her hands and bowed her head in prayer. There was a long awkward moment as we scrambled to be respectful of her silence.

As soon as Nicolette raised her head, William cleared his throat. "Nicki's been going to church lately. Learning how to be grateful."

I made my way around the table, offering bread, salad, wine. Everyone ate in silence for long minutes. I kept my eyes trained on Lucas, but he was spearing lettuce leaves with gusto. I'd played the role of the happy hostess. But

I'd fallen down on the conversation part of the job. Resolved, I dove in. "Lucas tells me you're in Tahoe," I said to William. "How do you like the area?"

"Nice enough." William said. His tone didn't invite much in the way of conversation.

Lucas put down his knife and fork with a loud clink. "How did you guys meet?"

"I was volunteering at the church. Will was in...one of the programs that meets in the basement," Nicolette said.

"I'm sorry I meant my mother and father," Lucas said, bordering on rude.

With that, we were off to the races. I'd tried to tell him that he should slow down. I'd tried to advise him to ease into it. You had to do that with some patients. If you asked flat out if a person drank alcohol or took drugs, their initial reaction was to recoil, the first answer no. But if you asked them if they'd gone to the new wine boutique on the Westside, or tried the flight pairing at the newest chic restaurant, the inevitable three glasses of wine a few days a week, or patterns of binge drinking would emerge. Lucas was a good clinician. He knew better. But from the furrow of his brow and the jerkiness of his hands, I could tell he'd tossed his good sense out the window in his quest for answers.

William looked from Laura to Nicolette and back in search of an answer. Laura took a large gulp of wine and spoke.

"I was at my family's place on Reno Lake."

"Is that in Minnesota?" Lucas asked.

Laura nodded. "Will was staying in a cabin with a group of guys. We saw them goofing around. Eventually, my mom and dad, aunts and uncles got tired, went to bed. Me and my cousins would take off in one of the cars and go to the local bar."

"Those were good times," William muttered, bobbing his head.

"I think we drank bad beer and sang worse karaoke those few nights. Will and I kind of hit it off, though. But he was passing through on leave, and we didn't keep in touch."

I wondered what she meant by "hit it off." Was she like Lucas and I, who "hit it off" in bed but nowhere else? I pulled back on the judgment. Maybe they'd had a deeper relationship. More in common than sex.

"And...?" Lucas prompted, interrupting my thoughts.

"We met up again at the beginning of the next season. Things were kind of overbearing at home so I went with him when his leave was over." Laura took a long pause, probably anticipating the next question. "We got married too young, probably. But we could only be together, really, if we were married."

"It was good those first couple of years," William piped in.

A look passed between Laura and William. For a moment the connection between them crackled. Nicolette sensed it and immediately grabbed for William's hand. "That's in the past, though. My man and I are going to get married anytime now," she said.

Though I found her very uninvited presence kind of annoying, I had to feel sorry for someone so insecure that the past made her avaricious.

"Congratulations," I said, trying to soothe her ruffled feathers, quiet her so that Lucas could hear what he needed, maybe heal that first trauma at least a little bit. Enough to stop him from obsessing about what could and would never be.

"I think I got pregnant in Norfolk," Laura said. "We hadn't been trying, but we hadn't exactly been not trying either."

I watched Nicolette shift in her seat. Her insecurity made me sad.

Laura continued, "When William got back from his tour on the...USS Albany, was it, Will?" Laura asked, flicking her eyes in his direction. I could see that it was hard for her to look straight at him, take him in.

"Yep, that was it. Old girl. Got decommissioned not long after."

"But you weren't exactly happy about it," Laura was speaking directly to Will now. "Coming back to me, I mean."

"I'd kind of gotten infatuated with another girl," William admitted.

"Who was married as well," Laura added matter-of-factly.

I'd heard this kind of story a hundred times in my practice. The details were different, but the basics were the same. I'd made the subsequent referrals to clinics and counselors as patients tried to sort out their lives.

"My CO caught on and we got assigned to Hawaii. I think he figured he could save my marriage and hers too if we got separated."

"Will's leaving out the fight he and that guy had in the middle of the NX."

"Fight?" I asked. "NX?"

"The exchange. The base grocery store. Will and I were in there shopping for...I don't remember...but Will looked at that girl...Cassidy...and her husband saw it. Next thing I knew, eggs and milk were flying. The MAs were there in an instant to break it up. And we left Hawaii not long after."

"That sounds like it solved the problem," Lucas said.

William shook his head. "I was kind of hard headed back in those days."

"There was another girl in Hawaii. She was off base this time. But I was pretty sure I'd made a big mistake. I'd gone against my parents' advice. I'd married and run away with a guy I hadn't known well enough. I'd dropped out of college. And given what had happened in Norfolk and what was happening in Kauai, I didn't think there was a future. I'd grown up in an in-tact family, a huge extended family. I wanted the idyllic life I thought my parents had. Sitting in soul-sucking base housing, pregnant and crying, waiting to see if my husband came home smelling like another woman was not how I'd imagined my future...my life."

"But you didn't want adoption, right Will?" Nicolette piped in.

That was news to me. "I thought both parents had to agree," I said, not letting William off the hook as easily as his new fiancé.

Everyone turned to look at William. "I signed the papers before I shipped off to Korea."

Laura's eyes pierced William. "You didn't want to sign the papers? You never told me that."

William shrugged. "I did. But you'd walked in on me and Aolani and I don't think either one of us heard much of what the other'd said."

Laura sat back. Stunned didn't quite cover it. She looked as if she were reconsidering a bunch of choices she'd made in her life. "But you went to Korea without me. You said you'd send for me when you got settled but never did."

"You said you needed time and space. I gave that to you."

"You were distant when you came back to San Diego."

"I grew up without my parents, Laura. I thought my COs were my parents, fellow sailors my brothers. I didn't know what it was to have a wife or a family. I figured I'd fucked it up way too much. I wanted you to have the life you should have had before I met you at the Red Fox."

"You remember the name of the bar?"

"I'll never forget it. I tried to reach for something I didn't deserve and it smacked me in the face."

That seemed as good a time as any to collect plates. All this emotion made me very uncomfortable in my own skin. I felt transparent like everyone could see through me. Except for Nicolette who was holding on to William for dear life, like he might slip through her fingers any second.

I passed dessert around the table. Everyone dug into the tiramisu-like ladyfingers were a refuge. Small talk resumed. Nicolette excused herself to go downstairs to get a better cell signal. Something was happening with her daughter that she needed to attend to right away. She was probably as uncomfortable as I was for an entirely different reason. When I turned back from giving Nicolette directions, William and Laura were leaning across the table, talking in low tones. Maybe they were catching up on what had happened in the thirty plus years they'd been apart.

I goosed Lucas from his chair. "Why don't you help me in the kitchen?" I suggested.

He reluctantly followed me the few feet from the dining room table to the counter. "Do you think they could get back together?" Lucas asked, inclining his head toward the two people at the table. His biological parents' hands had crept across the broad expanse of walnut and had met in the middle. It was a very sweet picture. One that I was immensely glad that Lucas had gotten to see. I wondered if Lucas and I would meet like that one day. Nah, we'd go our separate ways sooner rather than later. Other than this time in our lives where we shared secrets, there wouldn't be much holding us together. No strings from the past. I shook my head. Didn't want to dwell on the end of us just yet.

Lucas took my shake of the head as an answer to his question. I schooled my face. "I think Nicolette would put a stop to that," I said. "She seemed very possessive."

"She'd be his third wife. The way they told the story, Laura sounded like his first love."

I almost said, first love doesn't last. God knows I'd heard the phrase a thousand times. But in my heart of hearts, I knew that wasn't true. I'd still be married to Andrew to this day if fate hadn't intervened. Instead I said, "Sounds like they have a lot to catch up on."

When Nicolette came back, I called a car and shuttled them off to one of those single letter boutique hotels popping up everywhere. Both Lucas and I hugged Laura, William, and even Nicolette hard.

Easing off my high heeled pumps, I propped my feet up on Lucas' couch when we got back upstairs. The whole evening had exhausted me more than a morning of sample sale shopping.

"Are you staying?" Lucas asked. He lifted my legs as he eased himself down on the couch and laid my feet across his thighs.

I tried not to let the question tense me up. I'd made my peace with the temporary nature of our relationship. We were definitely lovers and maybe friends who had gotten into a complicated thing together. Relationship wasn't even the right word, not in the way people used it now. "Do you want me to stay?" I asked. We were both playing an ambivalent game. I'd blinked first before. Laid my heart out there only to face the ultimate rejection. Now that I knew everything was time limited, I was waiting for the other shoe to drop. Waiting for him to decide I wasn't worthy of his time. Waiting for the time I'd have to figure out the way to start act two of my life.

"Of course I want you to stay," he said. He took one of my feet in his hand, pressing his thumb against my arch. I bit back a groan. The silence grew as he massaged one foot, then the other. Part of me wanted to pull him down on top of me. Kiss him. Make love to him. But another part wanted to push him away. End the pain his inevitable absence was going to cause. Sooner rather than later would be better. I could start getting over the pain faster.

Mentally obliterating all thoughts of the future, I asked him, "Were you satisfied with the answers you got tonight?"

His hands stilled. It was a long time before he nodded. His eyes didn't meet mine, though. "I think so, yes."

Finally, I thought. I asked, "Have you called your family in Vermont?"

"No, but I should do that," he said, talking to the wall across the room. "They've been with me through everything. I wouldn't want them to think I don't love them."

"Do you forgive Laura and William?" I asked. "I think they were a couple of young kids who bit off more than they could chew."

Finally, he turned toward me and said, "The situation was more complicated than I thought."

"I think it always has to be."

"It sounds like he probably had a hard childhood. Maybe he was still running away from his demons."

"You said she'd walked in on him. She saw this fight. She watched the father of her child fly out of the country after your adoption. Maybe he wasn't ready to be a father. Laura picked up on that reticence before she was that statistical welfare mom fighting to make ends meet."

Lucas nodded like he understood. "If they'd talked it out? If she'd enlisted the support of her family…"

"It could have worked, Lucas. William could have grown up. Laura's family could have stepped in. None of that happened. Reality isn't a movie of the week or a Nicholas Sparks novel. There's no riding off into the sunset or happily ever after. Life is messy and hard. And sometimes the choices are forever."

Done talking, I pulled Lucas' mouth to mine. I wove my fingers in the curls at the nape of his neck. When I pulled back, desire sparked in his eyes. I closed mine and pressed my face into his neck. I inhaled that mixture of soap, aftershave, and man that was all him. I bit at his neck, soothing the red mark with my tongue. I kissed the stubble along his jaw expressly to push away the inevitable: the end of us.

With a stone cold certainty I knew Lucas would never forgive me because I could never forgive myself. He was right. He was inevitably, inexorably right. I'd made the wrong choice eleven years, three months, and six days ago. And there wasn't a single thing I could do about it.

30 Lucas

The baggage claim carousel spun lazily when I approached. For an unguarded moment, I looked at Matthew
Tucker, the man who raised me. He was sitting, legs
crossed, wool pants leg lifted to reveal mismatched socks.
Even from over here, I could tell the socks were knit from
mom's hand-dyed yarn stash. Probably leftovers from
school. I'd had many a pair during my life.

I looked down at the generic Macy's socks I was wearing and regretted not pulling something of Mom's from
the drawer before I'd boarded the plane.

"Dad!" I called and strode over to the bank of chairs
against the wall.

"Surprised you still call me that," he said.

That hurt. A lot. "You and Mom will always be my parents. You know that," I said, pulling him up and in for a hug. He remained stiff in my arms.

"That your bag?" he asked, pointing to my black weekend bag slowly turning on the black rubber pads.

Reluctantly, I let go of him and went to retrieve my bag. He jingled his keys and led the way to the parking lot. "New car?" I asked, pointing to the shiny new Subaru.

He nodded, squinting at the key fob and jabbing at buttons. The rear of the Forrester popped open. I placed my bag in the empty trunk and helped myself into the passenger seat.

"Looks like there are some upgrades from my Outback," I said.

My dad made a big show of looking at the map on the screen and weaving through the speeding Boston traffic. I should have offered to drive. If Los Angeles had given me one thing, it was a crash course in traffic navigation. "Dad, you want me to drive?" I offered in the middle of six lanes of traffic.

"I can still do that, Lucas," he said nearly sideswiping a van.

I shut up and let him drive. In a few minutes we were in New Hampshire. Once we got past that initial crush of suburban traffic, things quieted down. My dad stopped white knuckling the steering wheel.

"You thinking of retiring?" I asked. Seemed like he shouldn't be out commuting on snowy or icy roads. Maybe he and Mom could sell their big house and move to a condo in Concord or Boston. Something safer than small town Vermont a good drive from anywhere.

"I'm not quite ready to put one foot in the grave," he said. His tone did not invite further discussion.

I pulled my phone from my jacket pocket and fiddled with it. No call from Nari. I wondered if she'd received the note I'd stuck to the back of her office chair. In a post-coital haze we'd talked about driving up to Ojai for the weekend. Maybe tasting wine, cozying up in a big king-size bed away from intrusions from her parents in her apartment or the memory of my birth ones in mine.

But before I could indulge in that kind of hedonism, I needed to square things back here. I'd left a post it stuck to her chair because I didn't want to tell her face-to-face that I was putting my tail between my legs. That I realized I probably needed to apologize to my parents. I snuck a look at my dad. He didn't look quite as unhappy as when I'd first met him in the airport, but his lips were still pinched. Little white lines etched his mouth, face, brow.

"How's your book coming?" I asked when the road emptied after the 495 and Dad's hands further eased their grip on the steering wheel.

"I may not finish this one," he said. That was news. Dad was as dedicated as anyone to social history. He'd proudly taken up the cause of students and adults knowing what had come before them. Not repeating those mistakes. Learning from the victories and defeats. He'd given all of us that same speech hundreds of times. I may have majored in biology, but I'd minored in history at his insistence.

"Why not? It's always been important to you."

"I think Howard Zinn has it covered," he said. "His people's history has sold thousands of copies—to lay people."

"But doesn't he have more of a slant?" My father had scrupulously stressed objectivity.

"Oh, nothing's unbiased anymore. I used to think I was the objective voice of history. Me, a privileged white man living in an enclave of people just like me. What do I know?" He paused for a long time as he maneuvered through the increased traffic around Manchester and Concord. "Did you read any of those Naomi Klein books I gave you?"

I thought about the thick paper wrapped hardcovers on the shelf in my home office. Between finding my parents and negotiating whatever I had with Nari, reading hadn't been on the top of my list. If I'd been at home or in New York, it would have been. Even if I hadn't had the time, I would have read it because I loved him and wanted to support him. It's what our family did. He'd read every paper—horrible and not so—that I'd written throughout high school and college. He'd come to every game, every parents weekend for all three of us kids.

"I've been busy," I said, trying not to let the guilt eat me alive. I had an entire weekend ahead of me. If I let it start out like this, I'd never make it.

"I thought you were down to four days now," he said, glancing at me, then the road.

"Watch out!" I yelled as a deer darted across the road. Dad swerved hard, but was able to correct himself in time. Before we were off in the berm, waiting for a tow truck. When the adrenaline cleared from my bloodstream, we were nearing the Vermont border. I'd have a talk with Mom before the weekend was over. Dad didn't seem quite himself on the road anymore. He'd never been an aggressive driver, but at least I remembered him confident. Was it age or was it me?

Had I made my own father nervous? I was his son. He'd known me nearly since birth. Determined to remove whatever stress my being here was causing him, I settled back in my seat and stayed quiet. My head turned toward the window and I took in the passing landscape, the remaining miles to home.

I'd missed this. Tall thick maples, pines, greenery. There wasn't much I liked about the desert landscape of California, except driving through it with Nari.

The house was warm when I scraped off my shoes and headed in through the mud door. My mom, the woman whose lap I'd lived in for the first few years of my life, was vigorously mixing something on the counter. My nose picked it up before my brain could register the smells of home.

Mom dropped the spoon and came over to hug me. She was a small person with a mighty grip.

"My love," she whispered in my ear like she used to before I fell asleep in my room as a child. Before she dimmed the hallway lights and left my door open a crack.

I cleared my throat of the emotion that overwhelmed me, nearly made me mute. "What's for dinner?" was all I could push out. I wanted to say, I love you too, Mom. Guilt was like a wad of gum in my throat keeping all the wrong words inside.

"Coconut vegetable curry." She brushed a hank of hair away from her face with the back of her hand. A smudge of turmeric-dyed sauce landed on her chin. I picked up a kitchen towel from the counter and wiped it away. Not that it made a difference. There were curry stains on her sweater and what looked like dye on the knee of her pants.

"Brooke still a vegetarian?" I asked.

"She's probably vegan, but I don't know. She still eats butter and cheese in my casseroles."

"I need to get my bags," I said. "Wanted to hug my favorite mom first."

"I didn't know if you'd still call me that," mom said with a quaver in her voice.

I sat heavily on the utilitarian round oak stools I remembered from my earliest days in this house. "Of course I'd call you that. You're my mom," I said.

Dad bustled by with my bag in hand. I stood. "I was going to get that. Let me take it upstairs."

I reached out my hand, but Dad had already walked past and was halfway up the back stairs before I could make my move.

"Would you like some water, maybe a glass of wine?" my mother said in a tone she usually reserved for guests.

"Why are you guys doing this?" I asked. "You're treating me like I'm not one of the family," I said.

"You *were* adopted," Brooke said, poking her head in from the study. Undoubtedly, she'd been in there looking at one of those anime comic books she liked so much. The kind she didn't like to read in front of her New Yorker magazine-reading friends.

The "you're adopted" joke that had been funny for much of my childhood wasn't anymore. Where other kids' brothers and sisters teased them with the idea of being adopted, it was a point of pride in my family. Or it had been. Where other kids didn't get along, hated their siblings, we'd been a tightly knit threesome because we were so close in age. Because our parents had made sure we didn't treat anyone differently based on their blood lines. But that bond had been sorely tested last Christmas when I'd finally spoken up about wanting to find my birth parents.

"Why are you freezing me out like this?" I asked. "I'm starting to think that I was right all along. That you've merely tolerated me as some interloper to the family. If I make you uncomfortable, I can make my way down to the Village Inn," I said, bending over to tighten my laces and feeling very, very sorry for myself. I was ready to make the walk if I had to. After that little Brentwood sojourn I was up for anything.

"Maybe that's not a bad idea," Brooke said, full body in the kitchen now. Her red and orange dyed hair matched the tiffany lampshade above the kitchen table. There was a time I'd have made fun of her hair colored like the characters she read about and everyone would have laughed good naturedly. But I didn't dare. Maybe those days were long gone.

"Brooke, that's uncalled for. Lucas was born before you. He'll be staying up in his room like always."

"But he treated you and Dad like you'd done nothing for him."

"I did not," I said. "I made a decision to look for my parents...my birth parents. I didn't do that to hurt Mom and Dad."

"We understood your decision, Lucas," Dad said, coming back down the steps empty handed this time.

"Why are you snowing him?" Brooke said. Tact and soft-pedaling had never been her strong suit.

"You may not use that tone in our house," Mom said, wiping her hands on her apron. "He's our son as much as you're our daughter, but his journey to our family was different. To pretend otherwise would be unfair to him." Always the diplomat, Joyce had been. She'd mediated thousands of family disputes with a calm hand. Nothing had changed there.

Brooke's eyes nearly caught fire. "Mom! You don't need to talk down to me like I'm one of your restless kids during the handwork class."

"Don't I get a pass?" I asked my sister. "*Your* parents didn't leave you on the proverbial doorstep, Brooke. Is it too much for all of you that I wanted to find out why someone didn't wrap me up and take me home?"

"But that's exactly it, Lucas," Brooke said, jabbing a finger toward my chest, not quite touching. "Some people did wrap you up and take your crying fuzzy blond self home. You were not raised in an orphanage or by wolves in the jungle."

"I never said they'd done anything wrong." I gestured toward the only parents I'd ever known.

"So why did you have to go find these other people?" Brooke looked like she was on the verge of tears.

"Because I wanted to know my own origin story. Why can't you get this? I've been on dozens of adoptee advocate websites and those people get it." I paused for a long time before saying quietly, "I just needed to know."

"Did you find what you were looking for?" Mom asked in a whisper-soft voice. I looked away from my sister and toward her. No tears spilled, but her eyes were red rimmed nonetheless. Her face held the same tension it did at her aunt's funeral.

I abandoned the stool for the long oak table. Fingering the hand-embroidered runner one of my mother's more devoted students had made for her, I didn't have to meet any of their eyes. "I could use that wine, Mom," I said.

The unsealing of the fridge door was the only sound in the room. Mom pulled out a deep yellow chardonnay. I'd have preferred something that packed a much bigger punch. Nari's method of dealing with things had some validity, I was learning. But I didn't say a thing and graciously accepted the cool wine.

"Nari and I went down to meet Laura. That's her name—Laura Wallace."

Brooke stood on tiptoe to pull another glass from the cupboard. She sat at the table and helped herself to a large glass of wine. "Who's Nari?"

"She's the girl...a woman...she's a doctor in my office," I finally stuttered out. "She drove down to San Diego with me."

"How was she?" Mom asked, pouring her own glass of wine. I tried not to be taken aback. I think I could count on a single hand the times I'd seen my mother drink anything stronger than herbal tea. "Laura, is that right?"

"She'd been looking for me as well, if that's what you're asking."

Mom nodded then took a huge gulp of wine.

"She's nice. After Nari and I left, she called my birth father. I met him as well."

"What's his name?" Dad asked.

"William Coates."

I gave them the Cliff Notes version about William being in the military and their marriage falling apart at the same time Laura was pregnant.

"Is it what you hoped it would be?" Mom asked.

No, it wasn't at all what I'd hoped. But I think I was starting to realize there was no perfect scenario that was going to make it all okay for me. "It was fine. Nari thinks they might get back together." I fobbed off my hopeful fantasy on my absent lover.

"Did they have other children?" dad asked.

"Nope. I was it. William dedicated his life to the military. I'm not sure why Laura didn't have more. I didn't ask."

"Why does this Nari think they're getting back together?" Brooke asked.

"We had them over for dinner at my place. When Nicolette, that's Will's girlfriend, stepped out, Laura and Will reconnected."

"This doctor Nari was at your apartment?"

"She helped me with dinner. As kind of a hostess, you know."

"Doctors have certainly expanded their roles," Brooke said, her brown eyebrows nearly meeting her red bangs.

"Stop acting like we're thirteen again. Nari and I have been seeing each other. Okay."

I knew I must have really upset things when my sex life was a more comfortable topic than adoption. "Is it serious?" my mom asked.

"No. We're just friends," I answered.

"Sounds like more than friends." Brooke again.

"We were dating, I guess. But we've decided it's not serious."

"Why not?" my dad asked. Uh-oh. As the father of a daughter he took strong exception to Christian and I treating women with anything less than the utmost respect.

"It's complicated," I dodged.

"Does she know," my father raised his hands in air quotes, "it's complicated."

"I told her there couldn't be a relationship," I said. "You always say we shouldn't lead women...down a path we're not ready to follow."

"And she's okay with that?" my mother probed.

"We've made a truce," I said, feeling very warm under their collective scrutiny.

"What's wrong with her?" Brooke asked. Of course she'd hit on that thousand dollar question.

"Our values don't align," I hedged.

"Spill it," Brooke said. "Otherwise I'll get Christian here to torture it out of you. He can be relentless."

Didn't I know that. There wasn't a family secret my brother Christian didn't know. Everyone caved to him because it was easier than him giving you the eye for days on end.

"She was married."

"Oh," Mom said, sitting back in the cane backed chair.

Brooke leaned forward, pressed more. "He said *was* married, mom. What happened to her husband?"

"He died," I answered, resigned to the interrogation.

Brooke put her graphic novel down, the thumb holding her place, forgotten. "Did she kill him?"

"I think she couldn't have kept her medical license if she were a convicted murderer."

"Did she kill her abusive husband? Get off on a self-defense? Do you have a problem with a woman who's killed before, even if it was to defend her life?" Brooke's questions continued unabated.

"Maybe you should write one of those comic books you still read," I said.

"They're called manga, Lucas," she corrected. Then she leaned forward with renewed interest. "Am I right?"

"No, you're not right."

"What was it then?" Dad asked, giving up his silence.

"Sorry I'm late. Glad you haven't started eating," Christian said, bringing the sound of wind, a sweep of leaves, the smell of pine with him as he slipped into the kitchen. He leaned down to hug Mom around the shoulders and kissed her on both cheeks. Not for the first time I marveled at their cheeks jutting at the same angle, the same dimple on the side of their chins. Before Mom's was more gray than not, they'd had exactly the same hair color. "What's what?"

There went any chance I could keep this one a secret. Christian Put The Screws To You Tucker was in the house.

"Lucas was telling us why he can't date Nari," Brooke said, accepting the hug and catching their brother up.

"You're dating. Her name is Nari. That's a cool name, I've never heard it before."

"It's Japanese. I think it means thunder or lightning. I can't remember, but I saw it somewhere."

"Is it because she's Japanese, Lucas," my mom said, frowning.

"She's not Japanese. She's Korean from California by way of New Jersey."

"Do you have a picture?" Brooke asked, snagging my phone from where I'd left it on the table.

I snatched it back. "No. We don't have that kind of relationship. Plus I'm not a teenager. I don't have her picture as my wallpaper or something like that." Not that I hadn't wanted to do it. Inappropriately my mind's eye remembered her nude body next to mine, snapping a picture of that for these nights I was going to be alone, then quickly scuttled those thoughts.

Brooke threw her hands up on mock surrender. "Oh, okay Mr. Prickly Pear."

Four pairs of Tucker eyes looked at me. "I told her I couldn't see her because she gave her baby up for adoption. Okay? I don't feel comfortable with that."

The silence stretched out—long.

Cringing at my utter lack of discretion, I spun out the long tale of Nari and Andrew. She'd kill me if she'd heard me talking—spilling all her carefully guarded secrets.

Mom's eyes were red rimmed, but for an entirely different reason this time. "That's so sad for her. I hope she finds someone she can spend her life with."

That hit me like a ton of bricks. Nari would eventually find someone else—a real life partner. Her friends with benefits fuck-buddy relationship would have to end. It could be sooner rather than later. She was smart and beautiful. If she made a small effort, I'm sure there was a guy who'd step in to help her heal, make her smile. And that guy wasn't going to be me. And yet, I wasn't quite ready to step aside.

"So you're taking up her time, but you don't have marriage or any kind of long term relationship in mind?" Dad asked. I knew from his tone that I'd violated the nice guy code he'd laid down for Christian and I years before.

I nodded and stood, walking to the counter. I moved the stack of plates Mom had put out to the table and pulled out cutlery, napkins. "Can I put this in a bowl?" I asked, lifting the lid of the big pot. Coconut scented steam filled my face, blotting out the judgmental faces around me. I dished out vegetables, brown rice, and mom's homemade kefir soda.

The best thing about being one of three was that the focus on any one of us came and went pretty quickly. Dad and Christian got into it about tenure and the treatment of adjunct faculty. That would keep them occupied for a long time. Time that allowed me to think about how I was going to quit Nari for her own good.

31 NARI

"I miss Loehmanns," I said.

Daisy looked up from the dress she was inspecting. It was blue with flowers. Sometimes I wondered if she were trying out for a tampon commercial. She had to have dozens of these fitted spring picnic dresses. Since she didn't attend alumni functions at Hancock Park mansions or Newport beach parties, I thought she should take her wardrobe in a different direction. But I didn't say it out loud.

Friendship may have been about telling the truth, but it was also about knowing when to share that truth. Now wasn't that time.

"I hated that place. Squeezing between racks of clothes. That shared dressing room. I never wanted to see that many naked women. I never want to see that many naked women again."

I couldn't help myself. "Says the woman who's looked at naked women every day for nearly a decade," I said.

Daisy looked at me for a long moment. Pursed her lips. She picked up another dress, this one a sheath with large pink poppies or camellias or something like that. It was a bridal shower, baby shower dress. I looked away from that train wreck. I was hitting Nordstrom and Bloomingdales today. Sorting the dreck from the good stuff was harder at these stores that tried to cater to everyone's tastes from socialite to mother-of-the-bride. But I couldn't beat their return policy. Those cute little boutiques on Melrose or Robertson were "all sales final" kinds of places.

"Are you going to buy that dress?"

"I'll think about it," Daisy said.

I looked over the racks and motioned to Eun-ji. "Let's get lunch then."

After we ordered, I looked at my cousin. "What did your parents say?"

"That I have to move back in to your condo." She shook her head.

I matched that movement. "We can agree that you living with me wasn't working for us. You want to date guys. A lot of guys. I think that's fair. You're in college. I think you should go for it. But I can't have college boys in my apartment." That first morning waking up with a half-naked seventeen- year old boy walking around had scared the crap out of me. It had been wrong on so many levels.

Not the least of which was him hitting on me. His half-naked skinny ass was out the door in no more time than it took to toss him his clothes. But I knew the floodgates were open. Another one would follow that one. Eun-ji was cute and had no boundaries. And I didn't want to raise her.

Eun-ji nodded in agreement. "But Dad says you'll do it because you owe it to him. What does that even mean?"

I sighed. I was tired of my secrets wielding power over me. "Do you remember the summer I came to stay with you?"

"I think so. I was eight or nine, right?" she asked, toying with her phone.

I turned her phone upside down, breaking her eye contact with that screen. "Oma, Apa, they sent me to Korea because I was pregnant and they didn't want anyone here to know."

"You were pregnant! Oh my God! What happened to the baby? Who was the father?" She looked at Daisy who was calmly pulling small bones from her miso cod. "Did you know?"

I eyed my best friend, signaling her discretion. Daisy only nodded. She was an old pro from Connecticut who was the very picture of decorum. Didn't scold me for only having found this out herself.

"I was married my last year in college," I said. As always, when I thought about Andrew I lost my appetite, but I didn't want to throw up or cry. So that was an improvement. Maybe the healing had finally begun.

I could see that I was blowing my adolescent cousin's mind. "You wanted to move out. You told me you were an adult. This isn't the kid's table."

"I know, Ajumma but…. Wow. I always thought you were perfect."

"No one's perfect. I did get pregnant by accident. But I loved Andrew and we got married."

"Why didn't you keep the baby?"

I pushed away the artfully arranged Chinese chicken salad. Someone would throw this perfectly good food into the garbage. So much of my life was a waste, time lost, too many clothes, uneaten food. Maybe I'd box it to go. "Ajumma?" Eun-ji probed.

"I came back to California before the baby was born. I gave her up for adoption. Then started medical school."

"Just like that?"

"There weren't a lot of choices," I said. Nothing in life was "just like that." But that wasn't a lesson I could or wanted to teach. If Lucas couldn't even understand it, how would Eun-ji?

"What happened to the boy? The guy you married?"

I tried to speak, but my throat had closed up. Irrationally I wondered if I had an allergy. Where was the nearest Epi-Pen?

"He died in a car accident during our senior year. A drunk driver hit him in New Jersey," I heard Daisy say.

"Ohh. I'm so sorry," Eun-ji said. "That must have sucked. That was that summer, huh?"

I could see my cousin's wheels spinning. She was filtering new knowledge through the lens of her memory. I wanted to tell her that her life would be filled with such moments. Revelations, facts you had to reassess. Things you discover were not exactly how you thought they were. Like the regret I was starting to acknowledge about Minnie. Something I'd never let myself think about.

"Why are you telling me this?" Eun-ji asked, pulling me back to the conversation at hand.

"Because I love you enough to know that you need to spread your wings. Because I'm going to tell your parents and mine that you're not welcome back in my apartment. Because your mom may let the cat out of the bag. But I'm over thirty and don't care about the wagging tongues of our extended Korean family or the judgment of the church family here. At the end of whatever happens, your parents will be happy to keep you where you are and away from my corrupting influence. And we can both agree with that, right?"

My cousin nodded her head. I was giving her what she wanted, her freedom. Even if it came about in this completely backhanded way, I knew she was going to take it.

The table vibrated. "Oh, my phone," Eun-ji said, picking up the saucer sized computer she'd laid on the edge of the table. A silly smile creased her face. "I gotta go. Thanks for lunch," she said.

She was out the door before I could ask if she needed a ride. But I guess the boy of the moment had a car and would pick her up and take her wherever. For a long moment, I missed that freedom.

"You ready?" I asked.

Daisy flagged down the waitress, paid the check. I ushered us out of there. We walked a bit through the mall, which had gone out of its way to replicate some small town Americana ideal right down to the streetcar. Daisy sat on a bench. I swiped at the dust on the wood slats before joining her. Then I braced myself for the explosion that was coming. Three. Two. One. Houston....

"Are you fucking kidding me?"

"I didn't know how to tell you," I said. My best friend had been too quiet, too accepting of my revelation. It was only a matter of time before her hurt feelings festered and blew up all over me. It had been too much to hope she was going to gloss over my lack of trust in our friendship.

"So now I'm right behind your porn star wannabe cousin?"

"Thanks for not saying anything at lunch about you just finding out. For not making that harder than it needed to be."

"Seriously? I'm an adult. The difference between adults and children is that we don't navigate our lives out loud."

"I thought she should know the why behind everything," I said, trying to gloss over the betrayal I could see in her eyes.

"Why like this? Why are you suddenly so candid now?"

"I told Lucas. And then Simon. You. I'm tired of hiding."

"I honestly thought we were friends. You know everything there is to know about me. Everything. But I feel like I don't know anything about you. You got pregnant? You had a baby? You told me you were in Korea that summer because you wouldn't be able to go back for a long time with medical school and everything."

"That wasn't the truth," I said, squinting at the memory of that drawn-out lie. The second or third of many such misstatements and half-truths in the last dozen years.

"Obviously."

"I still can't believe you told Lucas before me." Daisy was trying to hide the hurt and insecurity. She was doing a piss-poor job. "You've known him for all of ten seconds in the cosmic scheme of things. I've known you, what, fifteen years now. It's like that counts for nothing."

"I...I don't know why I told him. But it doesn't matter anyway."

"Why? Where is he anyway? I thought you guys were...I don't know...back to dating or something."

"That's over," I said. He'd as much as said so weeks ago. "It's not exactly dating. More like sex without strings." I made a gesture with my hands passing by each other. "Lucas and I are different planets in different orbits."

"Maybe?" Daisy lifted her shoulders in a shrug. But it was clear she didn't believe in a future for me and Lucas. She was throwing me a bone.

I shook my head very slowly. "No chance."

"Wow," she said. "I know you wanted there to be something. I'm sorry, but you deserve better."

"I'm feeling very judged right now."

Daisy was quick to push up her sunglasses, and really look at me. I pushed up my own. This was one of those moments when I wondered if men served a purpose on this earth. Because I could see the love she had for me. That she'd be there through thick and thin, marriages, sickness and death and divorce. I couldn't say the same of a single man in my life.

"I've never been in a position to judge anyone. You know that. I'm sure you did what you needed to do in that time and place. I'm a little sad that you didn't think you could trust me with it. But that's about me. And not everything is about me." My best friend paused a long time. I could see her throat working to hold back recriminations, swallow tears. She pinched at her nose. But the movement didn't work. Daisy pulled a tissue from her purse and dabbed at her nose. Finally, she spoke. What did Simon say?"

"That he was sorry I couldn't tell him at the time."

"I kind of thought you liked Lucas."

"I kind of really did. I wanted to come out of hibernation for him. But maybe I put too much stock into that.

Thinking that a guy was going to come in and save the day."

"Don't. Just don't let the mess with him push you back into the dark. I'm glad that you're coming out with the truth. The reason doesn't really matter." We watched children wave to us from the trolley. "Where is the catalyst of all this honesty anyway?"

"I have no idea. We were supposed to drive to Ojai for the weekend. But he called off work Friday and who knows..."

"You haven't texted him."

"From talking to patients I think men are bad at break ups. They sort of melt into the ether. It's not like he didn't tell me it couldn't work out. I'll spare him the nagging injured party texts."

"So why were you going to Ojai?"

"If sex in the city was good sex in the mountains would be better, right? Isn't that what drives the human race?"

Daisy matched my formality. "Then maybe you should seek that out elsewhere."

As if on cue a man who could have been from central casting as the "hot guy" walked by. He actually lifted his shirt and wiped sweat from his brow. Noticing us, he nodded his head in greeting and said, "Ladies."

I couldn't help myself. Laughter shook my whole body, escaping in an inelegant snort and giggle combination. Daisy was right there with me. I joined our elbows and we stood to go.

32 LUCAS

"How was your weekend?" I asked, coming into Nari's office without an invitation. I glanced at the clock on her desk. We had a good twenty minutes before the first appointment, though I was sure I'd seen a couple early bird patients warming the waiting room chairs.

"Are we seriously going to do this?" she asked.

I had a weird sense of déjà vu with that question. "Do what?"

Nari threw back her head in what only could have been exasperation. "Pretend that there's anything between us. Invent reasons to talk. Lucas, I got your message loud and clear. Now if you don't mind, I need to look through these reports before nine."

Feeling something inappropriate looming, I pushed the office door closed. "What message?"

"Silence can be deafening."

What the heck was she talking about? I'd been on a plane two of the last four days. She knew about the alphabet soup of TSA, NTSB, FAA and the long list of regulations regarding cell phones on planes, right? "I was with my parents."

"That's lovely, Lucas."

Lowering my voice, I said, "I'd have rather gone to Ojai with you."

"Can we not prolong this? You said you couldn't be with me. We made plans to go to Ojai, and you disappeared off the face of the earth or went to Vermont. Either way, I think we need to cut this short before we hurt each other any more."

The proverbial light bulb went on. "You didn't get my note."

"Note? Are we in eighth grade? No, the popular girl in the front didn't pass back your latest missive."

I got it then. She was hurt or pissed or both. She cared. I kind of wanted to smile, except that would have hurt her or pissed her off more. Instead I walked behind her chair, her eyes on me the whole way. There it was, flipped upside down, the note I'd taped to the back. Carefully, I removed the small rectangle that held my handwriting in addition to an ad for an anti-stroke drug.

I spun her chair around and handed the note to her. "Here."

She snatched it out of my hand. Read it. Placed it carefully down on her desk, all without a change in expression. "I have a nine o'clock patient. I need to look at her test results. If you don't mind."

I left her there. Because I didn't know how to say what I wanted. I needed to go work up the courage.

Ten hours of seeing her walk by with efficiency, talking to nurses about clinical matters, nearly sent me over the edge. I'd missed a weekend of going to sleep with her, waking up with her, being with her. I followed her out.

"Nari!" I called as she walked to her truck.

She paused. I could practically see her vacillation from fifty yards away. She stayed put and I loped over to her, hoping I didn't look as goofy as I felt. "Can you drive with me to Tahoe next weekend?"

"Tahoe?"

"Will and Laura wanted us to come up for the weekend."

"Us?"

"You were expressly invited. I'm extending that invitation."

"This can't be a regular thing, but I'll see it through with you."

Those four intervening days were torture. But I manned up and muddled through.

The green machine and I picked up Nari for the short ride to the airport. That ride, parking the car, the shuttle ride, and the quick flight to Reno were all in polite silence. I was nervous. I didn't really know what to say. Nari was as cool as a cucumber. Her big designer tote was filled to the brim with brightly colored fashion magazines. She paged through, made notes, and added sticky tabs like a professional shopper. But I had to admit she looked spectacular. The lace peeking between the buttons of the silky blouse she was wearing made me shift in my seat more than once. I'd have begrudged her those magazines if she hadn't been so damned good at making casual look sexy.

If she didn't have something to say to me, I wondered more than once on the trip and the ride to the bed and breakfast why she was there with me. If Laura hadn't asked me to bring Nari, maybe I'd have taken her up on the idea that we stop seeing each other. Being this close and knowing there was an end in sight was starting to be torture.

When we pulled up to the rustic-looking lodge, I started doubting myself big time. I'd looked at the website a thousand times. I had vacillated between the two-room suite and the room I'd eventually booked, a three hundred square foot room with the king sized bed and whirlpool tub. I expected an objection when I checked in. When the innkeepers took us up two flights to the room. When Nari plopped her black leather weekend bag on the bed. But I got nothing. We got a lesson on how to light the river rock fireplace. How to use the whirlpool came next. Then we were alone with a big pine bed and a view of the lake.

Nari rubbed her arms. I blinked slowly before I realized there was a chill in the room. My mind and body were so

overheated that the forty-degree temperature hadn't registered.

"Let me light a fire," I said. My phone rang and I
pulled it from my pocket. "It's William."

After a brief exchange of pleasantries, my biological father got to the point. He wanted us to meet them in the
morning. I scribbled down an address on the pad near the
desk and hung up.

"They want to meet after breakfast," I said.

"Okay." Nari said. "I guess we need to see this
through."

I pressed a button on the phone. "You up for dinner?"

Nari crossed her legs. Laceless Converse sneakers covered her feet. She removed a bobby pin from her hair.
"Can we order in?"

"I'll be back." Turned out we couldn't order in, but
twenty minutes later, I had take-out from the Italian restaurant down the road.

"You didn't have to do all this," Nari said as I set out
steaming plates of Portobello mushroom ravioli and vegetarian lasagna.

"I wanted to," I said.

"I think this needs to be our last weekend together,"
Nari said.

I set down the cutlery very carefully. This had been
coming. I knew it, but unrealistically thought we could
skirt the issue. I couldn't ask why because I knew why. I
was stuck where I was and the facts of her past weren't
going to change.

"But I love you," I blurted out. I hadn't meant that to come out now or in that way. "I think I'm falling in love with you," I amended. I don't know why I'd said that. I hadn't even fully worked it out in my head. I'd been thinking it on the flight back from Vermont. Every day I'd seen her in the office. When I'd picked up the dinner. But I'd never *ever* meant for it to come out. It's wasn't fair to her. To me. To us.

Nari stood from the table. She'd changed into some soft looking pajamas when I'd been gone. She stepped out on the terrace. I sat and ate some of the ravioli, and a bit of the lasagna. By the time I took a first bite of the *torta della nonna* and she hadn't come back. I looked and she was standing there, looking at the huge lake. The moon shone through the trees, highlighting her hair.

I made my way through the sliding glass doors. "Are you hungry?"

"I'm never hungry, Lucas. I don't think I've been hungry in years. I know how human physiology works. I eat to live. Given my metabolic rate, it takes seventeen hundred eighty-four calories a day to survive."

"How many have you had today?"

"That coffee and muffin at the airport. About six hundred."

"Come eat," I implored. I wrapped my hand around hers and gently tugged her back in the room. I closed the door and turned up the fire. She ate mechanically, brushed her teeth and pulled back the covers. I tucked the remaining food in the fridge. I took my time unpacking a few items, showering the day's stress away. I pulled on a pair of fresh boxers and came back into the room.

I turned out the light and joined Nari in the bed. Shadows danced along the ceiling and wood-paneled walls as the firelight flickered. I extended my arm. Almost as if by instinct, she moved closer. In a matter of moments, she tucked herself into my side, her nighttime loose hair spilled against my chest.

I traced the fine hairs along her hairline. Rubbed the pads of my fingers along her brow. Nari's breathing quickened a bit as I moved to the band of her pajama top. I slid my hand under the loose fabric. Toyed with the bones of her hips, the hollow of her navel.

A puff of breath pursed her lips. I couldn't resist the invitation. I ran my tongue along first the top lip, then the fuller bottom.

Nari had never been about teasing or soft touches. She cupped the back of my neck and pulled me close. Our breath mingled, then our mouths melded. Her tongue met and dueled with mine. When I broke contact, we were both winners. I lifted the top over her head, skimmed off the thin knit pants. I tried not to fall on her naked body like a dog on a bone. But I was hard. I pulled one nipple taught with my thumb and forefinger, watching it harden. The firelight bathed her body in a reddish orange glow, only heightening the flush of arousal staining her.

A moan like a cry escaped Nari, echoing off the pine-paneled walls. I couldn't wait any longer. I pulled a condom from the shaving kit on the bedside table, sheathed myself and tried not to crush her with my weight. I ground my cock between her legs, against her clit. In moments, we were both out of breath.

I wanted to hold off, make this last as long as possible. But I couldn't. "Nari..."

"There's always this, Lucas. Always this. Please. I need you inside me."

I didn't wait to RSVP. I tried slow, but slammed in fast. With each thrust, high pitched moans escaped Nari. Her responsiveness nearly made me explode. But I gritted my teeth, fitting my hand between us, pressing a thumb to her center until she lost the rhythm. The tiny quakes and tremors made me lose control. With two or three more thrusts, I emptied into her. I think I'd probably declared my love for her again. But I'm not quite sure what had come out of my mouth. It had been disconnected from my brain for a minute or three.

I lay my forehead against hers for longer than I could count, trying to gather my wits about me. Bracing my elbows on either side of her, I lifted slowly.

"I'm sorry," I said. My hair had rubbed an abrasion onto her chest.

"It'll heal."

One shove and I was up. I placed a hand on her hips, bracing her while I pulled out. I took a long time in the bathroom, cleaning up, washing my hands. Looking at the man facing me in the mirror.

Nari hadn't put her little sexy pajamas back on. She'd turned on her side. Firelight flickered along the long smooth skin of her back and side that wasn't concealed by thin bits of knit and lace. I lay back down, turned to her.

"You know what totally sucks?" she asked.

"What?"

"I think I love you too."

Something like adrenaline flooded through me. Though I lay perfectly still, I knew if I stood up and left the room, I could have completed a run around Lake Tahoe without missing a step. But I didn't move, didn't run that victory lap. Because that wasn't what I'd thought falling in love would be like. Even in my movie and television-free household, common themes on love snuck in. Fairy tales had always ended in happily ever after. Chick flicks my sister had twisted my arm in driving her to always had happy endings. Even action stars rode off into the sunset. But Nari and I weren't doing any of these.

We were two people in love and it sucked. Big time.

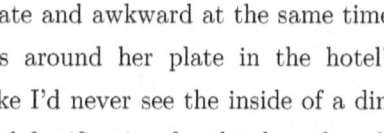

The morning was intimate and awkward at the same time. Nari pushed some eggs around her plate in the hotel's breakfast room. I ate like I'd never see the inside of a dining room again. I needed fortification for the day, though. William had been very quiet and I was waiting for the other shoe to drop, some kind of bombshell like another kid or cancer. I didn't know which would be easier to take.

"Do you have the address?" Nari said, lazily flicking through her phone. I don't think she'd ever done that before. Ignored me. She wasn't one of those people who was with you, but wishing she were somewhere else until now. I wondered where she wished she was. No, I didn't want to know. The answer probably contained the name Andrew.

"I have an address, but I'm not quite sure where it is." I passed a paper over to her.

"Let's go. I'll plug it into my phone."

She was up and in the parking lot before I could blink. I downed the remainder of my grapefruit juice and thanked the owners for breakfast.

When we passed the notice about entering federal land, Nari tapped her foot. "Do we need a permit to be here?"

"If we pass a ranger or whatever, I'll ask what the deal is."

"Fine."

The road, if it could be called that, wove through tall pines. The smell almost reminded me of home. I pulled into a lot where the road ended. "What does the GPS say?"

"This is it." Nari lifted her leg, eyeing her three inch heels. "Maybe these shoes aren't going to work." I tried not to think about last night. About how the whole package "worked" for me. I was amazed at the way she always looked wonderful no matter what. Today was some fitted dress with a little fur collar and sunglasses. It was classic Jackie-O. Or more like classic Nari-Y.

Nari shoved the shoes in her purse and I helped her from the car. "You really going barefoot?"

"Doesn't seem like another option. I'll be fine."

She made her way down the path a little ways before slipping. I grabbed her right hand in mine and tucked the other around her waist. The path spilled out on the sandy lakeside and there was Laura, Will, and a woman wearing a suit.

"We're so glad you found it," Laura said, hugging each of us. Something poked through my shirt. It was then I noticed she had a bouquet in her hand.

"Are you getting married?" Nari asked.

Laura was too choked up to talk, only nodded. William came over and shook my hand, kissed Nari on the cheek. "We walked and talked nearly all night after we left your apartment."

"We found what we'd been missing," Laura said, finding her voice. "We can't thank you enough for bringing us back together."

"Your guests are here. Are you ready?" the suited woman said.

They both nodded, and Nari and I stood back, a little apart from the threesome near the water.

"What you taught me, Laura, is about forgiveness. Forgiving you. Forgiving myself. I loved you then. I love you even more now." William's words were heartfelt. They hit me in the gut making me think I could use a little bit of his compassion.

"I accept your forgiveness. I forgive you and myself. Now that we know Lucas turned out fine, I think we're ready to love each other again," Laura said through tears.

The officiant did the regular "death do us part" stuff, and then it was over. Just like that, my parents were married again. It was like every kid of divorced parents' dream -come-true.

"We're having a brunch with Will's friends. We'd love for you to be there."

"Absolutely," Nari said. "I wouldn't miss it for anything."

In nearly every aspect, Nari was perfect for me. And I was going to lose her like Will lost Laura.

33 NARI

Everyone always says that love is infinite. You can love ten children as much as one. That you can have love for parents, and siblings, and friends and our hearts have space for more. But I didn't know if that was true. I didn't know if I could hold space for both Andrew and Lucas. My breath was constricted because there wasn't room for the two of them. I slid open my closet. The heavy door rumbled on its tracks. It was time to make space, leave room—say good-bye to Andrew.

Or rather, the memory of him. Our actual last good-bye had been hurried.

"Do you have your tux?" I'd asked. On one of the touring gigs, Andrew had forgotten his clothes. The other guys in the group were still joking about it two years later.

Andrew unzipped the garment bag. I fingered the lapels, felt for the pants. "Tie and cummerbund?"

"I'd be naked without you," Andrew said, grabbing me and starting a little waltz. I pulled away and found the hanger in his closet with the missing red silk pieces. I placed them in the pocket. "I'd like to be naked with you."

I looked down at the tiny baby bump I didn't hide around Andrew. My baggy school sweatshirt that had become a uniform was on the floor. "I look like I swallowed a baby burrito whole," I said.

"It's the sexiest burrito I've ever seen." Andrew's hand traveled up my abdomen and started fiddling with my bra.

I batted his hand away. "We don't have time for that. Everyone else has left. You should get on the road."

"You sure you don't want to come home with me?"

"We've talked about this. Us trying to tell my parents with both of us there was a disaster. I think you should tell your parents alone about the marriage and the baby. We tried the ambush approach and that didn't work. I'll come another weekend. One where I don't have an exam or a doctor's appointment looming."

"You're probably right. My dad's gonna blow a gasket at first. But Mom will be okay. She'll bring Dad around."

"I think I'd rather skip the gasket blowing," I said, sitting on the bed. I had to pee, but wanted to hold it in until I saw Andrew off.

"No matter what they say, we're a team, you and me." He held up his fist. I stacked mine on top. Andrew picked up his car keys. "You gonna walk me to the car?"

I gestured toward the window. Rain had started coming down while we were packing. "I'll wait here with your bags. You get the car."

"Ah, right."

He loped out of the room. I heard his sneakers slapping on the stairs. I used the communal bathroom without remembering to put on my sweatshirt.

"Wow," said one of the guys on the hall. I didn't know him well. "You got a baby in there?"

"It isn't a tumor," I said, hoping he'd forget he saw me. But my hopes were quickly dashed when he asked, "Is Andrew the father of that?"

"It's my time of the month. I'm really bloated," I said in deflection. He recoiled sufficiently at the mention of menstruation. "Can you help a pregnant girl with some luggage?" I said, taking advantage of his discomfort.

Fortunately for me, his manners won out over his curiosity. It was usually that way here. Under all those hormones and bravado were polite boys. "Yeah, what do you need?"

I retrieved my sweatshirt, then directed him toward the bags next to the bed. "Got 'em," he said, following me down to the huge front room.

Andrew pulled his Honda up and dashed out of the car without an umbrella. I hoped he wouldn't be too cold on the ride home.

He hefted the bags. Then he leaned down and kissed me, dripping water all over my shirt. "Our little family will be out in California in the summer. Promise I'll be back for that doctor's appointment. Okay?"

I nodded, then went back to the room I shared with Daisy. I worked on a bio ethics paper. Turned down a midnight run to the a.m. p.m. mini mart for snacks.

I shook my head, stopping my run down memory lane. There was nothing but bad memories after that. The phone call. The funeral. The lingering morning sickness that reminded me daily I had choices to make.

For what was going to be the last time, I pulled out the scrapbooks and dragged them to the living room. I pulled down candles from above the washer-dryer unit. The lighter came out of the drawer. I closed the blinds and curtains. Turned out the lights. Artificial dusk made the room dark. Dust danced in the remaining shafts of light. The little specks of hair and skin and lint mesmerized me for long moments. There was no time machine. I'd never go back to being that young naïve college senior. That girl whose options were infinite. That girl whose life was filled with love and possibility.

I stood for one last memorial. I lit the candles, flipped through the albums. Cried for the last time. I didn't know if it would ever get easier, but I was ready to grow up. Andrew was dead. I was alive. I was ready to reach for the

opportunities that might remain. It may not be with Lucas. But that was okay. Now that I knew I could love
again, fall in love again, I was ready for the future.

There was a knock on the door. I glanced at my watch.
Exactly on time.

I stood, walked to the door and let Daisy and her
awkward bundle into the apartment.

"What is all this?" she asked, taking in the smoking
candle wicks, the pictures, the dim room.

"It's my Andrew Clarke shrine," I said baldly.

My best friend's eyebrows shot to her hairline. But her
words didn't belie her shock or discomfort. "Um, okay."
She took off her shoes by the door, then came in and sat
cross-legged by the coffee table. With a light touch, she
brushed her hand over everything. "How often do you do
this?"

"Every year on the anniversary of his death."

I watched Daisy doing the math. "But you were in
Hawaii last year."

"It's portable."

She swept her hand in an encompassing motion. "You
brought all this with you?"

"It's what I took instead of you."

"Oh. I'm sorry I didn't realize the date. I thought you
didn't want me there for some other reason."

I *hadn't* wanted her there for another reason. But I decided my honesty didn't need to go that far. I wasn't
ashamed of those drunken hookups, but I wasn't proud of
them either. "I need your help."

Daisy's eyes shifted. No way she could have guessed what she was going to walk in on today. "Okay..."

"I need to pack this stuff away."

"I picked up the boxes and acid free tissue paper you asked for," she said gesturing to the large rectangular bag she'd left by the door.

"I can't do this by myself. But I think...no." I closed my eyes. Then opened them again. "I *know* I'm ready to put it away."

Daisy stood, squared a box, making it three dimensions from two, and started wrapping items. I watched her do it, no hand shaking, no reminiscing. One by one she tucked them in. She added tissue paper on top for extra protection. Tape appeared from her Coach purse. I had to smile at that. It may have been black and as attractive as a doctor's bag, but with work I'd gotten her to buy one or two designer items she considered tacky and frivolous. Daisy pulled at the ends and with a loud ripping noise, sealed one end of the box. She flipped it over and did the other side.

"What do you want me to do with it?"

"Let's take it down to storage," I said. Searching through a kitchen drawer, I found an extra set of keys. We made the elevator ride down in silence.

It took two tries to insert the key in the rarely used lock. A few more jiggles to get it to turn. Finally I got it open. There wasn't much in the small, dank space. A bicycle I'd used for a couple of years. Rollerblades too. The other boxes held designer purses and clothes I planned to consign when I finally had a moment to sort, and match receipts and labels with the original items. Daisy deposited the box on top of another.

"Let's go," I said, turning my back on the space. Only by turning away could I ease the crushing guilt of consigning my first marriage and child to a single solitary box.

34 LUCAS

"What's in Ojai?"

"My best friend, Daisy."

"What's her boyfriend's name?"

"Raphael."

I was unreasonably nervous about spending the weekend with Nari's best friend. But I figured she'd invited
them along in case I stood her up a second time. It was
like going on a two day-long job interview without the
prohibition of inappropriate personal questions. Given how
Nari and I had finally gotten together though, I could see
why she'd kept us apart. Nobody introduced the rebound
hookup guy to their friends. I nearly shuddered at my
characterization. I *wanted* to be more than that.

"What does he do?"

"He's a standup comedian. He's got a TV show called *The Brothers Kim* on CBT."

Some of our patients were on television. I always felt bad because they leaned forward on the examination table and eyed me with a half-cocked grin. The first two or three times I wondered if they were looking for a secret handshake or narcotic samples. But Margie clued me in after she'd nearly fainted when a young male patient had closed the door behind him.

Now, I knew they were looking for a spark of recognition. While asking them questions, I usually examined their chart carefully for hints of the actor or performer. A few had asked me flat out if I recognized them, usually followed by a request for some schedule III drug. First I broke out the Waldorf background, how my family didn't watch television. Then I said no to unwarranted prescription drugs.

Of course, I'd never seen Raphael's show.

"Have you seen his show?" I asked. It was what I'd done for years. Ask other people about TV and films, then take my cues from that.

"I went to a taping. It's the usual, kind of like a cross between *Three's Company* and that Margaret Cho show from eons ago."

I'd seen dozens of episodes of that old sit-com during a string of nights I'd sat by a dying patient's bedside. Margaret something or other, I'd never heard of. No hints there. Fortunately, Nari didn't seem like she really wanted to talk about the show.

I tried to guess what a friend of Nari would be like. Did she let this Daisy in on her innermost turmoil? What did *she* think about the baby, the adoption—Andrew? I wondered what her boyfriend Raphael would think of me.

Bah! I was too old for this. I looked out at the brownish green hills and held on for dear life as Nari wound her way up the 33 highway like it was the autobahn. Maybe one day I'd take her to Germany. Her lead foot would fit right in over there. My heart sunk to my toes. The future. A future with Nari. I wanted it so bad I could taste it. Only I didn't know if I could have it.

The minute I walked into the Ranch House restaurant with Nari that evening and she pointed to the table with her friends, I realized three things. Dinner was going to set me back a pretty penny and leave me hungry, Daisy was rich, and Raphael was Korean.

Nari's friends both stood when we got to the table. I shook Raphael's hand. "Lucas Tucker," I said. Then I awkwardly bussed Daisy on the cheek, careful not to disturb her headband. If Nari was wound tight, this Daisy was wound tighter. This pair made the frat boys at Dartmouth look like Seal Beach surfers.

We sat and looked at the menus in silence. After the waiter introduced himself but before he could launch into the day's specials, I asked, "Can we have a bottle of proseco?"

Four glasses came back full and sparkling. "I propose a toast," I said. Three sets of eyes looked at me expectantly. I immediately wished I hadn't said that. I didn't have a damned thing to toast to. "To a great meal with great friends," I finally said. The customary clinking of glasses took the focus of my lame toast.

"Nari tells me you have a TV show," I said. Great opener. I wanted to take Nari back to the hotel, make love to her, talk about our future. But I forged ahead with the small talk.

"*The Brothers Kim.*" Raphael stole a glance at Daisy. "It's pretty cool."

"How long have you known Nari?" I asked Daisy.

"We met in college."

"You lived together?"

"The last three years, yeah." Daisy looked at Nari. "Did you tell him about your freshman roommate?"

Nari shook her head, a small smile playing around her lips. "You were more sane."

"You didn't say that last year." To me Daisy said, "We lived together for about eight years between Olde Haven and Los Angeles."

Oddly, I couldn't see Nari with a roommate. "You lived together here?"

"That second bedroom that doubles as a small Robertson boutique. It used to be mine," she said.

"Eun-ji's room?" I asked.

"You haven't been in there, have you?" Daisy asked.

"Um, no," I admitted.

"Before you get involved, you may want to know a little bit about her shopping habit."

"Shopping habit?" I asked.

"Maybe it's a Korean thing," Raphael said.

I shifted in my seat, a little uncomfortable. The waiter came back to the table. Raphael ordered a pork chop. Nari chose a salad. I started to say something to her about getting her appetite back, but the server looked at me. "For you and your lady," he said, looking between Daisy and I.

"She's not—"

"We're not—"

"Oh. Right. Sorry. If you're undecided, scallops are a great choice," he said.

I ordered the beef tenderloin and left the seafood to Daisy.

Raphael grabbed Daisy's hand, rested them atop the linen. Squeezed it. The other couple gazed at each other for a long moment. The connection between them made me uncomfortable. I stood, excused myself. I took a long walk around the patio and out toward the woods. It was terribly rude, but between Laura and Will and Daisy and Raphael, I was terribly jealous. Green with envy. I wanted what they had. Love, a relationship with low barriers to entry.

"Hey there, Lucas?" I turned around. It was Daisy standing a few feet away. "I thought I'd tell you the food's on its way out."

"Thanks."

"Is loving Nari so hard?" she asked. I kept my head trained forward, but I heard the click-scuff of her shoe on the slate beneath us.

"No. Yes," I admitted.

"You know what? I found out about the baby after you."

"You haven't always known?"

"It was a secret from everyone, Lucas. Can you imagine having to carry around something as big as that for so many years? I was hurt, no, pissed she didn't tell me. Because I share nearly everything with her. She couldn't tell me something, she felt compelled to tell you."

"I don't get it," I said.

"What is there to get, Lucas? She trusts you. Probably loves you. I don't know if she regrets what she did, regrets keeping all those secrets all those years. But I do know that she hasn't been with anyone in more than a decade. That's gotta count for something."

I didn't correct Nari's friend's perception. But maybe I was the wrong thinking one. Nari had surely been with different men. But she hadn't let anyone into her heart, or share her secrets until me. Finally, I said, "It does."

"Underneath all those designer clothes and that bun, Nari's got a big heart. I love her. And I'm going to tell her not to waste it on you."

"You'd do that?" I said, not very much liking her interfering friend at this moment.

"Yes, Lucas. I'd do that. Unless you can forgive Nari and love her for who she is. Let her go so someone can."

I didn't sleep much that night. For once, Nari and I didn't have sex. It was as if seeing the real thing in front of me acted as an antidote to my libido. I held her while she slept. My mind raced nearly the whole night. I fell asleep near dawn and woke two hours later, knowing what I had to do.

"Did you bring your hiking boots?" I asked the next morning after both of us pushed fruit and eggs around our plate.

Nari produced beautiful brand new looking Merrells from her overnight bag. She added padded socks to her feet and laced up. I hoped the mud crusted on my five-year-old Timberlands didn't ruin the carpet in the room. We hiked and talked about Daisy and Raphael. It was a lot easier than talking about us.

They had to be the most unique couple I'd met in a very long time. He so clearly loved her and wasn't afraid to show it in everything he did for her. I was having a hard time reconciling what I'd seen last night with what Nari had told me about his playboy background. Weird. I didn't think I'd ever understand other people's relationships. I watched her walk ahead, hips swaying. I didn't even understand the one that I was in. The only thing I really knew was that I wasn't ready for it to end.

We weren't exactly alone when we got to the top of the park. Lots of couples, people with dogs, and teenagers were there for the sunset. We sat on a sandy spot near the edge of the hill. I pulled Nari into my chest and looped my arms around her waist. I leaned down to rest my chin on her hair and watched the sun come down over the valley and disappear behind the hills. They glowed pink and red just like the bed and breakfast brochure had promised. As soon as dusk fell, the crowd thinned out considerably.

When there was no one within the sound of my voice, I took a deep breath and spoke. "I'm sorry."

She sighed, leaning further into me. I scooted back an inch or two so the curves of her body didn't distract me from the speech I'd rehearsed all the way up the trail. "What for, Lucas?"

"For being a narrow minded asshole," I said.

"About what?"

"About you and Andrew and Minnie. I know making the decision to give up your daughter couldn't have been easy. I'm sorry that I made it out to be that way."

"I think I'll make contact with her."

I tried not to stiffen my body in shock. "Really?" I said, making my voice as normal as I could.

"Not today or tomorrow. But when she's eighteen I'll reach out in whatever way I can. I don't want her to think she was unwanted. Or was conceived out of anything other than love. It's more important than I thought it would be to a child. I had no way of knowing that until I met you."

To say I was shocked was an understatement. Nari finally got it. She finally seemed to understand my drive to find answers.

"Thank you."

"I'm doing it for her and for me. I hope I can answer questions and make that closure."

"I love you, Nari," I said.

She didn't reciprocate, and that was okay at this moment. "I want to apologize for what I said in Brentwood that day. It was unfair." Nari's breath hitched then held. I chose my next words carefully. "I want to be with you. I understand the decision you made eleven years ago and I won't bring it up again unless you want to talk about it."

"Okay." Breath puffed from her lips, blowing against the hairs on my arm.

"I only have one other thing I want to ask," I said. I'd thought long and hard about this. But on this one thing, I couldn't bend.

"What, Lucas?"

"I need to know if you can..." God, I felt like a supreme and colossal ass for bringing this up. But I didn't want to be second fiddle to a dead guy. It wasn't a fair fight. "If...Damned if I couldn't even figure out the right words.

"Is this about Andrew?" Nari asked as if reading my mind.

"Yes...I—"

"I will never stop loving Andrew. He was my husband. The father of our daughter. But what I said to you in my apartment that day isn't entirely true. I'm not in love with him anymore. I'm in love with you."

I didn't need to see her face at that moment to know that she was lit from within like that last time. But this go round, that love, that light was for me.

I held her tight. I'd never let her go.

ABOUT THE AUTHOR

I write crazy, beautiful love stories because I believe story-telling is magic. I love complicated heroines with secrets, strong heroes who fall hard, and a long winding road to happily ever after. When I'm not writing, I love to travel to witness the diverse tapestry of humanity, photograph the beauty of the world, visit museums, and watch live theater. I live in West Hollywood, California ten miles from the nearest airport.

I haven't found my own happily ever after, but I'm not done trying. Join me at Fifty First Dates, the Podcast, as I try to find my Mr. Right or maybe Mr. Right Now.

#50firstdates #joliemoore #crazybeautifullove